PSI EMERGENCE

PSI EMERGENCE
The Alex Fuller Chronicles

S. D. Knight

Knight Owl Publishing Company

Knight Owl Publishing Company

7371 Atlas Walk Way, # 230
Gainesville, VA 20155-2992

This is a work of fiction. Names, characters, places and events either are the product of the author's imagination or are used fictitiously. Any similarity to real persons, living or dead, business establishments, events or locales is coincidental and not intended by the author.

Library of Congress Control Number: 2015915283

ISBN 978-0-9968119-0-3

Edited by Crystal Liechty and Kelsey Down
Cover design by Melchelle Designs
Print layout by Booknook

Printed in the United States of America

For Jasper

Contents

1. PROBATION

Alex watched Amanda pull her silver Audi A5 Cabriolet into an empty parking space. It was Monday morning, just before school. Alex was seated in his usual spot under the large maple tree in front of Prestige Preparatory High School.

From here, he had an unobstructed view of the parking lot, which sat adjacent to the great lawn—commonly referred to as the Quad by the students. This parking lot was reserved for faculty members, but exceptions were made for a few students whose parents made sizeable donations to the school, like Amanda.

Amanda slammed the door closed with a metallic clap as she exited her car. Only the head cheerleader could make their drab school uniform look this good. The white shirt she wore under the grey school jacket was open down to the third button, exposing a plunging neck line. The unisex striped tie hung loosely under her shirt collar, and formed a large knot under the first fastened button. Her plaid, pleated skirt showed off her long, skinny legs, which seemed to magically lengthen with every step she took in her Mary-Janes. Her honey-blonde hair fell just below her shoulders, cascading in the light spring breeze. He watched as her skirt danced playfully around her legs, while she walked from the parking lot and across the Quad.

Alex had been committing mental images of Amanda like these to memory since the seventh grade, when they first met at Braemar Academy Middle School.

Back at Braemar, he and Amanda had become friends by chance. Alex had just moved to Northern Virginia with his mother, who was trying to get away from a defunct government funded research lab she used to work for in California. On his first day of school, the homeroom teacher had paired him up with Amanda, who was supposed to show him around until he became familiar with his surroundings and class schedule. Although Alex had told Amanda that she didn't need to show him around if she didn't want to, she had insisted on fulfilling what she called her civic duty as class president. However, when Amanda fell ill after first period, Alex carried her to the nurse's office and stayed with her until her nanny arrived. While they waited, Amanda had tried to convince Alex to return to class because he would receive a demerit for each class he missed. He received two demerits that day, but told her he would have risked expulsion just to make sure she was okay. After that day, the two were inseparable.

But even at Braemar, Alex knew that Amanda belonged to the upper echelon of society, from her fancy clothes to the car that dropped her off every morning before school, which came equipped with a personal driver. Yet, every day she made it her responsibility to usher the new boy around, even after he became fully capable of getting around by himself. Long after the other students got over his 'new kid on the block' status, he and Amanda remained friends—until they got to high school.

Prestige High was a preparatory school for college that sat on sixty-five acres of lush, green land in McLean, Virginia. In addition to the five buildings that housed the school's core academic departments, the campus also boasted two libraries, two gymnasiums, multiple sports fields and courts, three computer labs, six science labs, an art and photography studio, and a performing arts and media center. Alex was fortunate enough to be the recipient of a full scholarship and stipend to cover his tuition, books, and fees, based on his stellar grades from Braemar and a glowing letter of recommendation from Amanda's parents.

Upon entering Prestige High, Amanda was immediately sought out by the popular kids to be a part of their inner circle, the Novies—members of Northern Virginia's Elite Society. The Novies had no need for someone like Alex— the son of a single mother, with no formal education, no connections, and no money. Although Amanda was never bothered by Alex's social stature, or lack thereof, her new friends were. Alex, on the other hand, did not want Amanda ostracized because of their friendship. So, he slowly withdrew from all public social interactions with her during freshman year. Undeterred by Alex's attempt to distant himself from her, Amanda continued to reach out to him, until he made it clear that he wished to sever all ties with her just before sophomore year.

Watching her gracefully glide across the Quad, Alex still felt the large, gaping hole in his chest that was left behind when he decided to end his friendship with Amanda. *This was for her own good*, he reassured himself. One person was already dead and he was responsible for it. He couldn't bear the thought of Amanda succumbing to the same fate. For now, this was how it had to be, until he completely honed his new abilities.

The summer following their first year at Prestige High was when Alex went totally mental—literally. Amanda was off to Europe and Alex's mother enrolled him into Camp APRICOT—Axiom's Premier International Camp of Technology. After a near-death experience, he started to exhibit several paranormal mental abilities—telekinesis, pyrokinesis, telepathy, and the occasional out-of-body experience. His abilities were not of the subtle kind, where you had to wonder whether he truly possessed them or not. No. His abilities were of the fly-in-your-face, flagrant kind, where there was no mistaking they existed—and were evolving. To this day, he didn't know exactly how or why it happened. All he knew was, it happened—all at once.

His unfamiliarity with his new powers, coupled with his inability to control them, led to the death of the only friend he made at camp that year. So for the last twenty months, Alex had been living with the guilt of his friend's death and four mental abilities that seemed to be on steroids. Throw in the demanding academic schedule he had at Prestige High and he had concocted the perfect recipe for disaster. Something had to give and unfortunately, his grades and his friendship with Amanda were the casualties.

His grades plummeted from a 4.0 to 2.6 during sophomore year because he just could not concentrate on his schoolwork while keeping his abilities in check. Whenever he was in class and attempted to focus on the day's lesson, his abilities would run amok. Objects would start to levitate, smoke would emanate from objects if he looked at them too long, and random thoughts of his would get projected to the wrong person at the wrong time. Lucky for him, the other students never suspected that it was his abilities that were doing these things. They just blamed him for everything. Unlucky for him, his teachers grew tired of his distractions by spring semester and sent him to the headmaster's office.

Frequent trips to Headmaster Theodore Anderson's office placed his scholarship and stipend in serious jeopardy of being taken away. Unable to tell Headmaster Anderson the truth, Alex attributed his conduct to the death of his friend. He knew it was wrong, but he had to tell him something, and that explanation made the most logical sense. The headmaster bought it and agreed to give him more time to grieve. But he insisted that Alex start seeing Verona Lucci, one of the school's guidance counselors. He also placed Alex on academic probation.

For students receiving scholarships, being placed on academic probation meant that they had to maintain a grade point average of at least 3.4, or their scholarship would be taken away. Realizing that Alex couldn't possibly meet this grade point average by the end of sophomore year even if he received all A's in his classes, Headmaster Anderson gave him until the end of his junior year to do so.

Alex brushed aside his thoughts of the last twenty months as he continued to watch Amanda from behind the pages of his physics textbook. She had just walked up to David Locke and his friends, who were standing outside the school's main building, waiting for the bell to ring. David was the captain of the football team and the typical jock —always two French fries short of a happy meal. Alex desperately wanted to know what was up with them. David was a senior; why the hell didn't he stick to the girls in his own grade? The rumor around campus was that the jock had a thing for Amanda. *Not that I blame the guy; but still*, he thought, *Amanda deserves more than a guy who spends more time looking in the mirror than she does.*

Although they had not spoken since the last time he hung up on her, he wondered if she had heard the rumors about his bizarre behavior, like his fascination with starting fires and throwing things. More importantly, did she believe them? He never cared much of what people thought of him, but Amanda's approval was still important to him. As he watched her giggle at something the jock had just said, he got up and pushed his way to the school's entrance when the bell rang.

* * *

"Is everything okay, Alex?" asked Verona Lucci. She'd been asking this question for a year now, ever since they started their counseling sessions.

"Everything is fine, Ms. Lucci," was Alex's usual reply.

"Everything doesn't seem fine. What happened on your Spanish quiz this week? I thought we were doing so well in that subject last semester." Her face was filled with genuine concern for the student sitting across from her desk. "How do you expect to get into a decent college with these grades?"

Alex turned away from his guidance counselor and examined her tiny office. Her desk and the floor surrounding it were cluttered with piles of paper. The file cabinet to his right was bursting at the seams with files. *A small fire could really wreak havoc in such a confined space*, he thought. Fighting the temptation, he turned his attention back to Ms. Lucci and said, "I don't know."

"Alex, this is your future we're talking about. 'I don't

know' is not going to cut it." Now she really sounded like his mother. "Clearly something's wrong."

"Nothing's wrong, Ms. Lucci," Alex said, almost in a shout, as he leaned forward in his chair. "Look, I'm here because you, Headmaster Anderson, and my mother decided I needed counseling. No one asked me whether I thought I needed counseling. There is nothing wrong with me."

"Alex, you have this all wrong. We're not saying anything is wrong with you," Ms. Lucci said softly, trying to calm him down. "But your grades are slipping again, and you still have not attained a 3.4 GPA. In your defense, they are a lot better than last year's. So that's a good thing. And good job on participating more in Physics and Mechanical Drawing, and not daydreaming as much. But Headmaster Anderson only gave you until the end of the year to get off academic probation. We're already halfway through the spring semester of your junior year, and you're so close. If you'll just focus more—"

Alex stared past Ms. Lucci, tuning her out and looking through the window behind her to keep himself from exciting the atoms in the objects—and person—in front of him to the point where they all burst in flames. This was one of the methods he developed to control his pyrokinesis ability —clear your mind of the current stressor and replace it with something more tranquil.

"If you need a tutor, I can get one for you," Ms. Lucci continued. "If you need someone to talk to *about anything*. Whatever it is that you're going through, you—"

"Is that all?" Alex interrupted.

Ms. Lucci sighed heavily, then conceded, "Yes, that is all."

"Okay," he said, as he grabbed his backpack and reached for the door.

"Don't forget, we meet again Friday," Ms. Lucci yelled as Alex disappeared out the door.

"Whatever," he said from the hallway.

* * *

Alex hated people trying to pry into his psyche. What if they had the same abilities he had? His mind would be like putty in their hands. As he exited the main entrance to Prestige High, he unconsciously headed to the football field behind the building. School had been over for about half an hour now, but there were still a few students standing around in the schoolyard.

Although he had nothing more pressing to do, he didn't like meeting with the toy shrink after school, twice per week. Why couldn't she keep their sessions focused on his grade, which he thought he had done a remarkable job of improving from a 2.6 to 3.1? Did she even know how much energy he had to exert into taming his abilities to the point where he could concentrate on his classwork to get those grades? You can't exactly relax your mind while trying to solve a polynomial equation. And now she wanted to talk about "whatever you're going through." *Lady, you know nothing about what I'm going through*, he thought.

He faced the football field, where the players were warming up to practice for tomorrow's game against a rival team. The cheerleading squad was also there practicing their routine for the game as well. Alex stopped breathing when he saw Amanda on top of a pyramid of girls. At the base of the pyramid were three scrawny girls positioned to catch Amanda when she free-fall off the top.

You better not make her fall, Alex accidentally projected.

Just then, all three girls simultaneously turned to look where Alex was standing, approximately 100-ft away, not realizing that Amanda had started her free fall off the pyramid. Alex gasped and then focused his energy on Amanda's falling body, which instantly slowed in mid-air, as if being lowered by a cable. Unsure of what had caused their distraction, the three girls returned their attention back to their post and stretched out their hands as Amanda plummeted into them. The girl in the middle caught Amanda under the arms, and the other two caught Amanda around the hips and thighs. Relieved, Alex watched as Amanda bounced out of the cradle and continued with the cheer, like nothing happened. Realizing the distraction he had created, Alex decided that it would be safer for everyone if he retreated from school grounds.

Walking across the Quad, Alex contemplated heading home. But home was not where he wanted to be right now. Ever since the emergence of his abilities, he had come to the resolution that as long as he and "they" had to cohabitate in the same body, he had better learn how to cope with them. After Camp APRICOT, he searched the internet, trying to find out as much information as he could about his new abilities. He found nothing that could explain how he went from zero to sixty on the paranormal phenomenon scale. Instead, he found hints of what he thought could help him cope with them. He learned that the more tense or anxious he became, the less control he had over them. If he exerted too much of his abilities, his nose bled. The key to honing his abilities was to relax—not necessarily his body, but his mind. As a result, Alex found himself engaging in various meditation techniques and breathing exercises when the opportunity presented itself throughout the day. One proven way for Alex to relax his mind was to get engulfed in a tranquil scenery—real or imagined.

During classes, he had to settle for envisioning imaginary sceneries, which some interpreted as him daydreaming. Right now he opted for reality, and took the city bus to the Meadowland Botanical Gardens. The Gardens always had a soothing effect on him. And after the little mishap at the football field, he needed to put his mind at ease. The one caveat with relaxing was, it facilitated his out-of-body ability.

At the admissions booth, Alex fished out his annual pass and made his way into the Gardens. This time of year, the Gardens boasted a robust assortment of flowers. The brilliant yellow daffodils bowed gracefully and smiled as he walked by them. Hues of vibrant red, pink, green, plum, and white danced before his eyes as he neared the tulips, Lenten roses, magnolias, flowering cherries, and Potomac Valley native wildflowers. Minor bulbs decorated rock gardens and carpeted the grounds surrounding the conifers collections. Alex found a bench in the shade, facing the picturesque landscape, where traces of zesty citrus, vanilla undertones, and subtly fruity fragrances floated in the air around him. While the wind massaged his face, he closed his eyes and allowed his head to fall back against the top rail of the bench. Slowly, he allowed his body to go limp and his mind to fade away into blackness.

Alex watched as his body lay unconscious on the bench below him. By now, he had learned that it wasn't safe for him to wander far away from his body when he was in this state, especially in public; but he couldn't help it. He propelled himself down to the edge of the lake, watching a group of ducks bathe themselves. Occasionally, he threw a glance over to the bench where his body lay, but then returned his attention back to the ducks, which were now frolicking in the lake. His fascination with the ducks was interrupted by a chubby, freckled boy, who gently placed a boat in the lake. The little boy retrieved a remote control from his backpack and started the engine on the toy boat. Alex watched as the boy chuckled with delight as he chased the ducks around the lake with the boat. Whenever the boat smashed into the ducks, the little boy rejoiced with glee. Alex was not amused.

What would be the best way to teach this little runt a lesson? Alex thought, when he saw the boat going after another brood of ducklings. Alex thought about reuniting with his body before confronting the little boy, but that would take more time than the ducklings had. With deep concentration, Alex focused his gaze on the tiny boat in the lake. A few seconds later, the boat burst into flames.

Alex's body jolted awake as he reentered it. He heard the chubby little boy scream and cry for his parents. He looked toward the pond, where the little boy cried in his father's arms as they watched the small inferno on the lake. Alex smiled and headed for the exit.

* * *

Alex arrived home at 6:53 p.m. He usually got home before his mother, even when he made the occasional detour after school. Today was no different. His objective for the next two hours was to do his homework, find something to eat, shower, and get into bed before his mother arrived. He hoped that the sight of him sleeping would be enough to deter her from lecturing him again about his grades.

Alex loved his mother, but you couldn't tell from the way he treated her over the last year or so. He acknowledged that his mother only wanted the best for him. But he didn't like the fact that she had to work those crazy, long hours at that law firm in DC to keep him in Prestige. He would have been fine with going to public school. A diploma from any high school, public or private, was still a high school diploma. Even a GED, or "good enough diploma" as he referred to it, performed the same function in his opinion.

Margaret Fuller refused to give in to her son's rationale to send him to public school. She would always rebut his argument by pointing to the law firm where she worked. A degree from a prestigious school meant that you got an office with a view and billed clients $350 per hour, whereas all others sat in cubicles and did more work than those with the offices, but got paid $35 per hour. She didn't care how much Alex resisted; he was staying at Prestige.

Alex walked into the kitchen and placed some penne pasta in a pot filled with boiling water. Then he walked over to the refrigerator to find something to drink, and the meat sauce his mother had made yesterday. Seven minutes later, he drained water from the pot, tossed some meat sauce on the pasta, and mixed it around. In three more minutes, dinner was served. Being the only child of a single parent who was rarely home, Alex had grown quite resourceful and independent.

He grabbed his backpack and walked into the dining area, pulling out his physics textbook and placing it across the table from his plate. He pulled out a chair, sat down, and turned his textbook to the day's lesson. After sprinkling parmesan cheese on his meal, Alex realized he had forgotten to get a fork. He turned his attention back to the kitchen and saw the cutlery drawer. Slowly, the drawer opened. From memory, Alex visualized where in the drawer the forks were. Just then, a fork emerged out of the drawer and floated over to the dining area. He grabbed the fork when it was within reach and scarfed down his dinner, while flipping through his physics textbook, making notes for his project on explosive devises.

His pyrokinesis ability had evolved to the point where he could create explosions. His sudden interest in explosions was to determine whether he could replicate the same amount of force in various types of explosive devices. After he was done with Physics, he spent the next hour studying his other subjects, but still found it difficult to concentrate on English Lit and Spanish—the two subjects he was least interested in.

In his bathroom, Alex turned on the faucet, letting the water run until a suitable temperature was achieved. Catching a glimpse of his reflection in the mirror as he undressed, Alex stopped and looked at himself. He watched as his pupils danced around in his eyes, as he reflected back on today's events at the football field and the Gardens. Alex liked to end each day with reflecting on what he learned about his powers and how he could better control them. This had helped because he was almost at the point where he could control them at will. But every so often, he got distracted or overly anxious and his abilities would take center stage again.

Today, he had made a thought slip from him to those

three girls. We must do better in this area, he noted. Did we really need to set that little boy's boat on fire to teach him a lesson? He struggled with an answer to this question. As he stepped into the shower, the only answer he could come up with was, maybe.

After his shower, Alex got into bed, just before his mother got home. The alarm system chimed when she opened the door to their small townhouse in Vienna, Virginia.

"Alex," she called. He didn't answer. He heard her climbing the stairs and walking to his bedroom. He heard when she stopped outside his door. There was no doubt in his mind that she was reading the sign posted on his door again.

NO TRESPASSING: VIOLATORS WILL BE SHOT.
SURVIVORS WILL BE SHOT AGAIN.

Quietly, she opened the door and walked over to his bed. Alex could feel her looking down at him. Slowly, she turned around and exited as quietly as she had entered.

Works every time, Alex thought, after his mother closed the door.

* * *

Alex was seated at the small island in the kitchen when Margaret came downstairs the following morning. He was eating cereal. He had even put on his mother's favorite brand of coffee to brew in her coffee pot.

"Alex," she said, tousling his long hair as she walked behind him.

"Mom," he responded, without pulling his gaze away from the newspaper in front of him.

Margaret retrieved a mug from the cupboard and poured coffee as she watched Alex shovel more cereal in his mouth. She shook her head and returned the coffee pot to the warming plate. Alex braced himself for the conversation yet to come, as Margaret pulled out a stool across from him.

"So, how are we today?" she asked.

"I'm fine. And you?"

"I'm good," was her response. Alex pretended to be preoccupied with the newspaper. "Anything of interest in there?" Margaret added.

"Not really; just your regular dose of political bullshit, corporate greed, environmental atrocities, and celebrity gossip."

"Oh, just your typical news of the day," she said, taking a sip of her coffee. "You know, we didn't finish our conversation from the other day."

No response.

"Your probationary period is almost up, and Ms. Lucci tells me that you're still a few tenths of a point shy of obtaining that 3.4 GPA."

"Mom, come on. Not that again," Alex said, throwing down his spoon in the empty bowl.

"Alex, tell me what else I am supposed to talk about," Margaret said calmly. "You know we need that scholarship."

"I know, Mom, and I'm really trying. It's just..."

"Are you seeing Justin in your dreams again?"

Alex stopped breathing when he heard the name of his deceased friend. Who would have thought that Justin was just as good a friend to Alex in death as he was alive? His

death had been the perfect cover story to conceal his abilities. He found it ironic that they were the same abilities that
led to Justin's death.

"Sometimes," he whispered, which was technically true.

"Do you think it's time we reconsidered getting some
more professional help?"

"No, Mom. The toy shrink will—"

"Will you stop calling Ms. Lucci that?"

"Sorry," he said. "The semester is not over yet. So I'll
just have to try a little harder."

"That's all I ask, kiddo," she said. "I don't like having
these types of conversations about your grades or Justin
any more than you do. But graduating from Prestige will
open so many doors for you. And as for Justin—" Margaret
put her hand on her son's shoulder as he tried to get up
from the island. "Sit down."

Alex complied, averting his gaze from hers.

"Tell you what," she continued. "I'll lay off the grades
conversations and wait until the end of the semester. But
you have to promise me—"

"I will, I will," he said, knowing she wanted him to
promise to study harder. "I'll find some way to get to 3.4, I
promise."

"And as for Justin, I know you miss him, sweetheart,
but he'd want you to move on too."

"Fine," he said.

"Will you stop saying that? Fine. I'm fine. It's fine," she
said, trying to lighten the mood. "I'm beginning to think
those are the only words in your vocabulary. And I'm not
sending you to Prestige to come out with the vocabulary of
a dolt."

"Very well, Mother," he said, mimicking some of his preppy classmates. "Is that better?"

"Yes … that's fine," Margaret said, imitating him.

Alex got up from the island.

"Hey, I'm not done yet," Margaret called after Alex, who was putting his bowl in the sink. "I need something in return from you, for *temporarily* waiving my parental right to pry into every aspect of your academic life whenever I feel like it."

"And what could that be, pray tell?"

Margaret walked over to Alex. Breaking down the collar on his school jacket, she said, "I need you to work on your social skills."

"That's it?" Alex asked.

"That's it."

"But my social skills are fine." Alex chuckled. "Lots of kids go through high school without making any friends and they turn out okay."

"Don't play with me, young man. Your social skills are not fine," she said sternly. "Networking is just as important as getting good grades in this town, if not more so. Don't forget, it's not only about what you know…"

"It's who you know," they said simultaneously.

"Got it," he said, grabbing his backpack and heading for the door.

"Do you want a ride to school?"

"No. I'll take the bus."

"Don't forget to get a haircut this week," she yelled as Alex closed the front door.

2. UNANSWERED QUESTIONS

Ever since his conversation with his mother, Alex made a concerted effort to focus more on his school work. Before he knew it, it was Friday and he was looking forward to the weekend. His mother had to work this weekend, which meant he could go back to the Gardens, or some other tranquil setting.

As he walked down the hallway toward his homeroom, Alex saw Ms. Sprung—his homeroom teacher—Ms. Graham—Amanda's homeroom teacher—and Ms. Lucci talking. When Ms. Lucci's eyes met his, she ended the conversation and headed in his direction.

Oh crap, the day hasn't even really started yet, Alex thought.

"Good morning, Alex," Ms. Lucci said as she walked by him.

"Good morning, Ms. Lucci," Alex responded, looking confused when she passed him.

What the hell was that all about? he wondered. *I guess I'll find out later during our session.*

* * *

Amanda got summoned to Ms. Lucci's office during homeroom. Leslie Knolls, a fellow cheerleader, chose to accompany her to the counselor's office.

"Why does she need to see you anyway?" she asked. "She's not even our guidance counselor."

"I don't know," Amanda replied.

"Weird."

Everything was weird in Leslie's universe if she couldn't figure it out, which happened a lot. If she couldn't find a word to rhyme with hoorah for a cheer, it was weird. If she thought she correctly answered every question on an exam, but scored only a 75, that was weird. If she couldn't figure out why David Locke was attracted to Amanda and not her, it was … you guessed it.

"I think this is her office," Leslie announced, as they stood before room 249.

"Yes, I think it is," Amanda said. "I'll see you later in Trig. This shouldn't take long."

Amanda walked into the small lounge area outside Ms. Lucci's office.

"Miss Bridgewater," Ms. Lucci said with a smile from behind her desk. "Please come in. Have a seat."

"Thanks," Amanda said, sitting down.

Ms. Lucci cleared her desk of the small pile of paper she had on her desk. *I guess Ms. Lucci didn't get the memo about Prestige's paperwork reduction efforts*, Amanda thought. She watched as the guidance counselor minimized the programs she had opened on her computer screen before turning to face her.

"So, how are classes?" Ms. Lucci asked.

"Classes are great. How's work?" Amanda retorted.

"Great," she answered, with widened eyes. "So, I bet you're just wondering why I called you here today."

"The thought did cross my mind."

"Well, I wanted to talk about your extracurricular activities."

That through Amanda for a loop. "What about my extracurricular activities?"

"I noticed that you're still on the cheerleading squad and the school newspaper, but you didn't sign up for the Big Sister program or offer to tutor this semester. Were they getting in the way of your studies?"

The Big Sister and Big Brother program was where juniors and seniors volunteered to mentor incoming freshmen of the same sex, to get them acclimated to life at Prestige High. The program was a huge success. It improved retention and promoted comradery among the student body.

"Not at all, Ms. Lucci. It's just that my little sister really didn't need me after the fall semester. Trust me, Kayla is as well-adjusted as any junior or senior I know. As for tutoring, I didn't sign up again because I didn't get anyone last semester due to the shortage of students needing—wait," she said as she thought for a moment. "Well, there was Dylan Bradshaw. And let's just say, he wasn't interested in being tutored in any subjects Prestige offers."

"Are you saying that if there was someone who needed a tutor, you'd be willing to volunteer?"

"Sure," she said. "Who's the student? And please don't say Dylan."

"Alex Fuller."

"Alex?" she exclaimed, nearly jumping out of her seat.

"Yes. Did I say something wrong?"

"No," she said calmly, taking her emotions off display. "It's just that I haven't spoken to Alex in a while."

"Yes, I've noticed. Did you two have a fight or something?"

Amanda wished they had had a fight, because at least then she'd know why Alex went all M.I.A. on her. At first, he wouldn't return her calls, then he hung up on her. He had totally ignored her the last few times she waved to him around campus. He had even moved and didn't tell her. Imagine how stupid she had felt when the new occupants of his old apartment opened their front door to find her there, holding a bunch of flowers as a peace offering for him. The absolute last straw was when she had invited him to her sweet sixteen party last year and he didn't even call to tell her he wasn't coming.

"No, there wasn't a fight." Just a whole lot of unanswered questions and frustration.

"Okay." Amanda heard the inflection in Ms. Lucci's voice and could feel the counselor's eyes on her. "If you don't want to do this, I'll understand. Although, I hope you'll agree to tutor him."

Amanda sat expressionless and still.

"The thing is," Ms. Lucci continued. "I'm running out of options here. As you know, Alex is a very private person. 'Social recluse by choice,' he calls it. He doesn't really let anyone into his world much. But you two were friends once. Your parents even provided a letter of recommendation for him to attend Prestige. I just figured that it might be easier for him to accept being tutored by you."

"Ms. Lucci, I don't think I can help you or Alex."

"You think, or you know?" she asked.

An answer didn't readily present itself to Amanda.

"Look, if Alex doesn't improve his grades by the end of the semester, he'll lose his scholarship."

"But if he loses his scholarship, he'll get kicked out of Prestige!" Amanda fired back.

"Precisely my point," Ms. Lucci said, sitting back in her chair.

"Okay, I'll do it."

* * *

Amanda walked along the empty hallway to first period, which had already started. Her heels gently tapped the shiny beige ceramic-tiled floor. She couldn't stop thinking about what Ms. Lucci had just said. Alex was on the verge of flunking out of Prestige. *How is that even possible?* Alex was one of the smartest people she knew. And his mother—this couldn't be going over well with her. Was this why he was avoiding her? Although she was still pretty mad at him, she didn't want him to flunk out of school. She would have to put aside her feelings and help her friend. Besides, if Alex was flunking out, there had to be a good reason. And she was determined to find out.

* * *

At 3:44 p.m., Alex arrived at Ms. Lucci's office to find her eagerly waiting for him. She seemed so excited.

"Come in, Alex," she yelled.

Alex walked through the door, taking off his backpack.

"You're late. Your gym class ended at 3:15."

"I know," he said. "I had another nosebleed after gym today."

"Did you go to the nurse?"

"What's the point?"

"You know, Coach Klutsky said you could have been an excellent athlete, if it wasn't for your nosebleeds."

Well, Coach Klutsky doesn't have to control four psychic abilities while having balls thrown at his face. "Yeah, I know," he replied.

"Sit down, Alex. This is going to be a short meeting today," she said, rearranging the documents on her desk. "I need to tell you something."

"I have something to tell you, too," Alex replied.

"What is it?" she asked.

He wanted to tell her about the agreement he and his mother brokered earlier that week, but decided against it.

"No, ladies first," he said, motioning to her. He was in a gentlemanly mood this afternoon.

"Remember our discussion Tuesday about getting you a tutor to help with your grades?"

"Yeah, I remember *your* suggestion to get me a tutor."

"Well, I think I found one for you," she said giddily.

"Uhh, about that…" Alex started.

"Amanda Bridgewater has agreed to become your tutor," she spouted.

Alex knew he had heard the name Amanda Bridgewater, but was unsure of the context. "What did you say about Amanda?" he asked, begging for clarification.

Ms. Lucci repeated her last statement, which caused Alex's mouth to drop open as he grasped its meaning. "Why … eh hem … why would Amanda want to tutor me?"

"Because I asked her," she replied.

Count, one, two, three, Alex said to himself. Why did the mention of her name send his heart into overdrive? Once he got his heartbeat under control again, he tried to mask his excitement behind a somber face.

"Did you hear what I said?" Ms. Lucci said, waving at him.

"I heard what you said, but I don't understand."

"Before you get all bent out of shape about this, I think this will be a good thing for you. Amanda is smart and sociable, and you two were friends before, right?"

Alex nodded.

"She will tutor you in the subjects you're having difficulty with, and hopefully, your interaction with her will provide you with an outlet to better cope with what you're going through." She paused to register the puzzled look on Alex's face, and then added. "This will only be temporary, until you get off probation. If it doesn't work, then we'll try something else. Okay?"

"Okay."

"Now, what did you want to tell me?" she added.

"Uhh, I forgot," he lied convincingly.

"Before our next meeting, I want you to get in touch with Amanda and work out a schedule with her for your tutoring session. You are free to use the lounge area outside my office for your sessions, or the study hall. You don't have to pay Amanda. She'll receive community service credit for this. That is all," she added dismissively.

Alex got up and head for the door. "Have a good weekend, Ms. Lucci."

"You do the same. And say hi to your mom for me," she called after him.

* * *

Alex walked out of the building, replaying the conversation he'd just had with Ms. Lucci over in his head. Amanda Bridgewater was supposed to tutor him. The same Amanda who was kind to him when he first moved to Virginia. The same Amanda whom he pushed away to save her from himself and his entourage of psychic abilities. Sure, it would be nice to talk and be around her again, but would it still be the same Amanda he had known? High school had a funny way of changing people—and not for the better sometimes. And let's not forget the way he had treated her for the last year and a half. What if she started to ask questions about his anti-social behavior? He wouldn't lie to her, but he couldn't tell her the truth either.

Why didn't he tell Ms. Lucci that he was going to try harder to get his grades back up as a part of his agreement with his mother? Now he was paired up with Amanda again and there was nothing he could do about it. Better yet, there was nothing he *wanted* to do about it. To prepare for the coming week, Alex decided to spend the entire weekend at the Gardens.

* * *

Monday morning, Alex took his usual seat underneath the large maple tree in front of Prestige. He hadn't spent as much time as he'd wanted to this past weekend at the Gardens. To his mother's delight, she hadn't had to work on Sunday. Margaret made it perfectly clear that she intended to spend the entire day with her favorite little man. They started out with brunch at IHOP after sleeping in late, and then ended the day with a Nationals' baseball game. Alex couldn't understand why major league players got paid so much money to play a child's game when most of them spent their time on the bench recovering from various ailments. Not wanting to thwart his mother's good intentions, he played along and tried to look surprised when the home team lost. So enthralled with his weekend memories, Alex didn't notice Amanda walking across the schoolyard toward him. She was right on top of him before he noticed her.

"Hey, you," she said, bumping him on the shoulder with her leg. "Love what you've done with the tree."

Alex looked up at her, realizing that she was referring to the red maple tree he was sitting under, which was in full bloom.

"Oh yeah, I had ole Acer here put on a new coat of leaves since you were coming over," Alex said, smiling.

"Acer? You named the tree Acer?" Amanda said with a laugh.

"Yeah. His full name is Acer Rubrum, which is Latin for red maple," Alex responded, giving her his full attention.

"I see. So you just go around calling trees by their Latin names and hanging out with them?" she added.

"No, just this tree."

"Why this tree?"

"You see this thin bark that it has?" he said, turning to face the tree.

Amanda nodded as she stepped closer to examine the tree and its bark.

"Well that makes it very sensitive to fire—"

"Yeah, it's a tree … made of wood. Of course it's going to be sensitive to fire," Amanda said sarcastically.

"True, all wood eventually burns when set on fire, but the red maple is a bit different. It is highly intolerant of fire. In fact, up until a century ago, they used to be restricted to swamps. But with modern fire suppression methods, these swamp things have been on the increase in northeastern forests, like those found in Virginia, and have even popped up on landscapes such as this," he said, motioning toward the school ground like a game show host. "My friend Acer here is a real ecological wonder. He doesn't require much water, nutrients, or even light to survive in a place like this."

"And the syrup his sap makes tastes great on my pancakes too," Amanda said as they both laughed.

"So, what else have you been up to besides hanging out with Acer?" Amanda asked.

"Nothing much. Just trying to do my time here at Prestige with as little interference from the warden or the other inmates as possible," he said, his head nodding in the direction of the Quad, which was filled with Novies.

Amanda smiled. "So, are you really going to make me wrestle this out of you?"

"Amanda, whatever do you mean?" Alex said in his best British accent.

"Well, a little birdie told me that you've been having trouble with your classes."

"A little Italian birdie, in heels and glasses, about yay high?" he said, holding his hand, palm down, about four feet from the ground.

"One and the same," she replied, tossing her hair to the side. "What's up with that?"

Alex shrugged his shoulders and averted his gaze away from Amanda, who had dropped her bag on the ground next to him, so she could sit on it.

"Ms. Lucci told me you were flunking out of school. That makes absolutely no sense and you know it."

Alex did not respond.

"She asked me to *tutor* you," Amanda continued. "I agreed, because one, I don't want you to flunk out of school; and two, if I didn't, she would have found someone else, and I know you wouldn't want one of your Novies friends doing it."

Getting no response from the boy next to her, she pressed on. "I also agreed because I've missed you. Once upon a time, we were best friends, but now we don't even say anything to each other."

Amanda paused, watching Alex as he continued to stare at the entrance to the school.

"Amanda, don't blame yourself for this. This has nothing to do with you," he said, finally returning her gaze. "You have always been a good friend, and I'm sorry for not returning your calls or telling you I moved. I just needed some alone time."

"It's been over a year now. Alone time is over," she said, pulling at his arm. "Listen, the bell is going to ring soon, but we need to get together and come up with a game plan to tackle your class work."

"Game plan? Tackle my class work?" he said laughing. "What are you—a cheerleader or the quarterback? And who told you that I'm agreeing to this whole tutoring thing?"

"This is not a request, Fuller," she said, shaking her head. "We are going to go over every subject you have and study the material until it oozes out of your ears and your grades are back up to par. Understand?" She watched as Alex smiled, but when she got no verbal response, she stuck her finger in his ear, twisting it around until he fell on the ground laughing. She didn't stop until he succumbed to her demand.

"Okay, okay," he said.

This was the Amanda Bridgewater he knew, and he was

glad to have her back. Just then, the bell rang. They got up, gathered their bags, and headed toward the main building.

"Ms. Lucci wanted me to work out a schedule with you for the tutoring sessions. She wants it by tomorrow when I meet with her after class," Alex said.

"I have cheerleading practice today during seventh period, but we usually run a little late, so I won't be done until 3:30-ish. Why don't we meet after that?" Amanda said as they neared the entrance to Prestige. "Are you going to be around here at that time, or do you want me to meet you at your new undisclosed home?"

"Why don't we meet at my house, so your friends won't see you hanging around the weird kid?" Alex said, looking at David and two of his steroid-prone buddies, who had not taken their eyes off him and Amanda since they left the cover of the large maple tree.

Amanda followed Alex's gaze. "Oh please, don't worry about them. Do you honestly believe I'm the kind of girl who cares what a jock thinks of her?"

"Correction, jocks like David don't think." They both laughed loudly enough for David and his goons to hear.

"Hi, Amanda," Leslie said, who now joined the three jocks at the bottom of the stairs. The inquisition in her face and voice was daunting.

"Hey, Leslie," Amanda said to her, and then returned her attention to Alex. "Okay, so see you later at your…"

"Townhouse," he responded, filling in the blank for her. "My mom got us a townhouse over in Vienna."

"That's awesome," she spewed. Amanda still remembered the tiny one-bedroom apartment he and his mother had shared in a not-so-nice neighborhood when they first moved to Virginia.

"I'll send you a text with the address."

"No problem."

"See you, Amanda," he said as he walked by the quartet on the stairs and headed for his homeroom.

* * *

Amanda acted oblivious to the accusatory stares she got after Alex left her by the stairs at the entrance to Prestige High.

David was the first to break the silence. "What's up, Amanda?"

"Hi, David. Did you have a good weekend?"

"Uhh, yeah," he responded. His face couldn't conceal his disappointment that Amanda had turned him down for another date to the movies on Saturday. "So, Fuller's your new BFF now?" he snickered.

"I'm surprised you even know his name," Amanda replied.

"Of course I know his name. They're always wiping up his blood from off the gym floor," David said, elbowing his friend Timothy Waltz, who stood closest to him.

Amanda rolled her eyes, and said, "Alex and I have been friends since the seventh grade, and we're still friends."

"Funny, none of us have seen you two hanging out lately," he said. "Can't be much of a friendship then, can it?"

"Yeah, well we've both been busy—"

"I guess being a freak is a full time job," Rafi al-Sharif, David's other teammate, blurted out, which caused an eruption of laughter from the quartet.

"You guys are idiots," Amanda said, pushing past them to enter the building.

Leslie rushed to Amanda's side and the two walked down the hallway together. "Please tell me I have nothing to worry about with you and freak-boy rekindling your old friendship."

"What does my friendship with Alex—or anyone for that matter—have to do with you?" Amanda retorted.

"Relax. I'm not the bad guy here. I'm just saying, your friend is a little creepy," Leslie said sharply.

"Creepy how?" she asked as the anger grew inside her.

"He's always by himself."

"I'm still waiting on the creepy part, Les."

"He ... he's always daydreaming."

"And?"

"I can't put my finger on it, but he's ... he's ... he's just weird. Plus, he's not typical Prestige material, if you know what I mean," she said dizzily. In an attempt to disguise her snobbery, she added, "If it makes you feel better, he is kind of cute though."

"No Les, that doesn't make me feel better," Amanda said as they stopped outside their homeroom. "Geesh, you can be so shallow sometimes."

"Look, I'm just being honest with you," she said, trying to sound sincere. "What kind of friend would I be if I can't speak my mind around you?"

"Thank you for your concern. Your objection to my friendship with Alex has been duly noted," she said, as they entered their homeroom.

* * *

Alex watched from his living room window as Amanda's silver Audi pulled into his driveway. The first time he recalled seeing her car was last October, the weekend after Amanda's sweet sixteen birthday party. Although he was invited to the birthday gala, he did not attend. A sudden feeling of guilt washed over him when Amanda stepped out of the car.

"Hi, Amanda," he said, opening the door before she had a chance to ring the doorbell.

"Hey, Alex."

"Come on in."

"Thanks."

Amanda stepped into the small foyer where Alex stood, looking over the space with an approving eye.

"I like," she finally said, walking down the short hallway to the kitchen and living area.

"Yeah, me too," Alex chimed in. "It's way better than that apartment we use to live in."

Without commenting on his last statement, Amanda asked, "Where do you want me—living room or dining room?"

"Uhh, the table in the dining area is fine." Alex grabbed his backpack from off the couch and headed over to the table. "Nice car, by the way."

"Yeah, I got it for my birthday last year," she said. "Speaking of which, why didn't you come to my party? I know you got my invitation."

Amanda had no way of knowing that Alex actually got her invitation after she placed it in the mail, but her way of getting the truth out of someone was to make a statement and wait for a reaction, instead of asking questions.

Wow, I walked right into that one, Alex thought. "I wasn't feeling well that weekend," was all he could come up with, as he sat down in the chair across the table from Amanda.

"Liar," she said, moving the fruit bowl that separated them. "Why didn't you come? It was my sweet sixteen."

"I'm sorry, Mandy," he said, searching for the right words to say. "I just wasn't up for it."

"Do you know you are the only person outside of my immediate family that I allow to call me Mandy?"

"Yeah, I remember," he smiled, honored to have such a privilege.

"Well, let bygones be bygones. I'm willing to forgive you for all your transgressions toward me over the last couple of years, but I will need an explanation … soon."

"Always a stipulation with you, isn't there?"

"Well, you shouldn't expect something for nothing," she said, taking out her laptop. "Now, what classes are you taking?"

"Algebra II, Advanced Physics II, English Lit, Advanced Spanish, Diplomatic History, and Mechanical Drawing, but I don't need any help in physics or mechanical drawing. And of course there's lunch and gym, but unless you were going to teach me how to hold a fork or dribble a ball, I think we can rule out those two as well."

"Ha ha, very funny. I've had everything except for Diplomatic History and Mechanical Drawing. What are those?"

"Mechanical drawing basically covers technical drawing used by architects and engineers."

"So you draw blueprints?"

"Exactly. Blueprints of small objects though, nothing as lavish as designing a bridge or car yet. Personally, I like to design interlocking mechanisms."

"You mean locks?"

"Yeah, but more like safes or vaults."

"Interesting. And Diplomatic History?"

"In that class, we study international relations between countries over time. But instead of focusing solely on events, we focus on the decision makers behind the events, like presidents, monarchs, and other high rulers, and how they employ diplomacy to resolve conflict. Think President Theodore Roosevelt and his Big Stick policy."

"What brought on the interest in that subject?"

"Mechanical Drawing?" he responded, knowing full well that was not the subject Amanda was referring to.

"No, your Diplomatic History class."

Amanda's father was a diplomat from England, or at least that's how he held himself out to the public. He had married her mother, a former beauty queen and heiress to a large fortune, only after she got pregnant with Amanda.

For some reason, Amanda's life intrigued Alex. He was especially intrigued by her father, who seemed to operate under a cloak of secrecy all the time. Although he'd been to her house on several occasions in the past, he still wanted to know more about what happened behind those tall wrought-iron fences when no visitors were around.

"Nothing in particular," he lied, and then added, "Just wanted to learn history from another perspective, I guess."

"Oh," said Amanda, looking a bit disappointed.

"Do you want something to drink?" Alex said, trying to change the subject after seeing the expression on her face.

"Sure. You have any Bling?" she asked absently.

The mention of the forty-dollars-per-bottle water caused Alex to stop in his tracks. "Uhh ... you know what, we just ran out," he said sarcastically. "Actually, my mom just used the last bottle to water the plants this morning."

Amanda must have realized her blunder, because she smiled and said, "I'll have whatever you're having."

For the next two and a half hours, Alex and Amanda drafted a schedule, detailing when they would meet and what subjects they would cover. They agreed to meet on Tuesdays and Thursdays, because Amanda didn't have cheerleading practice those days, and one day on the weekend, depending on her schedule. Because Amanda had never taken Mechanical Drawing or Diplomatic History, it was Alex's job to teach her what he had learned. Amanda believed that in teaching her these subjects, Alex would develop a better understanding of them. They then went over each subject, focusing on areas that he was having difficulty understanding. Amanda declined from giving Alex a quiz today, realizing that the clock in the kitchen was inching its way toward six. Instead, she packed up her books and laptop as Alex placed their empty glasses in the sink.

"Next time, we should focus more on Spanish," Amanda decided. "That's the subject I think you need the most help with, especially the proper use of your verbs."

"I can't thank you enough for agreeing to do this. I owe you big time."

"De nada, mi amigo," she responded, with a huge smile on her face.

As Alex walked her to the door, she added, "Oh, I meant to ask you if you're coming to the lacrosse game Friday night."

"Lacrosse game?" he asked, a bit surprised. "You cheer for the lacrosse team too?" he added with a snicker.

"Why not? They are a part of our school," she retorted, punching him in the arm for the condescending remark. "They need love too. Besides, what would we do in the spring, when it's off-season for football and basketball? It's not like we can cheer for the baseball team."

"I guess you're right."

"So, you're coming, right?"

Alex stopped just short of the door. "I don't think so, Mandy."

"Why not? Give me one good reason why you won't come to the game."

"It's just not my scene. Plus, I don't want to draw anymore unnecessary attention to you."

"Well, make it your scene and stop worrying about me," she said, facing him. "Now give us a hug."

Alex grabbed Amanda in a bear hug, lifting her off her feet to meet his six-foot stature. Overcome by the inebriating smell of her hair, Alex carelessly allowed a thought—*the smell of your hair is so intoxicating*—to slip from him.

"Well, I'm glad you like it," Amanda responded.

Shocked by her response, Alex released his grip on Amanda, causing her to fall to the ground.

"Alex, what the hell?" she yelled, as she landed on her backside on the floor.

"I'm so sorry. I didn't mean to…" was all he could say, as he watched her scramble to her feet.

"You didn't mean to do what?" she said, looking at Alex, perplexed by his cowering demeanor.

"Nothing," Alex said, opening the door for her. "Good night, Amanda."

Amanda stopped and looked at Alex, who had become ghostly pale.

"It's no big deal," she said. "In fact, I fall all the time in cheerleading practice," she added, obviously trying to put Alex at ease, but failed miserably.

"Thanks again for coming," he said, opening the door even wider, just in case Amanda didn't get the hint.

Unsure of herself, Amanda quietly said good night. Standing on the porch, Amanda turned around and looked at her friend, who now seemed devoid of any sustenance. "Alex, if something was wrong, you would tell me, right?"

Unable to meet her gaze, Alex's eyes fell on the brown leather bag Amanda had slung over her shoulder. He kept perfectly still, without saying a word or returning her gaze. Amanda stretched out her right hand, placing the palm against Alex's left cheek.

"In your own time then," she said, as Alex hastily closed the door behind her.

* * *

You idiotic moron! What the hell were you thinking? Alex scolded himself as he walked toward the kitchen. *Your hair is so intoxicating? I thought we agreed no weird stuff; no more accidental projection. This was a bad idea. I should have never agreed to let Amanda tutor me,* he thought, leaning against the counter in the kitchen. *There's no way this is going to end well. I have to get Ms. Lucci to change her mind about this,* he decided. *And if she refuses, I'll just have to change it for her,* he added, referring to his telepathic ability, which had evolved to include full-blown mind compulsion.

Content with the resolution he came up with, he started his daily ritual of hunting for dinner. A sandwich would have to do, because he didn't feel like cooking pasta again. As he gathered the ingredients to make his turkey sandwich on rye bread, he thought about Amanda. Amanda was incredibly inquisitive. Having her around tutoring him would constantly put his abilities at risk of being discovered. And what if she found out? Then what? She'd freak out, that's what. She would either end up in an asylum trying to convince some shrink of what she'd discovered, or she could end up dead in a river gorge, like Justin. The look in Justin's eyes as he fell to his death reemerged vividly in Alex's mind. He closed his eyes, hoping that the tears that welled up inside would wash away the image. Amanda could never suffer the same fate.

"Well, that's decided then," he said, as he ate his sandwich, watching the evening news, then an episode of *Family Guy*. As he climbed into bed later that night, one of his day's reflections puzzled him. He had spent almost three hours studying with Amanda, yet he didn't have to exert any energy at all to keep his abilities under control. Interesting.

* * *

Alex got to school eight minutes early the next day, and as usual headed for his tree. Several yards away, he realized that there was someone already sitting under it. Alex stopped and looked around him to make sure no one was watching. Satisfied, he turned his attention to the figure under the tree. Before he could mentally persuade the figure to leave, it got up and stepped out of the shade of the tree. It was Amanda.

"Hey. Acer and I were wondering when you'd get here," she said with a smile.

"So now you're hanging out with trees?" Alex said, and

then shook his head. "I knew I'd be a bad influence on you." He grinned as he walked toward her.

"Honestly, Alex, I'm not that easily swayed."

"So what are you doing here?"

"Just wanted to make sure we were okay."

"Don't you mean—if *I'm* okay?"

"Whatever. I just don't want you to go beating yourself up for nothing. I fall on my ass all the time in practice."

It's just like Amanda to make light of the less important subject matter, while ignoring the more serious ones for my benefit, he thought. But sooner or later, she always came back around to the serious matters.

"Yeah, I'm sorry about that again. I just don't know what to say."

"It's okay," she said, punching him in the arm. "It's no big deal." Looking over toward the main building, Amanda saw her fellow cheerleaders. "I have an impromptu meeting with my squad before school starts, but we'll catch up later during our study session."

"What you said, lady," he feigned agreement.

"Bye," she said as she ran to meet up with her friends before the bell rang.

* * *

"Absolutely not."

"But you haven't heard me out."

"There is nothing you can do to convince me to make Amanda stop tutoring you," Ms. Lucci said to Alex.

"But I've changed my mind," he protested.

"Well change it back," she snapped.

"Please, Ms. Lucci…"

"Just last week, you sat in that same chair and agreed to let Amanda tutor you. Now, four days later, you waltz in here and ask me to make her stop," she said, fuming from behind her desk. "Now you listen to me, I do not have time for this. It's a good thing Amanda stopped by this morning and told me about this little stunt you're pulling."

"What did you say?" he asked.

"You've only had one session … one single, solitary session, and you're ready to call it quits already." She sighed heavily, then mumbled, "I did not sign up for this sh—" catching herself before she finished the word.

"Ms. Lucci, what did you say about Amanda stopping by?"

"She stopped by during her lunch break to thank me for pairing you two together. She said you guys had a lot to work on, but she was confident that by the end of the semester your grades would be back at a satisfactorily level. And then she said, and I quote, 'If Alex tries to get you to end his tutoring early, don't. He's just scared and needs time to warm up to the idea.' And in you walk, less than three hours later, asking me to do exactly what she told me not to do." Ms. Lucci paused to catch her breath. "Now you listen to me, young man—"

At that moment, Alex zoned out of the conversation. Convinced that Ms. Lucci was not going to change her mind without a little persuasion, Alex focused his energy on her head, which was bobbing up and down to add emphasis to the words that spewed out of her mouth. It was totally quiet now in his head, as he massaged his left temple. He waited until Ms. Lucci's body jolted upright and sat perfectly still in her chair. She had stopped talking and wore a blank, trance-like expression on her face. He then mentally explored her cerebrum and implanted his desires into her frontal lobe.

In a whisper, he said, "Ms. Lucci."

"Yes, Alex," she replied drily.

"I don't want Amanda to tutor me. Do you understand?"

"You don't want Amanda to tutor you," she repeated like a zombie.

"You will call Amanda and tell her she is no longer required to tutor me."

"I will call and tell her."

In what appeared to be a flash of light, Alex exited Ms. Lucci's mind, layer by layer—first the frontal lobe, then her cerebrum, skull and skin. He watched as Ms. Lucci's somber face transformed back into the highly animated facial expressions she usually wore, as she continued with their conversation, oblivious to any interruption.

"Now, Alex," Ms. Lucci said, "if you don't want Amanda to tutor you anymore, I won't force you. I'm really struggling within myself about this, but in the end it's what you want that matters."

"Thank you for understanding, Ms. Lucci. I think this is best for everyone involved." *And God help me if I'm wrong,* he thought. "Will that be all for today?"

"Yes. I need time to think of what else we can do to improve your grades. This is not how I had planned to end our meeting today. So I'll see you Friday."

"Thanks again, Ms. Lucci," he said as he walked out of her office.

* * *

Alex walked through the lounge area outside Ms. Lucci's office, down the hallway, and pushed the door open to the staircase. Once there and out of sight, he threw himself up against the wall, then allowed his body to slide down to the floor. He had promised himself never to do that again. *Never, ever take away someone's free will,* he had vowed. And now to suit his own personal, selfish whim, he had done it again.

Alex considered himself a moral person. To have abilities like his, one had to have some morals. Like most people he knew, religion was Alex's moral compass. Although he wasn't deeply religious, he recalled attending mass on a few occasions back in California. One thing Alex remembered quite clearly from one of the sermons he heard was the three powers of the soul—memory, intellect, and will. The soul is believed to be sacred and the very essence of a human being. As humans, we should be free to obey our conscience in doing what we think is good—this is free will. However, what he had just done to Ms. Lucci was contrary to all that he believed. He had interfered with her free will and planted his own desire into her conscience.

But what other choice did he have? He didn't want to be placed under Amanda's watchful eyes. Plus, being around her was dangerous. He distinctly remembered that his recent slip-ups had occurred when she was around—first at the football field with the three girls and last night at his house. Now this thing with Ms. Lucci came about only after Amanda was involved. He felt bad about what he did to Ms. Lucci, but he wasn't going to change it.

* * *

Alex was lying on the couch with his algebra textbook open on his chest and his notes from today's lesson open on the floor next to him when he heard the doorbell ring. He wasn't expecting anyone. He glanced over at the clock on the DVR that sat next to the television. It said 4:48 p.m. The bell rang again.

It has to be Mrs. Osaka from across the street, he thought. *Maybe she needs help again to find her cocker spaniel. Why the hell doesn't that old lady keep her gate shut?* he wondered. He set his textbook down on the couch and walked toward the door. The bell rang again, this time for a longer duration.

"All right, all right. I'm coming," he shouted at the door.

Not bothering to look through the peep hole, Alex unlocked the door. Just as he turned the knob, the door flew open, knocking him off balance. As he struggled to remain on his feet, Amanda stepped inside the house, looking like a wildcat.

"You sneaky, selfish little bastard! I knew you would go crying to Ms. Lucci. I just didn't think it would be this soon."

"Amanda, calm down," Alex tried to reason with her.

"Don't tell me to calm down! Don't you dare!" she said, inching her way further inside the house.

"Amanda, I did this for your own good."

"My own good? Don't you dare make this about me," she shouted. "You did this for yourself—so you can be alone in your own little world, with all your little secrets. You ... you..."

"Say it, Amanda! Weirdo! Freak! That's the word you're looking for."

"Coward! How about that word? You are a sniffling

little coward. I can't believe you. How could you? You know what, I don't even know why I bothered. It's clear you don't want to be friends. Message received. I'm out of here," she said, turning to go back through the door.

"Amanda," he called after her.

"What!" she snapped, turning back around.

"I'm sorry."

"Is that all you can say? Is that all you're going to say to me—that you're sorry?"

"I don't know what else to say. I didn't mean for this to happen."

"You never meant for anything to happen," she shouted. "Well, you know what, Fuller, you can take your sorry and shove it up your ass." She stormed out of the house.

* * *

Amanda was so upset she could barely see the road in front of her as she drove to her house in McLean. *That was the final straw*, she thought. Initially, she had befriended the shy little boy back at Braemar after he incurred two demerits for taking and staying with her at the nurse's office. But as they hung out together, she found him very easy to talk to. She didn't have to mince her words with him. It didn't matter what it was, she knew she could always talk to Alex. Like the time when she told him about her first period. He wasn't grossed out by it. His only concern was whether she was going to die from all the bleeding and all. The memory brought a smile to her face, but it was not enough to subdue the anger that was raging inside her.

She had never liked the idea that they had grown apart.

However, her first year at Prestige was so turbulent—at home and school—that the few sporadic calls she made to Alex were the best she could do to salvage their friendship. She was hurt by the fact that Alex had stopped taking her calls. She searched her memory of all her conversations with him, trying to figure out whether it was something she had said. She knew she was outspoken and that bothered a lot of her friends, but not Alex. He had always encouraged her to speak her mind. So what was the cause of the current predicament?

Alex had a secret—that much she knew. But could it really be that bad, that he thought he could not share it with her? *We all have secrets.* Heck, she'd had a secret crush on Alex for years now. *Who wouldn't be attracted to Alex?* she thought. He was so hot, and didn't even know it—tall, California-sun-kissed skin, lean, with a six pack to die for. And his hair—long, fluffy spiral curls that hid his big, beautiful, brooding light-brown eyes. Then there was that chiseled, square jaw and those soft, perfectly formed lips. But somehow, she had never told anyone how she felt about him. She was too afraid that the one boy she'd ever liked, but who was totally oblivious to her presence, would not return the same feelings for her. They'd known each other for over four years and he'd never asked her out.

She hated herself for yelling at him. And for calling him those horrible names. *Oh, how could I have called him those horrible names?* she thought, as she rested her forehead against the steering wheel at a red light. Amanda lifted her head from the steering wheel, trying to pull herself together. What was she supposed to do now? Although she regretted her choice of words, she could not forgive Alex for going behind her back to end their tutoring sessions.

3. COFFEE RUN

Alex hadn't gotten a good night's sleep since his last encounter with Amanda. Two whole days went by and he had not seen her at school. He knew she was there because her car was in the parking lot. Was she deliberately avoiding him? Who could blame her? Although he certainly didn't want his ass handed to him again, he still cared about her and wanted to make sure she was okay. Just a glimpse of her would suffice.

During his meeting with Ms. Lucci today, he told her about the agreement he and his mother had made about improving his grades. Ms. Lucci listened with skepticism. They ended the meeting with Alex agreeing to conduct his self-study sessions in the lounge area outside her office. Every day after school, he would go straight to her office after gym and spend the next two hours studying. This would dramatically reduce the amount of time he spent at the Gardens, but he would've agreed to anything to alleviate the guilt he now felt in Ms. Lucci's presence.

After their meeting, Alex started his self-study session outside her office. Two hours later, he was finished studying, but didn't feel like going home. Once outside the building, he remembered that there was a lacrosse game today. He knew Amanda would be there. Suddenly, the idea of watching the game intrigued him. Maybe this was his chance to see how she was doing. He headed over to the field, where the game was already in progress. The score was 5–3, Prestige.

Alex took a seat high up and toward the back of the bleachers, close to the exit. From here, he could see her without being noticed. He watched as the players swung their lacrosse sticks to catch, carry, and pass the small, solid rubber ball. He frowned as the opposing team scored another point, after Prestige's futile attempt to dispossess them of the ball. Having never watched the game played outdoors before, he fully understood now why helmets and padding were necessary. *It is like playing football with weapons*, he thought. There was no way he could play this sport without losing a quart of blood.

The highlight of the game came in the last quarter, when the opposing team was desperately trying to make a comeback before the game ended. The score was 11–9, Prestige. One of the opposing attackers unleashed the ball at a slightly off angle, thrusting the ball approximately 60 mph toward an unsuspecting cheerleader on the sidelines.

"Oooh!" the crowd erupted, as the ball smashed into the cheerleader's face.

That's going to leave a mark, Alex thought as the cheerleader went down. He watched as one of the other cheerleaders helped their fallen comrade off the field and headed for the exit. So enthralled with the game, Alex didn't realize that it was Amanda who was helping her fallen comrade off the field, until she was looking straight at him from the bottom of the bleachers. When he returned her gaze, he saw anger blaze in her eyes before she went through the exit and headed for the gymnasium.

With a look like that from Amanda, Alex debated whether he wanted to stick around until the game was finished. He certainly didn't want to run the risk of seeing her again with such disdain in her eyes for him. So he took up his backpack and left the field.

* * *

The following day, Alex thought he caught a glimpse of Amanda near the staircase on the third floor. She was in a hurry to get through the doors that led to the stairs. At first he couldn't be sure it was her, but was reassured when he saw Leslie and Katt staring at the doors in astonishment. Leslie and Katt were always with Amanda, so it left very little doubt in his mind that she was the one who had fled the scene. When Leslie and Katt looked around to see what had spooked their friend, they saw Alex, who looked just as confused as they did. Katt gave him the finger, as Leslie dragged her through the doors to follow after Amanda.

What was that about? Alex wondered. Katherine Zimmerman, who went by Katt, was a staff writer on the newspaper and another one of Amanda's Novies friends. Alex never had any interaction with this girl before, so he couldn't figure out why she had made the obscene gesture. The bell rang and the idea of Katt became inconsequential.

* * *

The locker room was empty now that eighth-period gym was over. The only person left behind was Alex. On days when his class played contact sports, he was not permitted to play because of his frequent nosebleed. Instead, he had the option of either sitting on the sidelines and learn the fundamentals of the games, helping with the equipment, or engaging in some non-contact sport of his choosing, like jogging or weight-lifting. Today, he opted for athletic equipment detail, which entailed retrieving the equipment at the beginning of class and storing it afterwards.

He had just dragged a mesh bag filled with basketballs back to the equipment room and changed into his uniform. He was sitting on a bench in front of his locker with his gym clothes next to him. The sound of a locker door being slammed shut at the end of the aisle drew his attention. When he looked up to see the origin of the ruckus, he saw David Locke walking slowly toward him and his two goons standing watch at the end of the aisle.

Oh great, just what I need, Alex thought. Although he was never afraid of David, or the other boneheads who gave him a hard time in school, Alex just wished they would leave him alone. He had always employed the policy of benign neglect when it came to the Novies, and had hoped they'd do the same toward him, but every now and then, the two collided.

"Hey, freak!" David yelled halfway down the aisle from where Alex sat.

Alex rolled his eyes at David and got up to hang his gym shirt on a hook in his locker.

"Hey! I'm talking to you, freak-boy."

"What do you want, Locke?" Alex said. Not being able to resist the urge, he added, "The full-length mirror is two aisles over."

"Did you say something, freak?"

"Are you deaf, too? I guess that comes from all the head injuries." Alex chuckled.

"What did you say to me?" David said, trying to look menacing.

"Okay, that was a cheap shot," Alex said, leaning against his locker. "But seriously, what do you want?"

"I want you to stay away from Amanda."

Amanda? That caught Alex by surprise. If he recalled correctly, Amanda had given him the impression that there was nothing going on between her and David.

"What about Amanda?" Alex inquired.

"She's been acting weird ever since I saw you two together. And the word is, she doesn't want to be anywhere near you; so stay away from her."

Oh, so that's what this is about, Alex deduced. "And what if I don't?" he countered.

"And what if you don't what?"

Alex laughed. "What if I don't stay away from Amanda? You really should get a doctor to examine that head of yours, because you're having difficulty keeping up with a simple conversation."

"You think this is funny? You think this is funny, you little punk bitch?" David yelled, motioning for his goons to join him.

Seeing where this was going, Alex closed his eyes to clear his mind.

"Yeah that's right, freak-boy. Say a prayer," David said, inching himself closer to Alex. He had only taken two steps toward Alex when the sound of something being smashed against the lockers could be heard behind him, followed by a thud. The sound came from Rafi and Timothy being slammed against the lockers simultaneously by an unseen force, which caused their bodies to hit the floor in a loud thud. David spun around to see his friends squirming around in pain on the floor. David joined in his friends' misfortune a second later when a strong unseen force knocked his feet from under him, and his body slammed into the floor, as he drifted in and out of consciousness.

Alex was careful not to step on David as he passed him, twisting around in agony on the ground. When he got to the end of the aisle, where the two other boys were, he saw a large container of liquid anti-bacterial soap in the dispenser mounted over the sinks. Mentally, he lifted the bottle out of the dispenser and emptied its contents on the floor where the three boys were still writhing around in pain. He then left the locker room and found the janitor.

"Hey Charlie," he said to the retired, elderly veteran, who now cleaned his school. "There's something slippery on the floor in the locker room. I just saw three guys slip on the stuff in there."

"I'll take care of it," Charlie responded.

* * *

Amanda was reviewing a news article Joshua Goldstein had submitted for publication entitled "Judaism: Religion or an Emerging Race?" She was reading the article on a desktop in the newspaper room. She wasn't the type to censor a student's free speech, but she knew the headmaster would not allow her to publish this article in their newspaper. Instead, Amanda started to put together a list of independent newspapers that would be Josh's best chance of getting his article published.

After she was done, she turned around and surveyed the newsroom. Eddie, the editor, and Katt were arguing over which two sentences they should cut from her article to make it fit in the newspaper's next edition. Brooklyn and Gavin were selecting pictures from the recent baseball and lacrosse games to run in the sports section. Chris, Lexi, and Chen were huddled over a desk, looking at something that Amanda couldn't see from where she sat.

It was 3:43 p.m. and Amanda could feel her energy level dropping. *Time for a caffeine fix*, she thought as she grabbed her purse.

"I'm going to the Brewery," she announced. The Brewery was the school's coffee shop. It had started out as a coffee break room for the faculty. However, as the student body's need for caffeine evolved, parents had demanded that the school provide their children with their daily fix of "go juice," despite the health warnings. Prestige had given in once they developed a ration program to regulate each student's daily consumption, and once the parents had offered to fund the conversion of the break room into a state-of-the-art café. It was originally called the Coffee Shop, but the students renamed it the Brewery because it sounded cooler. Besides, if Novies wanted an authentic coffee shop experience, they'd just hop over the pond and head for Amsterdam.

"Anyone need anything?" Amanda asked.

"Hazelnut latte for me," Eddie said.

"Mocha frappuccino for me," said Gavin.

"Me too," Chen chimed in.

"Caramel frappuccino, please," said Brooklyn.

"I think they ran out of caramel after lunch, Bea," Eddie added.

"Vanilla then," said Brooklyn.

Amanda repeated the order to confirm she had gotten it right. "Anything else?" she added. The remaining newspaper crew members shook their heads and Amanda left the room and headed for the main building, where the Brewery was located. Although classes were over, the Brewery stayed open until five o'clock for the benefit of the faculty and students who had after-school programs and extracurricular activities.

* * *

Ms. Lucci was standing in the doorway to her office when Alex ran into the lounge area.

"Good afternoon, Ms. Lucci," he said in his most polite voice.

"Late much?" was her sole reply as she walked back into her office.

Alex set down his backpack and was about to take his books out when Ms. Lucci returned with her pocketbook.

"I'm off to a status update meeting with the headmaster," she said. "It shouldn't take long, so I'll see you in a bit."

Alex pulled out his algebra textbook and his notebook. Sometimes he felt like he was the only student who still used a paper notebook rather than a laptop. He had only studied for a few minutes when he realized how thirsty he was after running from the gym to Ms. Lucci's office. He pushed aside his books and walked to the first floor, in search of the vending machine that stocked all sorts of refreshing sports beverages. The machine was standing in a large alcove off to the right of the hallway that led to the exit nearest to the gymnasiums and media center. There was another machine in there that contained bottled water.

This hallway was deserted at this time of the day, especially since no games were being played today.

Alex stepped inside the alcove and took a dollar and quarter out of his pants pocket. He slid the crumpled dollar bill into the vending machine, which it refused to accept. He finally gave up after the fourth try. Alex stared at the dollar bill, which he held with pincer grasps at both ends. As his eyes swept across the dollar, its creases ironed themselves out, leaving the bank note as crisp as the day it was printed. He easily slid the crisp note into the bill acceptor slot, but when he attempted to insert the coin, it fell to the ground and rolled under the machine.

Alex knelt down on the floor to look for the coin. He saw it to the far right of the machine in the back. There's no way his hand could fit under there, much less reach that far back. Instead, he propelled the quarter forward and watched as it flew from under the machine and levitated about a foot off the ground before he grabbed it.

He stood back up and dropped the coin into the machine. After making his selection, the dispenser pushed the bottle forward, but it failed to fall. Alex frowned at the bottle.

"You guys really want me to die of thirst today, don't you?" he said. With a flick of his fingers at the vending machine, it shook, causing the bottle to fall instantly. A moment later, the bottle emerged from the retrieval slot and flung itself into Alex's hand.

Alex turned to leave but stood frozen in his tracks when his eyes locked onto Amanda's. She was standing in the hallway with her eyes and mouth wide open. Alex looked at the bottle in his hand, then back at Amanda. The expression on her face left no doubt in his mind that she had seen everything. It seemed like an eternity that they stood there frozen, staring at each other, not saying a word. The whole scene was reminiscent of an old western duel. At any moment now, one of them would have to draw their weapon and fire. And it was Amanda.

She bolted down the short hallway to the exit from which she came. Alex instinctively took after her. Amanda burst through the door and out into the open air. Alex followed behind a few seconds later. She didn't seem to have a particular destination in mind; just as long as there was open space, she ran.

"Amanda, stop," he yelled, but she kept running.

"For the love of God, stop," he yelled as she entered the track and field area. Alex could feel his heart banging against his chest cavity, as if at any moment, it would break free.

Amanda easily cleared the tracks and was headed for the clearing in front of the woods that separated Prestige from the rest of McLean. Alex thought about using his abilities to make her stop, but decided against it, out of fear that it may further traumatize her.

When she neared the woods, Amanda veered left and ran along side of it. *How could she run so fast in those shoes?* Alex thought, as he looked at Amanda's blurred, inch-high Mary-Janes. He made a mental note to engage in more cardiovascular activities because his non-participation in gym was putting him at a serious disadvantage with the head cheerleader, who was required to work out three times per week.

Alex's eyes were so fixed on Amanda's long hair blowing in the wind that he didn't realize that she was headed for the largest of the three ponds at Prestige. He watched as she turned her head slightly to look back at him.

"Stop," he shouted, stretching his left arm toward her. Then he saw the pond and his pace slowed. He became mesmerized by the water. Gradually, his pace slowed even more to a light jog, then a walk, then stopped. The water was still, lifeless—calling him, mocking him, reminding him.

"Noooo," he screamed as his knees hit the ground. A wail rose from the pit of his stomach, shuddering his vocal cords as the sound ripped from his mouth. He clutched his stomach, doubled over on the ground, and cried.

"Not again, not again," he said, his eyes blinded by tears. "Justin, I'm so sorry. I'm so sorry."

He continued to repeat the phrase "I'm sorry" over and over, as he clutched his head and rocked back and forth.

"Hey," he heard a voice say from above him. Then something touched his shoulder. He looked up and saw Amanda leaning over him. He sat on the ground and pulled his knees near his chest. He stopped crying and wiped away his tears with the back of his hands.

Amanda knelt down on the ground in front of him, waiting for him to regain his composure. When his breathing returned to normal, he stared at the ground between his feet, refusing to look at her.

"You okay?" she asked. Alex nodded his head.

"You want to talk about it?" she added. He didn't answer.

Amanda turned around and sat on the ground next to him and pulled her knees to her chest. They stared at the pond. She wrapped her arms around him, and he rested his head against hers. The smell of freshly cut grass, pine, and strawberry filled his nostrils.

"You still smell of strawberries," he said.

He felt her body shake as she chuckled. Several minutes passed, then Alex's phone vibrated in his pants pocket. He took out the phone and looked at it. He didn't recognize the number, but the area code and line number suggested it was coming from a phone inside Prestige.

"Hello," he said.

"Ms. Lucci," he yelled as he stood up. "I just went to get something to drink." He listened.

"Yes, ma'am. I'll be there in five minutes." Alex turned around and looked at the main building in the distance. "Make that ten minutes," he reassessed and hung up the phone.

"I have to go," he said to Amanda. "Ms. Lucci is back at her office and looking for me."

"I'll go with you," she said, getting up from the ground. "I think I dropped my purse somewhere along the way." Alex looked at her apprehensively. She started walking toward the building, leaving the debate of whether he wanted her to accompany him moot. Gauging the distance they had to cover in ten minutes, he started to jog, and she kept his pace.

When Alex opened the side entrance door to the main building, he saw Amanda's purse on the floor. He stepped inside the hallway, picked it up, and handed it to her.

"Thanks," she said. "And I think this is yours," she added as she walked over to the bottle of sport beverage Alex had dropped when he gave chase after her.

"Thanks," he said when she handed it to him.

"So," he continued. "How much of that did you see?"

"Uhh, I think all of it," she said. "I saw when you stepped into the vending machine room. My intention was to sneak by, but then I saw that you were having difficulty with the dollar. I was about to give you some quarters, but then the dollar straightened itself out. And then the quarter was floating, then the bottle." Her voice trailed off at the end.

"Pretty scary stuff," he said, picking at the label on the bottle.

"Not really," she said shrugging her shoulders.

"You don't have to pretend for my benefit."

"I'm not."

"But you ran."

"Yeah, but not because I was scared per se."

"Then why?" he asked, puzzled.

"I don't know, maybe out of embarrassment."

"You were embarrassed?" he blurted.

"Yes, embarrassed," she replied. "You know that feeling you get, when you see something you know you should not have seen—like catching someone masturbating or your parents having sex—"

"Okay, now that's gross."

"Exactly. It's that sense of you invading their privacy. That's how I felt when I saw you. But I was so fascinated by what was happening, that I couldn't convince myself to look away. Then you saw me, and I panicked. So I just ran."

"Oh, I see."

"Is that … is this why you've been staying away from me?"

Alex nodded his head.

"But now that—" Amanda started, but was interrupted by the vibration of Alex's phone.

"It's Ms. Lucci again," he said, after fishing the phone out of his pocket. "I have to go."

"But we are going to talk again, right?" she added, as Alex started to walk backwards away from her.

"Yeah, and I'll explain everything."

"I'll wait for you in the parking lot, after I finish with the newspaper."

"Okay," he said, disappearing into the staircase.

* * *

Ms. Lucci was not happy with Alex when he entered the lounge outside her office. She lectured him for the first five minutes when he arrived about him being tardy, then ditching his studies to get something to drink, which she didn't buy. The vending machine was on the first floor and no matter how much he had dilly-dallied, she didn't believe it should have taken that long for him to return to her office. Alex added that he had also stopped by the library to borrow some books on explosives to finish up his Physics project, but they were already checked out. Ms. Lucci was equally unimpressed by this explanation and told him that if he needed to go to library, he should do so before or after his duty sessions.

"I don't like being toyed with." She paused for her words to register with her listener. "I would hate to think that you're throwing away the opportunity the headmaster gave you by shirking your studies. Now, I'm going to give you the benefit of the doubt and assume that whatever it was that you think you had to do is now resolved, correct?" she asked, furrowing her brows.

"Correct," he answered.

"And from now on, you're going to be a good student, who will not allow any distractions during his study sessions, correct?"

"Correct."

"Now, I have an appointment tomorrow after classes, so that means you don't have to come here. However, I fully expect you to carry on with your studies and take some time to think about what I just said."

"Thank you, Ms. Lucci," Alex said, getting up.

"Don't thank me yet," she warned. "Now, get back to your studies."

When Alex closed the door behind him, he heard a text come in on his cell phone. He fished it out of his pocket and saw that Amanda had sent him a text. It read:

> Got 2 go. Mom called. Needs me home now.
> C U 2morrow 7:30 under Acer.

* * *

Later that night, Margaret surprised Alex when she arrived home before eight o'clock.

"What happened? Did the building burn down or something?" he asked, obviously assuming that only a catastrophe could account for her getting home this early.

"No. Satan and his bride have to be in Houston by morning for some depositions," she answered, referring to the hiring partner and the office manager at Stanley & Gable, LLP (SAG)—the law firm she worked for in DC.

"So they took off earlier this evening, as did the admin staff.

"Lucky for you," Alex said from the table in the dining area, where he was finishing dinner—mac and cheese and the rotisserie chicken Margaret had bought at Walmart.

"Yes, very lucky," she said, walking into the kitchen to fix herself a plate. "I've been meaning to talk to you about my latest conversation with Ms. Lucci," she added, as she sat across from him.

"Mom, I thought we had an agreement—I'll study harder and you won't talk about my grades until after the semester."

"Calm down, I'm not going to talk about your grades. Although, I am hearing good things since you started your study sessions at her office."

"So what then?"

"Have you ever talked to Ms. Lucci about your father?"

"No, why?"

"Nothing. Just something she mentioned that made me wondered."

"What? Did she ask you where he was or something?"

"Yes, she did."

"Mom, she's a shrink of sorts. She's supposed to ask asinine questions like that to get a better understanding of my home environment. If I were you, I wouldn't worry about it. Personally, I never met the guy, and from how he treated you, I don't want to."

Margaret knew that Alex didn't ask or talk about his father out of consideration for her feelings.

"Ms. Lucci also told me that she got Amanda to tutor you, but you got rid of her," she said, changing the subject. "What's up with that?"

"A miscalculation on my part," he said. "But Amanda and I are cool now."

"Define cool?"

"We're on speaking terms again."

"Uh-huh," She smiled.

"What is that supposed to mean?"

"Nothing. I didn't say anything," she protested.

"Okay, I'm done," he announced, getting up and walking into the kitchen to put his plate, glass, and fork in the dishwasher. "Anything else you'd like to insinuate before I get ready for bed?"

"Nope."

"Fine. Good night then," he said, kissing her on the cheek and headed upstairs.

"Good night … Prince Charming."

"Whatever," she heard him say from the stairs.

* * *

To be honest, Margaret hadn't thought about Alex's father much since she moved to Virginia. However, two months ago, his existence had threatened to derail her friendship with Molly Tinker.

Molly had been Margaret's roommate and best friend when she moved from her hometown of Boron, California to San Diego to volunteer at Allied Research Institute, or ARI for short. ARI was one of the laboratories that had conducted research for the now defunct, government-funded Stargate Project. Alex's father, Dr. Karl Vaughn, was one of the psychologists at ARI.

For the three years she lived with Molly, Margaret never told her about her involvement in the Stargate Project until

Molly was about to relocate to Virginia. She also told Molly about her brief relationship with Dr. Vaughn, who had moved to Fort Meade, Maryland, after she told him she was pregnant with Alex.

"So what are you going to do now?" Molly had asked her.

"I don't know," she had replied.

"Well if you decide to keep it, you need to tell him. Don't let that asshole get away with not paying child support for the life he helped to create."

"I know."

"You already know what state he's moving to. And with me in Virginia, I could help you file all the paperwork with social services."

Margaret knew Molly was right, but if the *good doctor* seemed unconcerned when she told him she was pregnant, she doubt he'd give a damn if she kept the child.

Alex was born shortly after Molly left for Virginia, and Margaret had decided to take care of him herself. A year later, ARI decided to abandon the Stargate Project altogether and Margaret was left unemployed. To complicate matters further, her mother died soon afterward in Boron.

For the next ten years, she bounced from one dead-end job to another. Molly finally convinced her to move to Virginia after a fire destroyed her apartment. Molly told her that they were hiring paralegals at SAG, where she worked, because of an influx of lawsuits they had to defend. Molly, who was a senior paralegal by now, had promised Margaret that if she enrolled in a paralegal certification course, she could get her a job as an administrative assistant, then as a paralegal once she completed the course.

Molly thought Margaret had moved to Virginia to find

stable employment and put the whole ARI chapter of her life behind her. However, two months ago, Molly had found a three-year-old *Washingtonian* magazine in Margaret's bedroom, featuring the *good doctor*, who had opened a private practice in DC.

"What is this?" she had asked Margaret, before they left for their girls' night out.

"A magazine," Margaret replied.

"I know it's a magazine, Marge. A three-year-old magazine, featuring Vaughn and his accomplishments. Why do you still have it, I guess, is what I'm asking?"

"I don't know. Maybe someday, I'll work up enough courage to tell Alex the complete story about his father. I thought the magazine could come in handy."

"For your sake, I hope that's all you plan to do with it, because it says here that he's married with three kids."

Margaret rubbed her eyes as she cleared her mind of all things Vaughn and her previous conversations with Molly about him. She got up from the table where she and Alex had dinner. After loading the dishwasher, she started it, turned off the lights, and headed upstairs for bed.

4. ACCUSED

Alex left home before his mother woke up. He was excited about seeing Amanda. All morning, he kept going over what he would say to her. How would he start the conversation? What would be the best setting? He was so consumed with his thoughts that he didn't realize that the Prestige school bus was already loading at the stop around the corner from his house. He ran down the block with his backpack slung over one shoulder and a Hot Pocket in his hand.

He took his usual seat at the back of the bus. Pleasant Street, on which Alex lived, was the last stop the bus made before heading back to the school in McLean. It was mandatory for freshmen and sophomores to take the bus to and from school, or be dropped off and picked up. Juniors and seniors also had these options, with the additional choice of driving their own vehicles, but had to park in the student lot across campus—unless an exception was made.

Alex had planned to get a summer job to purchase a car by junior year, but those plans were permanently shelved when his grades dropped and Margaret insisted on him going to summer school. So here he sat, at the mercy of Prestige's school bus, and sometimes the regional transportation system.

Alex always kept his eyes glued to the window, so he was never aware of what went on inside the bus. That's probably why he didn't realize that Brooklyn Larkin was sitting in the seat across the aisle from him. Normally, he would have the entire back row to himself. His mere presence back there was enough to send the other students searching for seats elsewhere. However, his renewed interest in his class work and participation in classroom discussions gave Brook the guts to approach him.

Twice over the last two weeks, she had joined him at his lunch table without being invited. The first time she did it, he was caught off-guard and accidently said hi back to her. Little did he know that his one-word response would propel the aspiring writer to share her entire life story with him for the remainder of lunch. The following day, she sought him out again. This time, he didn't exchange any greetings with her, but she joined him nonetheless. As Brook delved into another chapter of her life, Alex had suddenly recalled why he preferred the life of a hermit. Unannounced, he had gathered up his belongings and headed for his fifth-period class, arriving twenty minutes early.

"Hi, Alex."

Alex knew who it was without removing his gaze from the window. Didn't she get the message the other day? He wasn't interested in her. *Maybe she is one of those people who seek out tortured souls to console*, he thought. Regardless of her motive, the fact remained, he was not interested in Brook, and he wasn't going to lead her on by building her hopes up. But then he remembered the deal he'd made with his mother about being more sociable. He sighed heavily as he contemplated what he was about to do.

"Hi Brook," he said, as he flew by the other students to

be the first one off the bus when it stopped in front of Prestige.

* * *

Amanda was already standing by the large maple tree in the schoolyard. She saw Alex far off and waved to him. As Alex approached her, she recognized Brooklyn from the news crew, who walked by them with a ridiculously large smile on her face. Amanda walked with Alex over to the tree and they took a seat in the shade.

"What happened yesterday?" he asked. "Is your mom all right?"

"Yeah, she's fine. Turned out that my dad was having some of his diplomatic friends over for dinner and they needed me for show and tell," she said. "Of course, Mother didn't tell me that was why she wanted me home until I got there."

"Of course."

"So, how did your study session go yesterday?" she asked, trying to put Alex more at ease before getting to the point of their meeting.

"It went well. Ms. Lucci lectured me for leaving to get something to drink. But after I was finished studying she said that my teachers were reporting progress in my behavior and classroom participation."

"That's great. Does she help you with your studies?"

"No. She just makes sure that I'm studying the whole time I'm there. She mentioned last week that she got some of my teachers to agree to give me extra credit to make up for my behavior from the beginning of the semester." He looked down at the ground and started pulling up some of the grass. "I could use your help with the extra credit work, but only if you have time."

"I'll see what I can do." Deciding to take the bull by the horns, she added, "So yesterday, you said you'd explain what happened by the vending machines."

He turned his attention away from the grass by his foot and scouted the area around them. "Yeah, I did."

"Sooo…" she prompted.

"I don't even know where to start," he said.

Amanda decided to stay quiet and let him proceed at his own pace.

"I have this thing that started the summer after freshman year," he said, dragging the words out more than absolutely needed. "It's kind of hard to explain."

"Take your time. I'm not going anywhere."

"It happened when I went to Camp APRICOT. I don't know how or why it happened, but … that's when it started."

"What started?" she asked softly.

Alex waited, debating whether this was a good idea after all to tell Amanda, especially since he could just wipe her memory clean of what she had seen yesterday, but he decided against it. It was time he talked to someone about this. And telling Amanda felt right.

"I started doing things with my mind," he said under his breath.

Unable to hear what he'd said, Amanda asked, "You started what?"

He repeated his last statement.

Confused, Amanda asked, "What type of things?"

He looked at her face, trying to read the expression he saw. Satisfied that she wasn't judging him, he continued.

"I can move things with my mind by exerting force on them," he said slowly, not taking his gaze from her face. He watched as her eyes danced around in her head, trying to understand what she just heard. When her eyes returned to meet his, he added, "I can also start fires with my mind."

He watched as her brows furrowed. It took a while for them to smooth back out. "I can project my thoughts into someone else's mind," he continued. "Well, it started out as mere projection, but now it sort of evolved to the point where I can mentally manipulate someone else's brain."

"What do you mean manipulate?"

"I mean, I can control the functions of someone's brain. I can project thoughts into their brains. I can change their minds. Anything you can think of that the brain does, I can manipulate it," he said, a bit out of breath.

"Can you read minds?" she asked nervously.

"Except for that," he admitted. "I've tried before, but I can't seem to make the link with what someone else is thinking, just imposing my own thoughts or taking over the functions of their brain altogether."

Amanda sighed a breath of relief. Then she thought for a moment, and said, "So yesterday, with the dollar—"

"That was my pyrokinesis ability. I simply added a little heat to iron it out."

"Pyrokinesis? So there's a name for this?"

"Yup. Or at least that's what Google told me."

"And the quarter and the bottle—"

"Telekinesis."

"That one I've heard about."

"Remember the night you came over to help me study—"

"Yes, the night you dropped me on my ass."

He smiled. "Sorry about that. So, you heard me make a comment about your hair, right?"

Amanda nodded.

"Well, that was me projecting my thoughts to you. I didn't mean for it to happen then, which kind of freaked me out and that's why I was acting so weird." He waited for her to wrap her mind around what he had told her so far. Finally, he asked, "So what do you think? Am I total freak or what?"

"Alex," she said, putting her hand on his thigh, "I don't think you're a freak or anything like that."

"There's one more thing."

"There's more?" she said, with her eyes bulging out.

"Just one. I can disconnect from my body sometimes."

"What do you mean disconnect?"

"Disconnect. Like … my spirit or soul, or whatever you want to call it, can leave my body, go for a walk, and come back."

"What happens to your body?"

"It just goes limp until I get back. It's like I'm asleep."

"So your heart and all your other organs are still functioning when you're not in it?"

"Yeah."

"Hold on a minute. Let's back up a minute. Now this all started—"

Suddenly, she saw Alex stand up with his gaze focused on something behind her. She turned around and saw Headmaster Anderson a few yards away, walking toward them with David Locke and his two friends, Timothy and Rafi. Amanda sprung to her feet as well.

"Miss Bridgewater," the tall, stout headmaster muttered.

"Good morning, Headmaster Anderson."

"Mr. Fuller," he said, disregarding Amanda's greeting.

"Headmaster Anderson."

"Please follow me," he said in a tone that was more of a command than a request.

Alex looked at Headmaster Anderson and the three boys behind him. Then, he looked back at Amanda. "I'll see you later, Amanda," he said, as he followed the headmaster back to the main building.

David threw Amanda a quick smirk and turned on his heel to follow the others. Amanda watched as all five of them walked into the building, although the school bell had not rung yet. Getting a bad feeling about this, she headed to Ms. Lucci's office.

* * *

Headmaster Anderson showed Alex into his office and told him to wait there. Outside, Alex could hear him having a discussion with the other three boys. Inside, Alex examined the Headmaster's large office. The walls were made of darkly stained cherry wood. Built-in bookcases that stretched from the floor to the ceiling covered two of the walls. The shelves were well stocked with books covering every subject under the sun. There were hardcovers, paperbacks, fiction, non-fiction, references, small books, large books, and voluminous textbooks, just to name a few.

The exterior wall had two large windows that faced the western side of the school yard, where one of the man-made ponds was, several yards away from the track and field. On the center of the wall hung a large oil painting of the current headmaster. His leather chair sat behind a large cherry wood desk. There were two more leather chairs on the other side of the desk. Alex assumed he would soon occupy one of these chairs. In the meantime, he continued his visual tour of the office, which was exactly how he remembered it from the year before. In the corner to the left was the small conference table with six chairs. In the corner to the right was the leather couch, an arm chair, and a small oriental rug.

Alex heard the door open again and in walked Headmaster Anderson, without David or his two friends.

"Sit down, Mr. Fuller," he said, pleasantly enough.

Alex took the chair on the right-hand side of the desk, which gave him the best view of the lake outside the window, just in case his abilities flared up.

"Mr. Fuller," Headmaster Anderson said, starting out the lecture standing, looking through the window on the left, "you have been here at Prestige for almost three years now. We had high hopes for you when you joined us. Because of your excellent grades from Braemar Academy and recommendation from the Bridgewaters, we granted you a full scholarship and you excelled during your first year with us. Fall of your sophomore year, your grades began to slip, except for your biology class. We took no action then, hoping that it was a short phase that you young people sometimes go through. Spring of that year, your grades plummeted further, again with the exception of your science class. Upon learning about your traumatic experience the summer before, I placed you on academic probation. So you remained at Prestige despite your subpar grades. Have I summarized your stay with us accurately so far?" he said, turning to face Alex.

"Yes sir, you have."

Turning his attention back to the window, Headmaster Anderson continued, "Prestige High has been around, in some form or another, for over one hundred and five years. Prestige prides itself on producing the future leaders of this country and the rest of the world. Only ten miles outside of Washington, DC, Prestige is the scholastic home to the children of many of our diplomatic visitors, congressional members, notable governmental agencies and affluent corporate heads. Every so often, we grant access to children in the surrounding communities, *like you*, in hopes of cementing our commitment to community development. We have never had an occasion to question our generosity," he said, turning to face Alex again, "until now."

"Now, Mr. Fuller," he said, walking over to his desk, and plunking down his large behind on the edge of the desk, "I'm going to ask you a series of questions. I want you to answer me truthfully. Do you understand me?"

What the hell is going on? Alex thought. "Yes sir," he said reluctantly.

"Your academic future depends on the next few minutes. Do you understand me?"

He didn't like where this was going. "I understand, sir."

"Did you attend your eighth period gym class yesterday?"

"Yes sir."

"After gym, did you return to the locker room to change clothes?"

"Yes sir."

"Did you see David Locke, Timothy Waltz, and Rafi al-Sharif enter the locker room?"

"No sir."

"You didn't see them enter the locker room?" he repeated suspiciously.

"No sir. I only saw them after they were already inside the locker room, sir."

"Very well. So you saw them in the locker room?"

"Yes sir."

"After you saw them in the locker room, did you have words with them?"

"Describe what you mean by 'have words' sir."

"Did you have an argument with them?"

"No sir."

"You did not quarrel with these boys?"

"No sir."

"Did you have any conversation with them?"

"I had a conversation with David."

"What about?"

"He wanted to talk to me about Amanda. He said that she had been acting weird ever since he saw her hanging out with me. I didn't know what he was talking about, so I laughed it off. Then he warned me to stay away from Amanda and I told him I would not. End of story."

"That's all you two talked about."

"Yes sir."

"So all of this was over Miss Bridgewater?"

"Yes sir."

"And you didn't do anything to provoke these boys?"

"No sir," Alex said, looking him in the eyes. "What is this all about, Headmaster Anderson? Are you accusing me of something? If you are, come out and say it to my face."

Headmaster Anderson sat up straight on the edge of his desk, allowing his chest to swell like a peacock. "Contain yourself, Mr. Fuller," he scolded. "I'm just trying to get to the bottom of what happened yesterday in that locker room. I've already heard Mr. Locke's and his friends' side of the story. Now I'm hearing yours."

There was a knock at the door. "Who is it?" Headmaster Anderson barked, obviously annoyed.

"It's Verona Lucci, Headmaster."

"Come in."

In walked Ms. Lucci, wearing her mother-hen game face. Alex saw Amanda's prying eyes as Ms. Lucci closed the door behind her.

"Can I help you, Ms. Lucci?" asked the Headmaster, who made no attempt to hide his annoyance.

"Yes sir. I heard you had Alex Fuller in your office and wanted to see if I could be of any assistance."

"Why would I need your assistance in talking to a student?" he asked condescendingly enough.

"Well sir, Alex has been in counseling sessions with me to get his grades back up by the end of this semester. I think he should be given the opportunity to finish the semester before any decisive action is taken."

"I see," Headmaster Anderson said, finally understanding why she was here. She thought he was going to expel Alex and wanted to get her two cents in before a decision was made. "Ms. Lucci, this meeting was not called to discuss Mr. Fuller's grades, although I'm very disappointed in them as well. This meeting was called at the behest of David Locke, who has accused Mr. Fuller of assaulting him and two others yesterday afternoon."

"Impossible!" shouted Ms. Lucci. "Alex came straight to my office yesterday after his gym class and spent the entire afternoon studying there." She purposely omitted his beverage break.

"Pipe down, Lucci. I was just in the middle of getting Mr. Fuller's version of the story when you walked in. Since you're such a great proponent of the lad, you're free to sit in on the rest of our meeting."

"Thank you, Headmaster," Ms. Lucci responded, taking a seat in the armchair near the leather couch.

Turning his attention back to Alex, Headmaster Anderson continued, "Now, Mr. Fuller, tell us what you recall about your encounter with Mr. Locke yesterday."

"Like I said before, I went to gym. Afterwards, I went into the locker room to change. I didn't see or hear them come in. In fact, I didn't know they were there until Locke started calling me names and telling me to stay away from Amanda. I told him I wouldn't. They fell. I left."

"They fell?"

"Yes sir," he said innocently.

"They just fell? You didn't do anything to cause their fall?"

"Sir, I never laid a finger on any of them," Alex said, avoiding the question asked.

"You never touched them?"

"No sir."

"Then how did they fall?"

"At first, I didn't know how they fell. I just saw their legs go out from under them," he said, hoping that he sounded convincing. "Then when I walked by them to get help, I felt this slippery liquid stuff on the floor. I almost slipped on it myself. It's a good thing I ran into the janitor as I was leaving the locker room, because I told him about the mess in the locker room and he said he would clean it up."

"Which one of the janitors did you see?" Headmaster Anderson asked.

"The older guy. His name is … Charlie, the ex-Army guy."

"Charlie Smalls."

"I think so."

"So, you never laid your hands on Locke or his friends?"

"No sir."

"Let me see your hands."

Realizing that his hands were in his jacket pockets, Alex pulled them out for the headmaster to inspect. Headmaster Anderson put on his spectacles, which had been in his top-left jacket pocket, and examined Alex's hands.

"Where did you go after you left the locker room?" he continued.

"I went straight to Ms. Lucci's office to study."

"Is that what you recall, Ms. Lucci?"

"Yes sir. As I mentioned in yesterday's status update meeting, he comes there every day now after gym and studies for two hours," she said, getting out of the arm chair and walking toward her boss.

"Ah yes. And you indicated that he was still on point to get off probation at the end of the semester?" he asked indignantly.

"Yes sir. His teachers are already seeing great improvement and some have even assigned him extra credit work. So there's no doubt he'll finish the semester with a 3.4 GPA, if not higher, sir."

"And you saw him yesterday after his gym class?"

"Yes sir."

"Did he appear disheveled?"

"No sir. He had his usual calm, sweet demeanor," she said.

Sweet? C'mon, Ms. Lucci, don't overdo it, Alex thought. *We want him to believe you, remember.*

"Mr. Fuller, do you have anything else to add to your defense?"

"No sir."

"I need to talk to Mr. Smalls about what he remembers. After that, I'm going to deliberate and see whose version is more credible. I'll render my decision Monday morning. So next Monday, I need you to come here before homeroom. That is all, Mr. Fuller. You may go."

Ms. Lucci smiled at Alex as he passed her, and patted him on the back.

"Lucci, you stay behind," the Headmaster ordered, taking his official seat behind his large desk.

After Alex left, Headmaster Anderson asked, "What is your take on all of this, Lucci?"

"Sir, I can vouch for Alex. He is not a violent person, and must be adequately provoked to even get a response out of him. And even then, he's more likely to walk away or ignore his pursuer than to attack them. Besides, there were three of them, and one of him."

"I know. The story did sound sensational to me too, but this is the Locke family we're talking about here, so I have to pay it some lip service."

"Isn't David a senior anyway? What would he be doing in the locker room after seventh period when it's not even football season?"

"I see your point," Headmaster Anderson said, rubbing his chin. "Well, this shouldn't be a tough decision. I just need to talk to Mr. Smalls first. That is all, Ms. Lucci. Thank you for your input."

"Thank you, sir," she said, then returned to her office.

* * *

When Alex exited the headmaster's office and stepped into the waiting room, Amanda rushed to his side, curious to find out what had happened.

Seeing the concern on her face for Alex, David became visibly angry.

"You're dead, Fuller! You hear me? You're dead!" David shouted from the opposite end of the room, as Timothy and Rafi tried to restrain him.

"Control yourself, young man," said Pearl Johnson, the headmaster's secretary.

Alex flashed a defiant smirk at David, as Amanda pulled him by the arm out of the room and into the hallway. The bell rang and the students, who were waiting outside on the Quad, started pouring into the hallways.

"What the hell happened in there?" Amanda asked.

"Locke told Anderson I beat up him and his two cronies yesterday," he told her as they walked toward her homeroom.

"When?"

"Yesterday before I saw you. By the way, you didn't see me yesterday afternoon, if anyone asks."

"Okay," Amanda chuckled. "So, did you beat them up?"

"Define 'beat up.'"

"Did you hit them?" she said, punching him in the arm.

"Technically, no. I never laid a finger on them."

"Why do I get the feeling there's more to this story than you're telling me?"

"You've always been very intuitive, Amanda."

Amanda stopped walking and twirled him around to face her. "What did you do to them?"

"I'll tell you later," he said, motioning to the prying eyes on them. Amanda looked around and saw that every student within a 10-foot radius was staring at them.

"You better," she said, shrugging off the onlookers. "I have cheerleading practice and a game tonight. Will you wait for me?"

"No."

"You ass! You're seriously not going to wait for me?" she smiled. "Is this because I couldn't wait for you yesterday?"

"No. I don't have my counseling or study session with Ms. Lucci today and I'm going to take full advantage of it. I have somewhere to go. I haven't been there in a while."

"Where's that?"

"Meadowland."

"The botanical garden?" she asked.

"Yeah."

"Why?"

"I'll explain that later too."

"Does it have anything to do with your—," she paused and drew closer to him, so no one would hear—"your *thing*?"

"Yeah, sort of."

"Okay. I'll come over to your house first thing tomorrow then."

"That works." He shrugged his shoulders. "Thanks, by the way."

"For what?"

"Getting Ms. Lucci. I think she may have saved my hind-end in there. We'll have to wait until Monday though."

"Wait till Monday for what?"

"That's when Headmaster Anderson will *render his decision*," he said, using his index fingers to signify quotation marks.

"About whether you beat up David?"

"Yup."

"That guy is really starting to get on my nerves," she allowed herself to admit out loud for the first time, because no Novies were around. She felt relieved as the words left her mouth.

"David?"

"Yeah."

"I thought you two were tight."

"Not," she said, bumping him with her hip. "David just wants some eye candy on his arm to go with his inflated ego. Plus, he's not my type."

"I see."

Amanda smiled. When they reached her homeroom, Alex saw Leslie's jaw drop when she saw him with Amanda by the doorway. Alex stepped in front of Amanda, so she could see his face clearly.

Brace yourself for the interrogation, he projected.

Amanda's eyes lit up like a firecracker. "Oh my God! I totally heard that, but your lips didn't move," she said, half believing what had just happened. "We so have to talk about this. This is like the coolest thing ever."

"Tomorrow then."

"You better not bail on me, Fuller. I know where you live now," she threatened.

"Yes ma'am," he said, saluting her as he walked away.

* * *

Leslie saw the dream-like expression on Amanda's face when she took her seat in homeroom.

"Amanda Bridgewater," their homeroom teacher called out, taking attendance.

"Here," Amanda responded.

"Now he has you wearing that same dazed expression on your face that he does," Leslie said, interrupting Amanda's thoughts of Alex.

"What?" asked Amanda, who really hadn't heard a word Leslie said.

"That freak, Alex."

"Leslie, don't call Alex a freak. You don't know him, that's all."

"I know you don't want my opinion about this, but I don't like you hanging out with him."

"Thanks for mentioning that for like the hundredth time."

"And what is this I heard about Headmaster Anderson taking the little freak into his office this morning?"

"If you insist on calling Alex a freak, rather than his given name, we're not going to have this conversation."

"Okay, fine. Why was *Alex* taken to the headmaster's office?"

"David told Headmaster Anderson that Alex beat the crap out of him, Tim, and Rafi yesterday."

"Shut up!" Leslie erupted, almost forgetting that she was in class, until several students shot her a piercing glance for the outburst.

"Leslie Knolls." The homeroom teacher continued down her attendance list.

"Here, Ms. Graham," she responded, then turned back to Amanda. "So is it true?"

"I don't know, but Headmaster Anderson is going to make a determination Monday."

"Who would have thought that your little pipsqueak could take on three football players and survive? That is so weird. But I have to admit, that is also kind of hot."

"You are such a hypocrite."

"Yeah, but I'm keeping it real."

5. SURPRISE

It was early Saturday morning, and the Fuller house was quiet. The meteorologist said it would be warm and sunny, but someone had forgotten to tell the clouds that now loomed over Fairfax County. It was the perfect weather for sleeping in. Given the type of day they'd had yesterday, Margaret and Alex could easily keep sleeping until noon.

Margaret dreamt she heard a door bell ringing, but could not find the strength to get her limbs to respond.

Ding-dong.

There it goes again, she dreamt, but remained motionless. A third ring. Suddenly, Margaret was awakened by a loud banging on the front door of her house. She jolted forward, feeling a sharp crick in her neck.

"Oh, I have got to change these pillows," she said, rubbing the sleep from her eyes.

Bang, bang, bang.

Who the hell is that and why are they at my house so early? Margaret pondered. She pulled on her robe and headed downstairs, as the loud banging continued. Like a bear that was prematurely woken from its hibernation, Margaret was visibly annoyed, and she projected the same notion as she flung the door open.

"What the hell do y—? Amanda?" she asked, as her eyes adjusted to the slightly familiar face that looked back at her in astonishment.

"Good morning, Ms. Fuller." Amanda smiled.

"Oh my goodness! Amanda. Is that you?"

"In the flesh."

"Get in here and give me a hug," she said, opening the door wider for the girl to enter.

"It's good to see you, Ms. Fuller," Amanda said as she stepped inside to hug Margaret.

"Look at you," Margaret said, releasing the teen to examine her. "You got so tall. And you're filling out."

"Ms. Fuller," Amanda blushed.

"But it looks good though. Very young-lady like."

"Thank you. And you look great, as usual."

"Oh girl, flattery will get you everywhere with me," she responded, as they both laughed. "Come have a seat. Let me get you something to drink."

"Thank you," Amanda said, following her into the kitchen.

In the dining area, Amanda took a seat at the table. Margaret walked over to the cupboards, pulling out two mugs.

"What will you have—coffee or tea?"

"Tea, ma'am."

"Oh, that's right. You're half Brit, aren't you?" Not waiting for a response, she added, "I have regular herbal tea and a few flavored ones?"

"Regular will do."

"One regular herbal tea coming up." She filled the kettle with water, placed it on the stove, and then walked back over to Amanda. "So how long has it been—two, three years since I last saw you?"

"Just about."

"Did you and Alex have a falling-out or something? He never really said."

"No. We just both got so busy with school. Plus, we didn't have any classes together anymore. And Prestige is so huge, compared to Braemar, we just didn't see that much of each other."

"I can see how that could happen. But it's like I always say, you will never have time for anything, until you make time. I'm not just saying this to you, but I've said it to Alex a thousand times." Margaret paused at the sound of her son's name. "Well, you're here now, and Alex could certainly use a friend."

"I hope I can be a better friend this time."

"Bite your tongue. No one has been a better friend to Alex than you," she said, referring to the fact that it was Amanda who had talked her parents into writing a glowing letter of recommendation for Alex to get into Prestige.

The kettle started to whistle profusely. Margaret got up and turned off the stove.

"Speaking of which, where is Alex?" Amanda inquired.

"Sleeping Beauty is still asleep upstairs," she said, pouring hot water into the mugs.

"Oh, I'm sorry about the time. I just want—"

"Don't worry about the time. We're glad to have you at whatever time works for you."

"Thank you." She looked around the house and added, "You have a lovely house."

"Thanks. It's certainly better than that old apartment

we used to live in," she said, bringing over the mugs. "Sugar and cream or honey and lemon?"

"Sugar and cream, please."

"A Brit to the very end," she said, returning to the kitchen to get the sugar. "Does Alex know you were coming over today?"

"Yes. I just don't think he expected me quite this early."

"Well, I know he'll be happy to see you, regardless of the hour," she said, settling back into her seat with the sugar and cream. "Have you seen his room?"

"No. Why?"

"Nothing," Margaret said, smiling to herself.

"Oh you can't leave me hanging like this. You have to tell me. Is it bad?"

"No comment," she said, sipping her tea. "How are your parents—Melanie and Geoff?"

"They're fine. My mother is her usual neurotic self and my father is ... well, he's my father."

Margaret recalled Amanda's parents quite well. *Neurotic* was one way to describe her mother, but *batty* was a suitable alternative. Although her father was polite enough, there was always something alien about him—no pun intended. Maybe it had something to do with his job at the British embassy; who knew?

"Well, give them my best when you see them."

"I will."

"So what do you two have planned for today?"

"Just hanging out. You know ... catching up. What about you?" Amanda asked, changing the subject.

"Molly is—You remember Molly, right?"

"Yes. Your friend from California."

"Well, she's coming over a little later, then we're going

into the office for a couple of hours. Just because we're supposed to be off today, doesn't mean the work stops piling up," she said, taking another sip of her tea. "And I guess Alex won't be joining me for breakfast this morning, so I can go back to bed."

"Oh no. You can still have breakfast with Alex. I don't want to—"

"Shush. Alex and I can have breakfast tomorrow. You two have fun today. Are you done with that?" she asked, pointing at the mug Amanda had set aside.

"Yes, ma'am," she replied, handing the mug to Margaret. "Do you mind if I go surprise Alex?"

"No, go right ahead."

"Where is his room?"

"It's upstairs, first room on your right," she said from the sink.

* * *

Amanda tiptoed from the staircase over to Alex's room, trying not to alert him of her presence. She read the sign on the door and chuckled. Slowly, she opened the bedroom door. From the hallway, Amanda could see Alex's bed and the outline of his body under the sheet. She could also hear music. As she listened more intently to figure out the lyrics, she realized, it wasn't music. It was the sound of the ocean. *That's odd*, she thought, as she stepped into his room, closing the door behind her.

The room was dark, because the blinds were closed. The low sound of the ocean was very soothing. As her eyes adjusted to the dark, she surveyed the room. It was an adequately sized room, with a window that faced the front of the house and the typical furnishings for a student. She almost missed the flat-screen television that was mounted on a swivel arm, which could either fold flat against the wall or extend out, so the television could be viewed from anywhere in the room. There was something on the walls, but she couldn't make it out given the poor lighting.

Amanda turned her attention back to the boy, who lay asleep on the bed. Carefully, she made her way to the head of the bed, where she found Alex's face buried in the pillows. She smiled with delight, looking down at her unsuspected prey. In one leap, she jumped on top of the outlined form on the bed, intending to find Alex's armpits. As Amanda's fingers made contact with Alex's body, she found herself airborne, flying across the room until she crashed into the wall and fell in a loud thud to the floor.

"Amanda!" she heard Alex shout from across the room, then his feet running across the floor. She felt the pain aching in her back and buttocks as Alex gently lifted her head from the floor.

"Amanda! Are you all right?"

She tried to verbalize a response, but all she kept hearing were groans and moans coming from her throat. Then she heard another set of footsteps, then Alex's room door burst open.

"What the hell happened?" Margaret said hysterically, walking over to Alex and Amanda.

"I don't know," Alex stuttered. "She just came in. And I didn't know."

Margaret opened the blinds, which now showed a partly sunny sky. "Well this is a fine start to your day together. What did you have planned next—throw her in the Potomac River and see if she survives the currents?"

"Mom! You're not helping," Alex said sternly.

"Okay. Let's get her to the bed." Before Margaret could give Alex a hand, he had Amanda in his arms and was heading for his bed.

Alex watched as Amanda's eyes fluttered, then eventually opened and met his. "Are you okay?"

"What happened?" she groaned.

I kinda threw you across the room, Alex projected.

"Oh."

"How's your head, honey?" Margaret asked.

Realizing that Margaret was in the room with them, Amanda downplayed her injury and responded, "My head feels fine," she answered honestly. *It's my back and butt that's killing me,* she thought, sitting up in the bed. "That's the last time I try to surprise you," she laughed.

"See. She's fine, Mom," Alex chimed in, edging his mother out of the way. "No need for alarm."

"Okay, okay. I can take a hint. I'll go back to my room." Turning to Amanda, she added, "Amanda, it was nice seeing you again. And if you guys leave before I get up, have a great day."

"Thank you, Ms. Fuller," Amanda said as Margaret walked out of the room.

"Are you really okay?" Alex asked.

"My back's hurting a bit," she said, massaging the nape of her neck. Suddenly, she noticed the walls. There was something on them. "What the—" was all that escaped from her mouth.

Alex's room was covered with a hand-painted mural depicting a tropical oasis. Half the walls and ceiling closest to the door depicted a deserted beach, filled with sand and various tropical trees and foliage. The other half depicted the ocean, which started out in a light aqua green color and subtly darkened, as it met the sky line on the opposing wall by the window.

"Wow," Amanda said, admiring the intricate detail of the mural. "How? Why? Where did you get this mural from?"

"I drew it."

"You drew this?"

"Yeah. Do you like it?"

"I love it. It's ... it's beautiful. And you drew this all by yourself?"

"You know, your confidence in my artistic abilities is so encouraging," he said.

"No offense. It's just so grand. I thought maybe you had it professionally done."

"Not on my allowance. Besides, I don't think anyone could have captured exactly what I was looking for anyway."

"It's really beautiful," she said, still admiring the mural.

"I know," Alex said, referring to Amanda, whom he hadn't taken his eyes off since he woke up.

"As much as I'd like to kick it here in your tropical paradise, we have a date today."

"A date?"

"Yes—a date," she said pulling him close to her, and then whispered, "Where you tell me everything about your mental abilities. And unless you want to tell me here, within a few feet from your mother's ever-so-attentive ears, I suggest we skedaddle."

"Got it," he said, pulling himself away from her. "Just give me a few minutes to shower and get dressed."

"Sure," she said, hopping into his bed and reaching for the remote.

Alex eyed her suspiciously. "The television in the living room is much bigger."

"I don't mind this one," she said, ignoring his insinuation.

Alex stood awkwardly in his room, as if he was trying to figure out what he was supposed to do next. Amanda started flipping through the channels, continuing to ignore his discomfort. She didn't care how uncomfortable he was in her presence; she wasn't going to let him push her away again.

"I guess I could make myself helpful and spread your bed," she said, hopping off the bed and throwing the pillows and sheets on the floor before Alex could protest.

Giving up on the idea of ousting Amanda from his room, Alex found a clean set of clothes and headed for the bathroom across the hallway.

* * *

How disappointing, Amanda thought when Alex returned to the room already fully dressed. She was lying on top of his neatly spread bed. He was towel-drying his hair when she spoke.

"I can't believe you still have this picture."

He turned around to see her holding the Braemar graduation picture she'd given him almost three years ago. He'd had it framed and had placed it on the nightstand next to his bed. He suddenly felt foolish for not insisting that she wait downstairs. What else had she dug up while he was showering? He didn't respond to her, but kept drying his hair.

She looked at him, wanting to say something, but kept quiet instead, realizing that she may have embarrassed him.

Satisfied that his hair was dry enough, Alex grabbed his wallet and said, "Let's go."

Amanda followed Alex, who was already heading through his bedroom door. Downstairs, Alex headed for the kitchen and asked, "Did you want something to eat before we leave?"

"No. I'm fine. Your mom made me tea earlier."

"Okay. Give me a minute," he said, as he grabbed a muffin and a small bottle of orange juice from the refrigerator. "I'm ready."

"Where are we going?" she asked, trying to catch up with him as he made his way to the front door.

"See you later, Mom," Alex yelled when he opened the front door.

"Bye, Alex," Margaret responded from upstairs.

"Goodbye, Ms. Fuller," Amanda yelled.

"Bye, Amanda."

Outside, Alex locked the door after Amanda exited. "Do you mind driving?" he asked, walking toward her car in the driveway.

"I don't mind, but I'd still like to know where we're going first."

"Meadowland."

"Meadowland? Didn't you go there yesterday?"

"Sure did."

"Did I ever tell you what a delight your allegiance to the mundane is?"

"Do you want to know my secret or not?"

"Okay, okay. Don't get your boxers in a bunch," she said, getting in the car.

"Here's the address," he said, handing her a brochure of the botanical gardens. He watched as Amanda punched the address into the GPS. Noting the pristine condition that Amanda kept her car in, he asked, "Can I eat in here?"

"Go ahead."

6. FULL DISCLOSURE

The two teenagers rode in silence for the first few minutes down Route 123. Alex was eating his breakfast, which he almost lost when Amanda took the sharp curves a little too fast. She blamed her erratic driving on her unfamiliarity with the narrow, winding road. He blamed it on her heavy right foot.

"What's so special about this botanical garden anyway?" she asked, as she turned left onto Beulah Road.

"It helps me to relax."

"Alex, when I need to relax, I don't drive miles to a botanical garden to do it."

"Your mind isn't like mine," he said, looking at her. "Trust me, I'd gladly drive to the moon if I had to, just to put my mind at ease."

"So, what goes on in your mind? Why can you do all these things?"

"I don't know," he admitted. "One day, I was this perfectly normal kid, and then the next day my mind just took over everything."

"What do you mean it took over everything?"

"It started consuming everything that I was. I would get these splitting headaches. Then my mind would just start doing all these things, like starting small fires, moving objects, without me really wanting it to. It took everything in me to keep it together those first few days."

"Okay, slow down. You said yesterday that this started when you went to Camp APRICOT."

"Yeah."

"Did they do something to you while you were there that triggered it?"

"No. I don't think so."

"So how did it start?"

"I had a near-death experience," he said, staring blindly out the window.

"Are you serious?" she asked, almost veering off the road. "Oh my God! What happened?"

"Well, maybe I should start from the beginning," he said, glancing over at her. "Summer vacation had just started and I was getting ready for camp. I remember feeling nervous, thinking that I wouldn't know anyone there. When I got there, it was just as I'd imagined—a lot of kids from all over the world that I didn't know. First, they divided the boys from the girls. Then they further divided us into groups of six. Each cabin housed six of us. The sleeping quarters in the cabins were simple enough—six beds with a shelved headboard and a foot locker at the opposite end. I don't remember any of my roommates, except for Justin Dunns."

"Who's he?"

"The only friend I made at camp that year," he said as Amanda drove down the small street that ran alongside the grounds of Meadowland Botanical Gardens. "Make a left into the second entrance."

Amanda found a parking space close to the entrance of

the park. They both hopped out of the car and walked over to the admissions booth.

"One please," Alex said to the attendant, then paid for the ticket. He handed the ticket to Amanda, as he flashed his annual pass and led her through the visitor's welcome garden.

"So you met Justin at camp," she said, eager to hear more. "Do you two still stay in touch?"

"No, we don't," he said, with a sad look on his face. "Justin was from California, so we had that in common. We shared sleeping quarters for a week before we ever said a word to each other. Turned out, he was even shyer than I was."

Amanda smiled and held his hand as they walked past the herb and formal gardens. "I can't imagine anyone being shyer than you were back at Braemar."

"He was. Anyway, it seemed that California wasn't the only thing we shared in common. One day, during a soccer game, both Justin and I got nosebleeds and had to sit out the rest of the match on the sidelines. I use to get a few nosebleeds here and there before all this, but it really got bad after my abilities showed up. Anyway, that's when Justin and I first started talking to each other. After that, we started hanging out."

"There was this big kid from Russia—Grigori Petrovskii. Grig was a bully. Anyone who tried to call him Greg, instead of Grig, got the crap beaten out of them. He was a year older than me and this was his third year coming to Camp APRICOT. He didn't like Americans, and as far as I could tell, the feeling was mutual. Grig got a kick out of tormenting the smaller American boys, whom he thought were weak and wouldn't fight back. He tried out his scare tactics on me during the first week, but when he saw that I didn't scare easily, he moved on to Justin—that's where he focused his attention. Justin was a petite fourteen-year-old. He never stood up for himself. He never talked back. He was the perfect target for Grig."

Slowly they strolled along the great lawn toward Lake Carolina.

"Grig made Justin's life at Camp APRICOT a living hell. He would trip Justin whenever he came within arm's length of him. Cut his hair while he slept. Placed worms and insects in his clothes, knowing that he was allergic to insect bites. Nailed his hiking boots to the floor. All sorts of horrible things."

"And no one did anything?"

"I helped Justin when I was around, but I wasn't with him all the time, especially when we got split up for our daily activities. And it seemed that Grig would sneak into our cabin when we were asleep or during the daytime when we weren't there. When Grig cut his hair, I told Justin to report it to the counselors, but he didn't want to. He didn't want to be known as a rat. Instead, he told me to cut off the rest of his hair to even it out."

"Was this before your mind could do those things?"

"Yeah," he answered. "That summer, the DMV area saw an unprecedented rash of heat waves and thunderstorms. The thunderstorms caused massive power outages and flash flooding across the region. Our camp was no exception. The power got knocked out around the end of the fourth week of camp and the small river nearby started to overflow its banks. The power company promised to have the electricity turned back on in less than three days, so the counselors decided that we would tough it out like the original settlers until then. So imagine it, no AC, and we weren't permitted anywhere near the river until the water receded and we were told it was safe."

Alex stopped a few yards away from Lake Carolina, lost in his memories.

"This is truly magnificent," Amada said, referring to the scenery, while giving Alex enough time to collect his thoughts. "Let's go sit on those chairs under the cherry trees," she suggested. Alex followed her around the edge of Lake Carolina and sat in one of the two chairs they found in the Cherry Walk.

"The night the power went out was absolutely miserable," he continued. "We had no air conditioning and it was so hot in our cabin, I couldn't sleep. Instead, I went outside, hoping that it would be a bit cooler—but it wasn't. That's when I saw Grig, coming toward our cabin with another boy. I guess they were there to inflict another round of assault on Justin. I ran inside to get a baseball bat from my foot locker, then went back outside before they entered the cabin. They saw the bat in my hand when I went back outside. Grig wanted to know what I was going to do with it. I told him to come closer and find out for himself. Then he said that I wouldn't be there all the time to protect Justin. He was right.

"The next day, we were supposed to stay near the camp site and play games because the ground was so saturated from the rain. I remember seeing Justin at breakfast, before we split up into groups. I made absolutely sure that Grig was not in his group before I joined mine."

Alex stopped and stared at the lake in front of him. Amanda was about to say something when he started again.

"We were in the middle of playing Jeopardy when we

heard someone shouting for help. It was the boy whom I had seen with Grig the night before. He was running from the river toward the camp grounds. He told us that someone had fallen into the river. I immediately started looking for Justin. When I didn't see him among the other kids in his group, I ran to the river.

"The banks of the river were flooded. By now, the counselors were all there and so were most of the kids. I saw Grig standing alone by himself—frozen—staring out at the water. I followed his gaze and saw Justin's head bobbing in the river. He was struggling to stay afloat. The counselors were yelling at Justin to hold on as they tried to find a rope. I didn't stop to think why the counselors were waiting to find a rope; I just jumped into the river, trying to get to Justin. I was only a few feet out into the river, when I felt the current pulling me downstream. I fought against the current, but it was too strong. It kept pulling me away from Justin, whom I could no longer see in the water. I panicked and starting screaming for Justin. Water started gushing into my mouth and the current kept pulling me under. I kicked and fought, trying to get back to the surface, but the current overpowered me. I saw death coming and there was nothing I could do.

"Resolute on my impending demise, I stopped fighting. The only thought that remained with me was that I desperately wanted to save Justin. Then I had a brief moment of clarity within my chaotic surroundings and that's when it happened. Somehow Justin's body made its way over to me and we floated to the surface. I don't know how it happened, but I saw it."

"What do you mean you saw it?" Amanda asked.

"I saw Justin's body being pulled from the bottom of

the river up to where I was. I grabbed him when he was within reach and then our bodies floated to the surface. It's like I imagined it and then it happened. Once we got to the surface, we were still caught in the currents. Then I saw a calm area of the river off to the side where our campgrounds were. Our only hope now was to get over there and away from the currents. It was a good thing that I still had one hand wrapped around Justin's body, because all of a sudden, his body started to drift over to the area that I saw, pulling me along for the ride."

"Wait a minute. Who saved whom? Did you save Justin? Or, did he end up saving you?"

"I wasn't sure at first. But over time, I learned that I can only move the objects around me, but not myself. I can't propel myself, like I can with objects or people for that matter. I have to depend on my own two feet to get around," he said, smiling at her. "So that's how it happened. My pathetic attempt to save Justin must have triggered something in my mind to make me into the freak that I am."

"Alex, you're not a freak," Amanda said a little too loudly, because the older couple that was strolling along the Cherry Walk looked over at them with a grimace on their face. Amanda hated that *children should be seen and never heard* look grownups tended to give teenagers—*as if we're not supposed to enjoy the world we live in too, just because we're kids*, she thought. Flippantly, she turned her attention back to Alex, ignoring them.

"You should be proud of yourself for saving Justin," she added.

"Save Justin?" he spat with disgust. "Amanda, I didn't save Justin."

"He drowned?" she exclaimed.

"Not that day. He survived the river incident. After they dragged us out of the river, they performed CPR on him. He had taken in a lot of water, but eventually they were able to resuscitate him before the ambulance arrived. They took him to the hospital to run tests and kept him overnight for observation."

"So what was going on with you?" Amanda asked.

"When I came out of the river, I knew something was different. First I had this tingling sensation all over my body. At times, I felt like my spirit wanted to leave my body, but something kept pulling it back in. Some of the counselors were standing over me, trying to get me to focus on how many fingers they were holding up. That seemed to reorient me and the sensation stopped. I told them I was fine, and that they should focus their efforts on Justin.

"As I watched everyone swarm around Justin, my senses started to heighten. Images became sharper. Sounds were clearer. Scents were more pungent, to the point where it felt like I could taste what I was smelling. And whenever someone passed within a foot of me, the hair on my body stood up.

"After EMS cleared me to stay, and took Justin, the counselors took me back to the small infirmary at the camp. The camp nurse, named Shannon, insisted that I spend the night there. I remember being so pissed at her for doing that, but looking back at it now, I'm glad she did."

"Why?" Amanda asked, looking on with great expectation.

"The first day with my abilities was the worst. When I got to the infirmary, which was really just another cabin with medical supplies, my senses were still up there. After having me change into dry clothes, Nurse Shannon put me to bed.

"Wait. So she just puts you to bed without saying anything about your heightened senses, or the sensation you felt?"

"I didn't tell her about my senses or the sensation. I didn't tell anyone—not the counselors, not EMS, not the other campers. No, that was something I kept to myself. Hell, I even tried to convince myself that it was just the adrenaline coursing through my body because of all the excitement. But deep down inside, I knew it wasn't.

"After I woke up in the afternoon, it was still pretty hot outside because I could feel the heat penetrating through the wooden walls of the infirmary. Nurse Shannon must have stepped away because I was alone in the cabin. My senses were back to normal and I felt better. I was still sitting in bed when my mind thought of Justin. Suddenly, everything in the cabin started to shake. I panicked, because I thought the place was haunted. That's when the shit hit the fan. Everything in the room, except for the three beds, started flying around the room—bed pans, waste baskets, overbed tables, clipboards, scale, privacy screen, bedside cabinet, you name it. As I watched the circus unfold before my eyes, the bed in front of me burst into flames. *Where the hell is Nurse Shannon?* I thought. Then the tingling sensation came back again and I felt my spirit trying to escape again, but my body refused to let it go."

"When you say your spirit was trying to leave, was that your out-of-body ability?" Amanda asked.

"It was, although I didn't know it at the time. The first couple of times that I had an out-of-body experience, or

OBE'd, I didn't like it. It felt like my spirit was being ripped out of my body, which left behind an immense tingling sensation, and I would get these god-awful headaches. But as time has passed, I've learned that if I relax, it makes the process a whole lot easier.

"So anyway, I heard Nurse Shannon calling my name from outside. Then, I heard her climb the four steps that led to the door of the infirmary. All I kept thinking to myself was, *how am I going to explain all this to her?* I just wished it would all stop because it was giving me a terrible headache. As she flung the door open with a vase of flowers in her hand, everything returned to its original position and the fire disappeared."

"What?" Amanda said, astonished.

"Yup. Just like that, everything was back to normal, except the sheets on the bed in front of me. Those were scorched. And that was the only proof I had that what I saw earlier had actually happened.

"Nurse Shannon ran over to me and said she heard me calling her, which technically didn't happen. That was my telepathic ability emerging. She placed the vase on the small table next to my bed and walked over to the bed in front of me. She examined the sheets, which had a burn spot on them. I lied to her and told her that I thought I smelt smoke and that's why I called for her. She couldn't account for the scorched sheets because there were no igniters in sight, so she easily dismissed it. She decided to stay with me after that, but the longer she stayed, the more exhausted I felt. I didn't know it at the time, but it was because I was trying to suppress my abilities—desperately wishing that every object in the room didn't come charging at us. Then my nose started to bleed. She helped me to clean up. Afterwards, I told her I was hungry and she left to get something from the canteen.

"Alone in the room, I let my mind rummage over what had happened earlier. And then it started again. Everything started to shake. There was a small table next to my bed, with the vase of flowers Nurse Shannon had placed there. As I watched it fall, I remember saying to myself, *please don't break*. And the vase stopped just short of hitting the floor. I was flabbergasted. I looked at the vase levitating about two inches above the floor, when slowly, it floated over to me. I held it and turned around to look at the other objects that were either still shaking or floating. But this time, they were slowly floating toward me. The closer they got to my face, I wished they would stop and they did. That's when I realized that maybe all of this was happening because of me. So one by one, I wished each object back to its original place, and they complied.

"When I was all done, I looked at the bed in front of me and wondered why it wasn't on fire. And sure enough, as I thought it, the bed burst into flames again. I heard footsteps on the stairs again and I wished the fire away. The flames disappeared as Nurse Shannon came in with my meal. Blood was dripping from my nose, so she helped me clean up again. She thought my nosebleeds were caused by the heated indoor air, so she said she'd get me a battery-operated fan to cool the air in the cabin."

"So that's how it started?"

"Yeah. The next day, I was placed back into the general population, where I learned that the hospital wasn't going to release Justin back to the camp until the electricity was back on, which was scheduled to happen the next day. With so many people and objects around me, it was hard to keep my abilities under control, especially since they were so new. As I tried to carry on with my day, objects would levitate or move as I walked by them. I had to force them back down to the ground or stop them before anyone realized what was happening. The fire from the gas stove that they used to cook our meals would dance uncontrollably as I walked by the kitchen. People started to respond to my thoughts and not what I said. I thought I was losing my mind. All day, my mind felt like a jigsaw puzzle that was taken apart, and it took everything in me to keep it together. It took so much concentration to keep my mind from running wild that day. And on top of that, the sweltering heat didn't do much to help put my mind at ease.

"The next day, Justin came back to camp." Alex stopped and took several breaths.

Desperate to hear more, Amanda asked, "What happened when he came back?"

"When he came back, he was fine ... physically. The hospital released him to the camp because his parent were vacationing in the Orients and didn't want to interrupt their travel to attend to their son. If only they had come home, none of this would have happened."

"What? What happened?"

"That day, we were supposed to go hiking at a nearby park. All morning, I kept to myself and lagged behind the group to avoid detection. But Justin kept checking on me. I told him that I thought I was going to be sick and that he should stay clear of me. But that made him want to stay with me even more.

"Once at the park, I went to the bathroom more often that I needed, to avoid Justin. I thought I had gotten rid of him by the fifth trip. When I came out of the bathroom, our group had already started their hike up the trail that followed along the edge of a river gorge. The river flowed past several jagged, rocky surfaces and high-walled cliffs. At certain spots along the trail, you could look straight down at the seventy-foot drop to the river below. At other spots, large boulders paved the way down to the river. I kept my distance from the group going up the trail.

"It was so hot that day. I was trying to keep my mind from obsessing about it because with the thought of heat comes the thought of fire, and poof one would start along the trail. So I stopped under a tree that was off to the side of the trail, closer to the river to cool down a bit. Or so I had hoped. But it was still hot even in the shade, so a small fire appeared. I put out the fire by mentally scooping up some dirt and heaving it onto the fire. I turned to rejoin the group, but Justin was standing there, looking at me pretty much the same way you did the other day.

"I took a few steps toward him and he backed away. I told him I could explain, but he kept backing away. I was so consumed with trying to reason with him that I didn't realize that as I was inching my way toward him, he was backing closer and closer to the edge of a vertical cliff of the gorge." Alex stopped and a tear rolled down his cheek.

"I didn't realize how close to the edge he was until he took that one fatal step backwards," he said sniffling. "He fell and I screamed, which alerted the others in our group and some other passersby. When I ran to the ledge, I saw Justin holding on to a small branch that had grown out of the side of the cliff, just a couple of feet down. Below him was the gorge, with several large, steep, jagged rocks protruding out of the water. I lay down on the ground, stretching my hand as far down as I could to Justin. But he hesitated. He seemed to be just as afraid of me as he was about falling. I begged him to grab my hand, telling him it would be okay. One of the camp counselors rushed over by then, and also stretched his hand down to Justin.

"Justin looked me in the eyes and for a moment he didn't seem afraid anymore. I watched him shift his weight in order to grab my hand, but as he did, the branch's roots gave way." Tears rolled down Alex's cheeks as he held his head down. Amanda sat on the edge of her chair, looking at him. Cautiously, she put her hand in his hair as he shook his head from side to side.

"He fell. He hit his head on a rock before his body fell into the river. The current dragged his body several miles down the river. When they found him, they said he was alive when he hit the river. That's the day Justin drowned," he said, choking on his tears. "I killed the only other friend I had in Virginia, other than you." He finally allowed himself to say it out loud for the first time.

Alex buried his face in his hands as he continued to sob. Amanda remained silent, crippled with shock. Now she understood why he had looked so tortured since that summer. Without thinking, she got down on her knees in front of him and put her arms around him. Alex fought to push her away, but she tightened her grip until finally, the resistance stopped. All she felt was the heaving of Alex's chest and the tears soaking through her T-shirt.

How do you console the inconsolable? How do you heal a heart that even time has failed to? She didn't know the answer. All she knew was, her friend was in pain, and she wasn't going to sit idly by and do nothing.

"Alex," she said, resting her head against his. "I know

you blame yourself for Justin's death, but what happened to him was a terrible, terrible accident."

Alex pushed her away. "I killed him, Amanda. It wasn't an accident," he roared ferociously, trying to get up from the chair.

"Yes, it was," she said, pushing him back down into the chair and turning his face to look at her. "You stumbled onto these powers. Powers that no one could have imagined, much less understood. You didn't ask for them. No one taught you how they worked or what they were capable of. It would be like me giving a person the key to my car and telling that person to go for a spin by him or herself, knowing that that person has never been inside an automobile before and has no idea how it operates. Can I really be surprised if that person runs down an entire family caught in a crosswalk? Of course not. It would be tragic— yes, but not that person's fault. It would be my fault. What I'm trying to say is, if there's anyone to blame for this, blame the person who did this to you and left you alone to fend for yourself."

"I don't know how any of this happened to me, much less who or what did it," Alex said hysterically.

"What about your mom?"

"What about my mom?" Alex asked defensively.

"Maybe she knows how this—"

"No way. I'm not telling my mom about this," Alex said, finally breaking through Amanda's barricade and walking further down the Cherry Walk.

"Your mother doesn't know about this?" Amanda asked, trailing after him.

"No, and she's not going to either."

"Alex, you have to tell her."

"No way!"

"She may know why this happened to you. Or it could be hereditary. Or she—"

"Are you saying my mom's a freak like me?"

"Of course not. And will you please stop using that 'F' word?" Unable to keep up with Alex's long strides, Amanda stopped to catch her breath. "Alex, could you please stop walking, so we can talk about this?"

Alex stopped and turned to face Amanda. "There's nothing else to talk about. I promised to tell you my secret and I've kept my end of the bargain."

"So that's it. You're going to just shut me out again? Is that it?" she yelled, as Alex resumed his walk. "Is that your big, fat, stupid plan? Well, I have news for you, buddy— you can't shut me out. I won't let you." Amanda was beside herself. She had to make him stop and listen to her. Suddenly, she got an idea. Ordinarily, she wouldn't stoop this low, but what choice did she have? Alex was already a few yards ahead of her.

As Alex entered the intersection between the Cherry Walk and the Cross Country Trail, he heard Amanda frantically bawling behind him.

"You've got to be kidding me," he said to himself. He stopped and turn around, shaking his head as a huge grin appeared on his face. Slowly, he walked back to the sobbing girl, who was trying desperately to squeeze a tear through her dark blue eyes.

"You are pathetic, you know that," he smiled.

"It worked, didn't it?" she laughed.

"I guess it did. I wasn't—" Alex was interrupted by the Lady Gaga ringtone coming from Amanda's cell phone.

"Just a second," she said to Alex, fishing the phone out

of her pocketbook. "Hello?" Amanda said into the phone. "Hi, Katt," she continued, holding the phone in one hand while sticking the index finger of her other hand into her ear to block out the noise around her.

Realizing that Amanda's conversation was going to take a while, Alex said, "I need to use the can. See you in a minute," then walked off.

* * *

Alex was still inside the restroom when Amanda got off the phone with Katt. Amanda liked Katt because she wasn't like the other Novies. Katt was not consumed with fashion, fame, or fortune; instead she had political inclinations. Amanda had hoped to spend more time getting to know her outside of school hours, but Katt had an even busier schedule than she did, with her extracurricular activities and working part-time for her father, a U.S. Congressman.

Although Katt had sided with Amanda when she was on the outs with Alex the other day, Katt didn't hold it against her for hanging out with Alex today. As long as Amanda was happy with the choices she made, Katt would be supportive.

Amanda was still standing outside the restroom when she saw a wedding party walking toward the gazebo in the middle of Lake Carolina. The photographer was busy positioning the bridesmaids and groomsmen around the happy couple.

"That's right," Amanda whispered to herself. "Keep that fake smile painted on your face and enjoy the one last perfect day of your life."

The institution of marriage didn't rank very high on

Amanda's list. *Whoever said that the nuclear family somehow cre-ates a healthier and more stable environment for children has never been to my house,* she thought. What a crock of matrimonial bullshit!

"Ready to go," Alex said from behind Amanda.

"Please," Amanda said anxiously.

Alex followed Amanda's gaze and saw the wedding party on the gazebo. "Stop hating," he teased her, recalling how her parents' marriage had soured her on the whole idea of marriage.

"To hate would suggest I actually give a damn."

"I cannot believe you still don't find marriage a won-derful thing."

"And you do?"

"With the right person, it can be."

"I don't understand you, Fuller. I have parents who are married. I see firsthand that it's not all roses. You, on the other hand, have a single mother, yet you believe in that crap."

"Ouch," he said, a bit perturbed.

"I'm sorry. I just don't get its appeal to you. Can we talk about something else?"

"Like what?"

"What happened in the locker room Thursday?"

"Oh, that." He smiled. "Well, David and his entourage were about to give me hell because he didn't like the idea of the two of us hanging out together. So I defended myself."

"How?"

"I threw Tim and Rafi against the lockers, knocking them out. Then I knocked David's legs out from under him."

"Let's go this way," Amanda said, motioning him to take the trail around Lake Lena.

This trail was more secluded than the others. It was dark and cool from the overgrown trees and plants that loomed over it. Satisfied that they were out of sight from the other visitors, she said, "Show me how you do it."

"How I move things with my mind?"

"That too, but all of the other stuff as well."

Alex looked around him to make sure there were no prying eyes. Satisfied, he stood close to Amanda. He saw when her cheeks turned pink, but it didn't register to him. "You still like roller coaster rides, right?" he asked.

"Yes."

"Well, no screaming this time, okay."

Amanda watched as Alex closed his eyes and inhaled deeply. In a split second, he opened his eyes and she felt her body slowly rise about five inches off the ground. Suddenly, she felt her body being pulled backwards along the trail they had just walked, and then shot up in the air among the branches in the trees. Just as she thought she was going to slam into the tall pine trees that flew by her, her body stopped in mid-air. A scream escaped from her mouth before she could stop it. Suddenly, her body propelled forward, taking the same path it had taken earlier, landing inches away from Alex again. When her feet touched the ground, she had a difficult time keeping herself balanced. Alex caught and steadied her.

"You okay?" he asked.

"Oh my God! That was so frigging awesome. Do it again! Do it again!" she said, bouncing up and down.

"Shh," he whispered, trying to calm her down. "I'm not

doing it again, especially because you can't keep your mouth shut."

"It was instinct. I couldn't help it."

"Well try. What do you want to see next?"

"Make a fire," she said excitedly.

Alex hesitated. He didn't like using his pyrokinetic abilities. It was the first ability he had worked earnestly to control after Justin's death. If only that fire had not started that day, Justin would be alive.

"What's the matter? You can't do it?" Amanda asked.

"Give me a minute," he said, looking around for the ideal spot. "Let's walk over there," he added, pointing to the left of them.

They walked across the boardwalk and past the Bog Garden. Alex stopped where they had a view of Lake Lena and no passerby would see them from this angle.

"Keep your eyes on the water," he instructed.

Amanda watched Alex close his eyes again, then something sparkled in the corner of her eyes on the lake. She turned around to see a small fire hovering over Lake Lena. She watched as the flame grew larger and its reflection danced on the water below it.

"Now watch this," Alex said. With his eyes still fixed on the fire, he held his hands out in front of him. They were about a foot apart, with his palms facing each other, like he was palming a basketball. He thrust his hands forward and the fire immediately took the form of a circle. Slowly, the circle swelled several feet in diameter, as did the flames inside.

"What is ... How are you doing that?" Amanda asked.

"Just a simple application of pressure to create a force field around the fire to contain it. Whenever I experiment with my pyrokinesis to create a fire or explosion, I use my telekinesis to create a force field around it to prevent it from spreading or getting out of control."

"A force field? Explosions?"

"Yeah, all my powers are evolving."

"Wow," she said, mesmerized by what she was seeing. Then, without warning, the large ball of fire collapsed and disappeared. She turned back around to face Alex, shaking her head in disbelief.

"What?" he asked, feeling a bit self-conscious.

"That was amazing."

Funny, Alex didn't feel amazing. For almost two years, he had tried desperately to keep his abilities a secret, afraid of what people would say if they knew about them. He never dreamt that one day he would reveal them, or that they would be met with such approval. But this was Amanda; she wasn't like everyone else.

"What about your mind-control abilities?" she asked.

"My telepathic abilities."

"I thought telepaths could read people's minds," she said, bringing up the subject again.

"I think that is the general consensus, but I can't. Or at least, my telepathic ability hasn't evolved that far yet. Come to think of it, I wouldn't want to have that ability. I don't fully understand my telepathic abilities, because I really haven't tested it quite as much as the others—except for projecting my thoughts into other people's minds, which you already know about."

"Why haven't you tested it?"

"I don't like controlling other people's minds. It's wrong and can be dangerous," he replied curtly.

"Have you ever controlled someone else's mind?"

He looked at her, but didn't answer.

"Did you ever control my mind?" she asked.

"No."

"Then whose?"

"Can't tell you."

"Come on. I thought you were going to share everything with me," she whined.

"Okay. Ms. Lucci."

"Ms. Lucci? Why?"

"You're going to get mad."

"No, I won't."

"Yes, you will."

"No, I won't. I promise."

"You asked for it," he said hesitantly. "I changed her mind about letting you tutor me."

"You did what?" she asked, tilting her head to the side and letting her anger seep into her facial expression.

Recognizing that look in her face, he reminded her, "You said you wouldn't get mad. If you get mad, I'm not telling you anything else."

Afraid that he would make good on his threat, Amanda resisted the urge to wail on him for the Lucci incident. "So how does that work?" she asked.

"You know about the three principal structures of the brains and their functions, right?"

"Vaguely."

"Well, depending on what I want the person to do, I mentally enter that structure of the brain and stimulate it like any of our senses would."

"I don't understand."

"Okay. Remember from biology where we learned about how our five senses send information to our brain and our brain in turn tells us how to react? Take the infamous hot stove example. When your hand touches a hot stove, the nerve endings in your fingers transmit the sensation to your brain, which interprets it and tells you to move your hand."

"Yeah."

"Well, like your senses, I can transmit messages to your brain. I can also block transmission from getting to and from your brain. For example, I could block transmission from your optic nerve, which would result in you becoming temporarily blind. I could also block transmission from your brain to—let's say—your heart, for example, which would make your heart stop beating."

"So, you could enter my mind, tell me to do whatever you want, then I just do it."

"I could, *if* I wanted to. But since I don't, I won't."

"Oh, come on. I want to see this one," she whined. "This is like the coolest power ever and you're not going to show it to me."

"Amanda, I don't like making people do things against their will."

"What if I tell you what I want you to make me do— then it won't be against my will, will it?"

Alex looked at her suspiciously. "What exactly do you have in mind?"

"Make me kiss you," she said, a bit too eagerly.

Alex stopped breathing for a moment. "You want to kiss me?"

"No," she said, trying to conceal her true intent. "It's just that, uhh ... kissing you would be the last thing on my mind, and ... uhh, the worst thing you could make me do

—against my will, that is. So if I gave you permission ahead of time, then we'd be cool. Does that make sense?

"No, not really," he said, shaking his head. "What if I make you feel like you just kissed a boy?"

"No," she exclaimed. "Just do it, and stop overanalyzing it."

"You're serious, aren't you?"

"Well, duh," she said, rolling her eyes.

"Okay," he said slowly. "What type of kiss do you want?"

"What?" she asked, looking confused. "A regular kiss. Geez Alex, you're acting like you've never kissed me before."

"That was years ago, when we were kids. We didn't even know what we were doing. And I almost puked in your mouth, remember?"

Impatiently, Amanda crossed her arms in front of her, stomping her foot. "Are you done?" she finally asked. "Are you through procrastinating, or would you like a few more minutes?"

"Okay, fine. I'll do it."

Alex fixed his gaze on Amanda.

"Wait!"

"What now?"

"I want proof," Amanda said, pulling her lipstick out of her bag. She applied a thick layer of lipstick to her mouth. "This way, I'll know exactly where you have me kiss you. Ready."

Alex smiled and repeated his earlier ritual. Once Alex entered her mind, Amanda's body stood erect. Instead of saying his commands aloud, he projected them into her mind. He watched her hesitate for a moment, blink her eyes once, and then walk over to him. Slowly, she placed her arms around his neck, tipped up on her toes, and kissed him. He felt her hand pressing his face against hers as their tongues playfully caressed each other. Suddenly, Alex felt a strange sensation as his mind reacted to Amanda's kiss. The feeling was euphoric. He had dreamt of this moment many times before, but this was not how it was supposed to happen. As much as he was elated that she had kissed him, he wanted her to remember it, so they could both share in the experience. So he exited her mind and relinquished control back to her. He watched as she awoke from her trance-like state.

"What happened? Did I kiss you?"

"You tell me," he said, pointing to his lips.

Pleased with what she saw, Amanda smiled and said, "Nice."

"You want to see the out-of-body experience?" he said, changing the subject and walking away.

"But of course," she said, following behind him, trying to figure out what had just happened to cause Alex to start acting so aloof.

"I just need somewhere to put my body," he said, avoiding eye contact with her.

"Actually, this part of the Garden is a bit scary. Why don't we head back toward Lake Carolina, where's there's more light?" she suggested.

"Actually, Lake Gardenia might be better for this one. The view from there is more serene and will make it easier for me to detach."

They doubled back past Lake Carolina. As they walked, neither one said a word. Although Amanda saw her lipstick smeared on his lips, she had no memory of the kiss. Alex on the other hand remembered everything about the kiss, but wished he could forget his journey into Amanda's mind. Amanda became bothered by the silence, but chose to remain quiet. When they reached Lake Gardenia, Alex found a bench that was donated to the Gardens by one of the many dignitaries that frequented the park.

"So how will I know that you really left your body?"

"My body will go limp, as if I'm in a coma."

"No, I mean—what proof will I have?"

"Oh. When you see my body goes limp, go into the woods, and do something silly. Then come back over to the bench."

"Got it."

Amanda watched Alex lie across the park bench, with his arms crossed on his chest. In less than a minute, his body went limp and one of his arms fell to the ground. Gently, she lifted his arm and placed it back on his chest. She waved her hands over his face, but got no response. Then she ran over to the Butterfly Garden instead, keeping her eyes on the boy who appeared to be asleep on the bench. In the Butterfly Garden, she scratched Alex's name into the ground, erased it with her foot, and then returned to the park bench. She watched as Alex inhaled deeply and his limbs came back to life.

"You don't take instructions too well, do you?" he said, referring to the fact that she had ignored his instructions to go into the woods, and not the Butterfly Garden.

"What did I do?" she said, laughing.

"You scratched my name in the ground over by the Butterfly Garden, then erased it."

"That is so cool."

"Glad you like it," he said absently. "It's getting late. Let's go home."

7. GALLERY PLACE

Sunday morning at 6:08 a.m., Amanda lay restless in her bed. She couldn't put her finger on it, but something was wrong. Yesterday, Alex had barely said a word to her as she drove him home from the Gardens. Come to think of it, he'd been acting weird ever since she kissed him. He had become distant and his words were short. Could his sudden change in behavior toward her really be over the kiss? She had told him beforehand that it would be okay for him to make her kiss him. Or did something else happen that she was not aware of?

Oh crap! That must be it, she thought.

She hopped off her bed, reached for the telephone and began dialing his number. Suddenly, she stopped. This conversation was not going to take place over the telephone. It had to be in person. She jumped into her favorite mini skirt, a tank, and sandals. What had she done to make Alex revert back to his distant self? What exactly did he have her do? Did she say something to him that she didn't mean for him to hear?

Oh dear God, please don't let it be that, she prayed.

She raced down the wide staircase of the enormous house she lived in—courtesy of the British government. In the sitting room to the right, she could see her mother curled up on a chaise lounge with the only man that gave her comfort nowadays—Jack Daniels. Amanda couldn't help but to feel sorry for her mother, who went looking for love in all the wrong places. Now she and Amanda's dad lived their separate lives under the same roof. The two only interacted when Geoffrey Bridgewater entertained his diplomatic cohorts in their home or when Amanda was the subject of discussion. Not wanting to be the only guest at another one of her mother's pity parties, Amanda left the house without waking her.

She pulled up to the Fuller house less than twenty minutes later, a feat she could never duplicate during the week, given the region's horrible traffic record. Once inside the Fullers' driveway, she pulled out her cell phone and started dialing.

"Hello," a groggy Alex muttered.

"Hey. It's Amanda. Look out your window."

"What?"

"Get up and look through your window."

A few seconds passed, then Alex appeared in the window above the front door on the second floor. He scanned the area until he saw Amanda, standing beside her car.

"Amanda, what are you doing here?"

"I need to talk to you."

"And you couldn't do that over the phone from *your* house?"

"No. Now come down and let me in."

Alex shook his head in disbelief. He knew this wouldn't be good. Reluctantly, he went downstairs and let her in.

"You do know that we have a doorbell that works, right?" he said sarcastically.

"I know. I just didn't want to wake your mother two

days in a row," she said, quietly closing the door behind her.

Alex led her into the living room and motioned for her to sit down. He plopped down onto the sofa, wedging a throw pillow under his head.

"This better be good," he said, yawning.

"What happened yesterday in the park?"

"Gardens," he corrected her.

"Whatever."

"Weren't you there?"

"Alex! Stop being mean and tell me what happened … when I kissed you."

Alex's eyes popped open and his heartbeat quickened. "I don't know what you're talking about," he lied.

"Yes, you do. You have been very … curt with me ever since I kissed you. Now the only thing I can come up with is that something happened when you made me kiss you."

"Wait a minute," Alex said, slowly sitting up in the sofa. "I didn't make you kiss me. You told me to make you kiss me. There's a difference."

"Okay, I told you to. Now, why have you been acting so weird since then?"

"I didn't realize I was acting weird, but from now on, I'll try to be on my best behavior."

"Alex, don't make fun of me. Now tell me exactly what happened yesterday. Starting with what you told me to do."

Alex shook his head. "This is exactly why I didn't want to do this to you." He took a deep breath and looked at Amanda, who was on the edge of the armchair, anxiously awaiting his explanation.

"Remember when I told you I didn't like controlling a person's mind?"

"Uh-huh."

"Well, I was very reluctant to do that to you."

"I know. That's why I told you what to make me do."

"Well, I didn't do *exactly* what you told me to do."

"Okay," she said, eyeing him curiously. "But I saw my lipstick on your lips."

"Oh, you kissed me all right. But that's not what I told you to do."

"What did you tell me to do?"

"Don't be mad with me, okay? I just didn't want you to do something you'd regret later."

Amanda sat quietly for a moment, debating whether she wanted to hear his explanation after all. "What is it?" she managed to say, bracing herself.

"I told you to remove all your inhibitions and do whatever you wanted."

Silence fell over the house as the two teens stared past each other. Amanda's mind was cluttered, and could not formulate a response. Alex appeared to be in deep thought, but his mind was blank. The silence lingered and the teens started to shift uneasily in their seats.

Where is Ms. Fuller when you needed her? Amanda wondered, looking toward the staircase. Finally, Amanda felt as if she was going to explode if someone didn't say something.

"So," she broke the silence. "Now that we've gotten that out of the way."

Noting her discomfort, Alex said, "It's no big deal. I mean, you used to kiss me all the time when we were smaller."

"Right," she joined in. "No big deal. Where is your mother?" she said, turning to look up the stairs.

"She's still sleeping. Do you want to go wake her?"

"No, I like breathing too much," she said, forcing a smile across her lips.

"How is your mom, by the way?" Alex asked.

Amanda's mind flashed back to the image of her mother on the chaise. She had obviously drunk herself to sleep last night after her husband called to tell her that he would be staying in Argentina two more days on business.

"She's fine. She was asleep when I left."

Alex interpreted her response to mean that not much had changed in the Bridgewater household since he was last there. Not wanting to make her feel uncomfortable, he changed the subject.

"So, what did you have planned for today?" he asked.

"Come to think of it, I really didn't have anything planned. But since I'm here, I'm pretty sure we can find something to do. Any ideas?"

"I don't know yet. Mom usually has something for us to do on Sundays."

"I knew I heard voices down here," said Margaret Fuller, walking down the stairs. "Good morning, Amanda."

"Good Morning, Ms. Fuller."

"Two days in a row," she said, walking into the kitchen. "Just like old times. So what's on the agenda for today?"

"That's what we were discussing when you walked in. I don't think we were able to come up with anything," Amanda said. She looked over at Alex for affirmation, but instead she found him staring at her.

"You guys should go check out that Crime and Punishment Museum in DC. I heard it's really awesome," Margaret suggested.

"That sounds like a great idea. Alex," Amanda said, throwing a pillow at him. "What do you think?"

"I've been there already," he said blankly.

"Amanda, have you been to this museum?" Margaret asked.

"No, ma'am," Amanda said, giving Alex her best pissed-off face.

"Alex, why don't you be a gentleman and take Amanda to the museum?"

Both women stared at Alex, getting ready to pounce on him if he didn't take the bait they had laid out for him.

"I thought we were going to do something together today," Alex said, looking at his mother.

"Alex, I'm so tired. I'm going to crawl right back into bed with this cup of tea and a good book. And if I feel like it later, I'll call Molly and we can go check out that new Brad Pitt movie. You're free to join us, but no puke noises when we swoon over Brad taking his shirt off."

"How do you know he'll take his shirt off?"

"It's Brad Pitt. No director is going to make a movie without Brad taking his shirt off, unless they want it to tank."

"Well, as tempting as your movie invite sounds, I think I'll pass. Amanda," he said, turning to face her. "Would you like to go to the museum?"

"Oh, only if you're up to it," she said coyly.

"Just give me a minute to get ready," he said, getting up off the sofa. Recalling the incident in his bedroom yesterday, Alex bent over and held Amanda firmly by the shoulders and quietly said, "You stay here."

Amanda flashed him a mischievous smile before he took off.

"Hi Alex," Amanda said, when he walked into his bedroom to find her lying on his bed. She had just spread his bed while he was in the shower. Casually, she flipped through a magazine he didn't immediately recognize. "Hope you don't mind, but your mom said it was okay for me to wait in here."

Alex clutched at the towel he had wrapped around his waist. "I thought I asked you to wait downstairs."

"You did, but your mom was going back to bed and she didn't want to leave me down there by myself. If you want me to leave, I can."

Alex looked perturbed, weighing the situation. "Yeah … why don't you do that? I think you might be more comfortable downstairs."

Amanda closed the magazine and hopped off the bed. She walked up to Alex, whose skin prickled from the close encounter. "You and I are going to have a serious talk, mister."

Alex grabbed her by the arm and said, "That's perfectly fine, but for right now—I need to get dressed. Now out you go." He gently pushed her through the door and closed it.

Amanda watched Alex walk into the living room, where she was watching television. He walked into the kitchen and opened the refrigerator.

"Can I have one of those bottles of orange juice you had yesterday, please?" Amanda asked.

A moment later, Alex gave her one of the small bottles of O.J.

"Thanks," she said, opening it.

"Are you ready?"

"Let me get my keys," she replied, as she walked over to the end table to retrieve them.

Outside, Amanda walked toward the driver side of her car.

"Why don't you let me drive?" Alex said from behind her.

"You drive?"

"Of course I do. Just because I don't have a car doesn't mean I don't know how to drive." Seeing Amanda's face covered with apprehension, he added, "I drive my mom's car when she's not using it. Besides, you drive like a maniac."

"Don't go there," she said, dropping the keys in his hand.

"Not only did I go there, but now I'm back," he said, bumping her out of the way. Amanda got into the car and they drove to the Vienna Metro station. Given the exuberant rates for parking near the museum, because the Horizon Entertainment Center was half a block away, they had decided that it would be better to drive and park at the Metro for free then to take the train into DC.

Alex used his SmarTrip card to pay for them to enter the station. SmarTrip was a farecard that commuters in the DC Metro area used to ride and transfer between the bus and train in the region. The teens enjoyed an uneventful ride to Metro Center, where they needed to change trains to get on the red line. At Metro Center, the station was packed with fellow teens. All of them seemed to be waiting for the red line to Glenmont, like Alex and Amanda. Alex held Amanda's hand and bore through the crowd to get them closer to the edge of the platform, where they'd stand a better chance of getting on the next train. As a bunch of rowdy teenagers headed their way, Alex grabbed Amanda around her waist and pulled her close to him. She reciprocated the move and held onto him long after the threat was gone and they were on the train.

They got off at Gallery Place and the crowd followed them up the escalator to the exit. Once aboveground, Amanda and Alex were caught up in a riptide that dumped them out in the sea of teens surrounding the Horizon Entertainment Center, commonly referred to as the HEC. The HEC was located right above the Metro station. Just then, Alex recalled that some female artist was having a concert there today. He had seen hundreds of fans sleeping outside the center for a week on television, waiting to purchase tickets. As he watched his peers, who chose to sleep on the filthy sidewalks in a city with one of the highest crimes rates in the country rather than use their iPhones to purchase tickets over the phone or Internet, Alex wondered whether the introduction of so many technological advances made his generation any smarter. Carefully, he navigated Amanda across F Street, toward the museum.

As they entered the museum, Alex walked behind Amanda, allowing her to tour the facility at her leisure, since he'd already been there. He watched as Amanda read about the atrocious torture humans had inflicted on each other in the attempt to preserve societal norms during medieval times. He read above her shoulders about how public hanging was a form of entertainment and how a man was severely punished for kissing his wife on the Sabbath. They read about the pirates of the high seas and infamous cowboys and law men of the Wild West. Alex stopped by one of the electronic stations to quiz himself on his knowledge of criminals during the Prohibition Era. Halfway through the quiz, he scanned the area, looking for Amanda, who was still over by the Bonnie and Clyde exhibition.

As he was about to finish the quiz, Amanda walked up behind him and asked, "What do you think of Bonnie and Clyde?"

Alex finished up his quiz, then turned to face Amanda.

"They were two criminals who got what they deserved."

"That's what I love about you, Alex—your unequivocal sense of right and wrong, black and white," she said, sticking her index finger in her agape mouth, pretending to make herself gag and making the sound to imitate it. "What about two people who loved each other so much that they were willing to die for one another? Or two people who never wanted to be separated from each other and chose to die together?"

"I thought you weren't too big on the whole love thing," he said, puzzled.

"It's not love that I have a problem with. It's marriage," she retorted. "Besides, Bonnie and Clyde were never married to each other. Theirs is a love story," she said dreamily.

"Do you even hear yourself? Here you have two criminals who terrorized the country for years with their robberies and killing sprees, but you would forgive them of all that," he said, placing his hands over his heart, "because they were in love."

"I didn't say that. I'm just saying—love can be a pretty powerful thing."

"And love can be a pretty stupid thing, too," he said under his breath. Alex smiled when he saw how agitated his statement made Amanda, which sent her racing to the next section of the museum.

When they reached the CSI section of the museum, Amanda quietly asked, "Have you ever thought about using your powers to commit a crime?"

"No," he said instinctively.

"I'm not saying actually having the nerve to go through with it, but just thought about it—even for a fleeting moment."

Alex stopped to reflect on her question. "I guess I did —once. But only for a second."

"Really? When was that?

"Last year when my mom came up a little short on the mortgage a month after she closed on the house, which wiped out her savings."

"Oh my God, why didn't you say something? I would've—"

"Amanda, don't," he said. "Our finances are not your concern. Besides, it was temporary and my mom sorted it out by the following month."

"So, what happened?"

"She went into the bank to explain our situation to the manager, who gave her a hard time and started throwing around words like foreclose and delinquent account. I thought about how easy it would be for me to enter the manager's mind, have him delete the late payment on my mom's account to show it as being paid, and then transfer a cool million to her savings account. Lucky for me, my mom is well versed in real estate law, so she called the manager's bluff and read him the riot act on homeowner's rights."

"Don't mess with Marge," Amanda said with a smile.

They made their final rounds in the museum and were about to exit when Alex remembered that he hadn't participated in his favorite part of the tour—the driving simulator. Amanda watched as Alex got into the driver's seat of a simulated police car and chased after the bad guys. For three minutes she stood there watching Alex run red lights and dodge racing cars and bullets, before crashing into a store.

The teens exited the museum and discovered that the crowd outside the HEC was gone.

"The concert must have started," Alex said. Amanda suggested that they have lunch at the restaurant around the corner from the museum before heading home. Alex agreed once he realized that they would still beat the crowd from the concert after they had lunch.

The restaurant had a cramped feel to it. The small tables, dressed in white tablecloths, were neatly arranged in rows. However, they were so close to each other that you had to be careful when you pulled out your chair, to avoid disturbing your neighbor. Alex motioned to the hostess to place them at a table next to the window, which offered a little bit more leg room. The hostess didn't argue, taking stock of Alex's height and good looks.

A minute later, the waiter came and took their orders. Alex ordered their infamous quarter-pound beef hamburger —topped with a remoulade-based sauce loaded with chunks of crab meat—Pepsi, and a side order of fries, while Amanda stuck to a Caesar salad with grilled chicken breast and light lemonade.

"Have you given any more thought to telling your mother about your secret?" Amanda asked.

"I'm not telling her."

"You are so stubborn."

"Look who's talking—the mule herself."

"I'm not a mule," she said childishly.

"I know you're not," Alex said with a smile. "I'm just teasing."

"Why do you like to provoke me?"

"Because it's fun."

Sitting less than three feet away from Alex, Amanda couldn't help noticing the handsome features of his face under his tousled brown hair. His eyes had the capacity to look both inviting and intimidating at the same time, if you dared to stare long enough into them. Why he never dated any of the girls at Prestige was beyond Amanda. Was he one of those guys that was waiting for the perfect girl? Or was he gay? Oh my God, could that be it? She had never considered that option. Amanda's heart sunk at the mere thought.

"Stop it, Amanda," Alex said, shattering her train of thought.

"Stop what?" she replied, trying to figure out if he had lied to her about being able to read a person's mind.

"Stop staring at me like that. It's making me uncomfortable."

"What—you don't like *girls* looking at you?" she said before she could stop herself.

Reading the insinuation in the inflection in her voice, he asked, "What is that supposed to mean? You think I'm gay?"

"Well, we never really discussed it and I've never seen you with anyone."

"So because I don't have a girlfriend, that automatically makes me gay?"

"I'm just saying—are you?"

"No, Amanda. I'm not gay."

"So why haven't you hooked up with anyone yet?"

"I haven't met anyone that I wanted to hook up with," he lied.

Amanda fell silent, a bit offended by his response. *Why doesn't he see me in the same light that the other boys at school do?* she thought. Was there something wrong with her? Were her thighs too big for his taste? Were her breasts too small? Was her butt too small to compete with the voluptuous asses she saw plastered in music videos? Maybe she wasn't as pretty as others led her to believe. Amanda suddenly felt undervalued and insignificant.

"Why don't you like me, Alex?" she asked.

"I'm sorry. What did you say?" Alex stuttered, stunned at the accusation.

Amanda couldn't find the courage to repeat her question. Instead, she sat back in her chair with her arms crossed.

"You think I don't like you?" he asked.

Amanda rolled her eyes.

"Amanda, you are the only friend I have outside of my mother—sad as that may be, but it's the truth." Realizing his words didn't do anything to lighten her mood, he continued, "I wouldn't be here with you if I didn't like you. You have been my best friend for so many years. Even during our little hiatus, I still considered you my best friend. You are so intricately entwined in my fondest memories that I can't imagine what my life was before you or what it would be without you."

"I wasn't talking about you liking me as a friend," she said.

"Oh," Alex said uneasily. "Well, I do like you in that other way too."

"You do?" she asked animatedly.

"Yeah, I do," he said a bit embarrassed, with his eyes fixed on the girl across from him.

"So why haven't you ever asked me out or say anything?"

"Amanda, you're the daughter of a diplomat and an heiress to the fortune of a pharmaceutical corporation."

"Don't make us out to be snobs like the other Novies. Have my parents ever treated you badly when we had sleepovers at our house?"

"We were kids then. I don't think Mr. Bridgewater would take too kindly to me hanging around his house now that we've hit puberty."

"Well, you'll never know until you actually do, now will you?"

"I like being your friend, Amanda—pleasantly annoying as you may be, I still like you. Let's not complicate things."

Just then, the waiter returned with their food. The smell from Alex's hamburger was tempting; he couldn't wait to get his hands on it. He raised the mouthwatering burger to his lips and took a huge bite. The juices from the burger titillated his taste buds, causing his eyes to roll back into his head in sheer delight.

"Do you know how many calories a burg—" Amanda started.

"Can I please enjoy my hamburger without you telling me how bad it is for me?" he interjected, with his mouth full. "You're beginning to sound like my mom."

"Whatever. It's your life."

"Yes it is. And if I were to drop dead when I step outside this restaurant, I would die a happy person knowing that this was my last meal. Now eat up your lettuce, bunny rabbit."

Amanda gave him the finger and kept eating her salad. The Alex she knew back in Braemar was more absorbed with staying alive than the one in front of her, she noted. Maybe Justin's death was what had brought about this new attitude about living each day like it's your last. She watched as Alex ate his hamburger, and then started on the fries.

"Alex."

Alex looked at her with raised brows and a mouth full of fries.

"So, yesterday when I kissed you, that was me acting on my own free will?"

Alex shook his head up and down.

"And you didn't initiate or have anything to do with it, right?"

Alex shook his head from side to side.

"You're not one of those guys that have to be married before they ... you know?" she asked timidly, looking around the restaurant for eavesdroppers.

Alex dropped the fry that he had in his hand and took a gulp of his Pepsi to wash down the food in his mouth.

"No Amanda, I'm not one of those guys." He smiled. "In fact, I'm a strong proponent of sex before marriage. But with all I have going on with my abilities and trying to get off probation, adding sex or a girlfriend to the equation may not be the best thing to do right now."

"You said sex or a girlfriend. Does that mean they are mutually exclusive in your book?"

"They can be, but—" he stopped short of finishing his sentence to look at her and smiled. "Is this what girls sit around and think about?"

"No, but you're the only guy friend I have whom I feel comfortable talking to about this."

"Well, I can only speak for myself. I don't like being rushed into anything just because other people are doing it. When the time is right, it will happen. Any more embarrassing questions you want to hurl at me?"

"No—not right now," she said finishing her salad.

* * *

After lunch, Alex and Amanda walked out of the restaurant and crossed the street to the Metro station. They were about to go down the escalator when someone called to Amanda. It was Krista, a fellow cheerleader, with a few of her friends. They were going to the concert but were running late because of car trouble. Alex told Amanda he would wait for her by the Metro entrance, while she walked with Krista toward the entrance of the HEC a few feet away.

As Alex waited by the escalator, he saw a ghastly, pale, thin man with an unusually large duffle bag approach the Metro station. He had tattoos on the nape of his neck and back of his forearms that were visible from the edges of his T-shirt. Alex would have no reason to notice such an odd person in a city like DC, except that the bag was so large and appeared to be very heavy from the way the man carried it. He couldn't help but wonder why the man didn't just buy a wheeled suitcase. Plus, the way he carried the damn thing, you would think he had a baby sleeping in there or something. As the man disappeared down the escalator, Amanda ran up to Alex and they headed toward the station.

Although the platform was not as crowded as earlier, there were still a lot of people there. Alex leaned over the edge of the platform to see if the train to Shady Grove was in the tunnel. That's when he saw the tattooed, thin man again at the end of the platform. He was seated on a bench by himself, with his duffle bag flush against the wall next to him so it was hardly visible. Alex watched as the man got up and walked toward him and Amanda.

When the man walked by them, Alex said, "Sir, you forgot your bag."

The man shot Alex a menacing look and continued walking out of the station as if he hadn't heard a word the boy said. As the man ascended up the escalator, Alex became even more perplexed by his behavior. Why would the man go through the hassle of lugging such a huge bag into the train station, only to leave it behind? Plus, the man had to have purchased a farecard to enter the station; why would he turn around and leave before the train arrived?

Alex felt himself drawn to the bag at the end of the platform. Before he realized it, he was walking away from Amanda, who was talking about her encounter with Krista. He walked a few feet past the duffle bag, and then turned around. In his peripheral vision, he saw Amanda walking over to him. Mentally, he unzipped the bag and took a step closer to see what was inside. He was expecting to see clothing, or worst-case scenario, a sleeping baby. He wasn't expecting, however, an object that looked like it had the face of a digital clock, counting down from 5:09 minutes. His eyes wandered over to the other contents of the bag, which included a bunch of multi-colored wires and several slender, silver cylinders stuck in beige, clay-like bricks. Alex desperately hoped that he was seeing things, but after closing his eyes and opening them again, the bag was still there with the clock now down to 4:58 minutes.

Amanda was about to say something disagreeable to Alex for leaving her talking to herself, when she saw the horrified expression on his face. She followed his gaze to the duffle bag on the floor and gasped when she saw the contents.

"Is that a bomb?" she asked.

"I think so. That guy I just spoke to left it there."

"Well don't just stand there—run!"

The two teens then sprinted toward the exit, yelling bomb as loudly as they could, while weaving through the crowd on the platform. They were almost at the top of the escalator on the second level of the station, when Alex realized that the people on the platform were not running, but instead looked at them as if they were crazy. Alex then ran to the first level of the station and found a Metro attendant in the booth by the exit and told him about the bag with the bomb.

"Where is the bag?" the attendant asked.

"On the Red-Line platform toward Shady Grove, to the left, near the end," Alex explained.

The attendant checked his video surveillance of the second-level platform, and realized that he wasn't getting any feed from the camera in that section of the station. "Okay, I have to check it out."

"No, you can't go down there. There's not enough time. You must evacuate the station."

"I'm not evacuating the station until I see it for myself. And God help you if this is a hoax."

Alex looked to his left and saw Amanda staring at him. "Get out of here," he said to her, before following after the attendant.

"What are you going to do?" she called after him.

"I don't know. Just go!"

Alex quickly overtook the attendant on the escalator down to the second level and continued to run ahead of him, in hopes of getting the attendant to hasten his pace. When they got to the bag, the attendant's jaw dropped. Alex looked down and the clock said 3:52 minutes.

"Everybody, exit the station," Alex heard the attendant yell behind him.

"That includes you too, young man," the attendant said to Alex, while he continued to usher people out of the station and radioed the station manager. Just then, Alex heard an alarm sound and the announcement for everyone to evacuate the station.

Alex started to leave the area, when he looked around him and saw that there were still a lot of people in the train station. He watched as the crowd cleared the platforms on all three levels of the station, but started to bottleneck around the escalators.

"There's not enough time," Alex whispered to himself. Just then, his mind ran on all the people inside the HEC, which would definitely be affected by an explosion in the station. *I can't leave,* Alex told himself. He had no idea what, if anything, he could do, but he still felt compelled to do something. There simply wasn't enough time and there were too many people. Suddenly, Alex turned around and started walking back toward the bag.

When he reached the bag, he looked to his left and saw that the platform was clear, but could hear the frantic cries from the crowd near the escalators, which was out of his line of sight. Satisfied that there were no onlookers, Alex returned his attention to the bag in front of him. Slowly, he mentally lifted the bomb out of the bag and placed it on the concrete bench where the tattooed, thin man had sat earlier. He was careful not to disturb any component of the bomb when he set it down on the bench.

From the research he had done for his Physics project on explosive devises, Alex immediately recognized the beige clay bricks to be C-4, a common plastic explosive that was 1.34 times more powerful than TNT. The good thing about C-4 was that it was extremely stable. Therefore, you couldn't detonate it by dropping it or setting it on fire— which is probably why the tattooed, thin man had chosen it over some other unstable explosive materials.

Alex quickly examined the bricks of C-4 and saw the small, silver cylinders inserted inside them. At the other end of the cylinders were the multi-colored wires that were connected to the digital timer. The silver cylinders, Alex assumed, were detonators. Despite its stable characteristics, C-4 would detonate when the right combination of extreme heat and a shock wave was added to it. A detonator could provide the heat and shock wave C-4 needed to explode. After all, a detonator was nothing more than a tiny, controlled explosion. Although it was not as powerful as C-4, the explosive material inside the detonator was very unstable and easily ignitable.

He looked at the timer again, which had just clicked over to 00:52 seconds. *Don't panic, don't panic,* he kept reassuring himself—*you can do this. Just think.* If he could prevent the C-4 from exploding, then the bomb would not have such a devastating impact. But that would entail removing the detonators from the C-4, he concluded. However, he wasn't sure whether removing the detonators would trip the timer, thereby hastening the explosion of the C-4. He also dismissed the idea of removing the detonators one by one, because if there was a tripping device, the removal of the first detonator could trigger it. *So, how am I supposed to remove all the detonators from the multitude of C-4 bricks in the little time I have left?* Alex wondered.

With 00:37 seconds left on the timer, Alex decided that he would have to remove all the detonators simultaneously. He then visually located every detonator and mentally yanked them out of the C-4 bricks. Alex watched as the colorful wires and the silver cylinders hovered over the beige bricks on the bench. He sighed with relief at the fact that the sudden removal did not disturb the detonators. Then something caught his attention back on the bench. It was the timer. It had just clicked over to 00:18 seconds.

He had forgotten about the timer, which was still connected to the detonators. Eighteen seconds was not enough time for him to figure out how the two were linked together. He then reflected back at his time in the Gardens, experimenting with his telekinesis powers to create force fields, and his Physics class discussions on the application of pressure on objects. His best bet at this moment was to create a force field strong enough to contain the pressure generated by the exploding detonators. This would create an implosion of sorts, reversing the effect of the explosion. However, from his school work, he faintly remembered that some bombs could explode from an implosion detonation. Although he didn't recall the specifics of this portion of his class work, he was fairly certain that these detonators would not have the capability to cause an implosion detonation of the C-4. Nevertheless, he decided to move the detonators to another area in the station, far away from the C-4, just to be on the safe side.

In one fluid motion, he mentally shot the detonators, their colorful wires, and the timer through the air, down the train tunnel, while chasing after them. He got to the end of the platform in time to see the timer click over to 00:02 seconds down on the tracks. He braced himself as his mind exuded a powerful force toward the bomb. The force was so powerful that the lingering trash on the tracks all flew toward the detonators and timer. Alex saw the gate that led down to the tracks fly open because of the force his mind was creating. He heard metal scraping behind him, but he did not turn around. Instead, he held on to the concrete wall in front of him for support.

As the timer displayed 00:00 seconds, Alex saw a burst of bright, white light, followed by what appeared to be fire. He couldn't be sure from where he stood, but he saw as the detonators burst into numerous tiny fragments from the blast triggered by the timer. He watched as the blast from the detonators collided with the force field he had created. The blast from the detonators appeared frozen in mid-air, as his telekinetic powers struggled to contain it. It looked like a large energy ball fighting to escape its boundaries. Alex could feel blood dripping from his nose as his mind worked overtime to contain the blast. If it wasn't for the fact that the blast could kill him, Alex would have sworn that the containment of the explosion was one of the most beautiful things he had ever seen. Beautiful or not, he could not contain it forever. He had to create more pressure ex-

ternally on the blast to overpower the pressure being exuded from the blast internally in order for it to implode.

Alex felt faint as he saw the blast swell a few inches,
which meant he was losing the fight. There was no way he
could let the blast win. Although not as potent as the C-4
that was sitting on the bench now behind him, this blast
had the potential to inflict significant damage; not to mention that it was still in close enough proximity to the C-4 to
detonate it. If that happened, then all would be lost—him,
all the people in the HEC, even Amanda, who was probably waiting for him upstairs. The thought of Amanda sent
a sudden surge of energy through his body, up to his head.
He then intensified the force emanating from his mind
onto the blast, which mysteriously collapsed in a loud bang
that caused a slight tremor throughout the station. The
bang and tremor were immediately followed by a strong
gust of hot wind that pulled him off the platform and onto
the tracks. On his back, Alex looked up at the tiny particles
slowly swirling over him. *It worked*, he thought. The wind
that pulled him off the platform must have been from the
suction caused by the detonators imploding. Slowly, his
mind slipped into unconsciousness.

* * *

Amanda stood, confused and unsure of what to do as she
watched Alex run back into the station. Her instincts told
her to follow him, but he had specifically told her to get out
of there. Amanda was about to dash back into the station
when she saw a little girl crying in a corner, near the ticket
vending machines. The girl could not have been more than

four years old. Amanda walked over to the little girl, whose cherub cheeks were covered in tears.

"Hi, pretty girl. What's your name?" she asked, bending down on one knee in front of the girl.

"Iulita," the little girl said.

"Iulita. That's a pretty name for such a pretty little girl. Can you tell me, where's your mommy?"

"Mommy's at work," Iulita said, sobbing.

"Your mommy is at work?" Amanda asked. Iulita nodded. "Where does your mommy work?"

"I don't know."

"How did you get here?"

"Nana took me."

"Where's your Nana?"

"She's in the box."

"The box? What box?"

"The silver box that goes up," Iulita said, annoyed.

Amanda looked around the station, trying to figure out what a child would consider a silver box that goes up in a place like this. Just then, she spotted the silver doors to the elevator. Amanda turned back to the little girl and asked, "Your Nana went into that silver box?" pointing to the elevator. Iulita shook her head. "If your Nana went into the box and you saw it go up, she's probably waiting for you up those stairs," she said, pointing to the escalators. "Would you like me to take you upstairs to see if she's up there looking for you?" Amanda watched as Iulita looked at her suspiciously before nodding her head. Amanda then scooped up the little girl in her arms and ran up the escalators.

Once outside, Amanda walked around, trying to see whether Iulita recognized anyone. She walked by the elevators—no one. Then she noticed that security guards from the HEC were ushering people out of the entertainment center and across the street. *The Metro attendant must have notified them*, she thought. Amanda crossed the street and had barely taken two steps onto the sidewalk when Iulita stretched her arms to the right of her and screamed "Nana!" Amanda turned to see an elderly woman wobbling toward them.

The woman grabbed the little girl out of Amanda's hands.

"Iulita! You scared your old babushka," said the elderly woman in a thick Russian accent.

She smothered the little girl with kisses all over her tear-soaked face. Amanda smiled at the heartfelt reunion. The woman interrupted her private moment with her granddaughter and looked at Amanda. She explained how she got separated from her granddaughter when they tried to board the elevator because of her bad hip. Iulita was accidentally pushed off the elevator as the doors closed.

"Zis ees all craziness," the woman said.

"I'm just glad she found you," Amanda said.

"I'm glad too. Zank you," she said, before hurrying off with Iulita beside her.

Amanda turned her attention back to the Metro station across the street. She watched as more passengers poured out of the hole in the ground. Traffic was at a standstill with all the people running out of the station, the HEC, and surrounding shops. Numerous drivers abandoned their vehicles when they realized they could not make a U-turn to avoid the impending disaster. People were stumbling over and pushing each other as they tried to exit the HEC through the narrow doors. Amanda watched frantically, hoping to see Alex emerge from the station's escalators. She paced the sidewalk aimlessly. Then she saw the Metro attendant whom Alex had followed back into the station. Her heart quickened and she started back across the street, hoping that Alex would not spend needless time trying to find her. She pushed against the flow of terrified passengers and concertgoers before she reached the other side of the street. She looked behind the attendant, but Alex wasn't there. *Did he use one of the other exits from the station?* she wondered. No—this would be the closest exit, she concluded. Besides, he knew she would be waiting for him here. So why wasn't he here?

"Where's Alex?" Amanda asked, grabbing the attendant by the arm.

"Who?"

"The boy who told you about the bomb."

"He's right behind me," he said, turning around and visually searching the area for the boy. "Well, he was right behind me," he said, when he finally realized the boy was not there.

"I have to go get him," Amanda said as she started for the escalator. Suddenly, she felt a hand lock on to hers.

"Oh no you don't. You're not going back in there," the attendant said, grabbing her and twirling her back into the direction she came from. "This station is closed. You get as far away from here as you can if you want to live." Then he forced her off the sidewalk into the street. Amanda waited a few seconds, then she inched her way back onto the sidewalk near the HEC. She kept a watchful eye on the attendant, until he became distracted by his colleagues on the radio, who were inquiring about the status of the emergency vehicles that were being dispatched to the scene. She

149

heard him say that they were almost here, because he could hear them in the distance. Casually, she made her way to the edge of the HEC building, where the Metro station escalators were in view. She quickly assessed her chances of getting to the escalators without being seen; they weren't good.

Suddenly, there was a loud boom and the ground beneath her feet shook. *Oh crap, it's starting*, she thought, as she sunk to the ground. She waited a few more seconds, bracing herself for what was to come, but nothing else happened. Half confused and half apprehensive, she stood up. Maybe she had gotten up too fast, because she suddenly felt lightheaded. Where was Alex? She didn't care who saw her now; she had to find him. Amanda then darted down the escalators, taking the stairs two at a time, without looking behind her.

Downstairs, Amanda jumped the turnstile and ran to the second-level platform. She walked down the platform, taking mental notes of all the debris she saw. She stopped and looked at the bench where the tattooed, thin man had sat moments ago. The beige bricks from the bag were all lying on the bench. To the right of the bench was the bag. Something was missing, she thought as she looked around. The timer and wires weren't there. *Where were they?* she pondered. Better yet, where was Alex? Then she saw a figure lying on the ground near the tracks.

"Alex!" she said, running down the platform, then jumping down onto the ground and over to the figure. She dropped to her knees to examine her friend. His eyes were closed and his face was bloody. *Is he alive?* she wondered. She put her hand over the left side of his chest and detected a heartbeat. She lifted his head and laid it in her lap. She called his name a few more times while gently patting his bloody cheeks.

"Alex! Wake up!" she said repeatedly. "You have to wake up." She saw his head sway a little. "Alex, we have to go. The cops and firefighters will be here any minute now and, unless you want to explain what just happened, we have to get out of here." She watched as Alex moaned a few times and continued to sway his head as if he were trapped in a nightmare. *Okay, Fuller, you asked for it,* Amanda thought as she pinched Alex hard on his forearm.

"Ouch!" Alex yelled as his eyes flew open.

"Welcome back," Amanda said, smiling down at him.

"What happened?" he said, trying to sit up. Suddenly a sharp pain ricocheted through his head, forcing him back down into Amanda's lap.

"What's the matter?"

"My head. It feels like it's splitting in two," he said, holding his head with both hands to the side and applying pressure.

"Yeah, and I think all the blood in there quirked out of your nose in the process," she said, motioning to his face.

Alex touched the base of his nose and looked at the blood on his fingertips. "Yeah, that still happens every now and then."

"Well you can explain that to me some other time, but right now, I need you to get up so we can get out of here. I heard the attendant say emergency vehicles were on their way. They should be outside by now."

Alex lifted his head again, with Amanda pushing him up by the shoulders. Gingerly, she helped him to his feet. She steadied him as he turned to look at something on the ground. She saw a small crater in the ground, surrounded by more debris.

"Is that from the bomb?" she asked, astonished.

"No, the detonators. Or, what's left of them."

"I don't understand. The bricks are still on the bench, but I heard something. I heard a bang. Did you—you stopped it?" she asked with a trace of admiration. "That little tremor I felt earlier, that was it? How did you—?"

"I'll explain later. Let's get out of here," he said, turning toward the platform he had fallen from.

"Let's use the other platform," Amanda suggested.

"Why?"

"Because this platform leads to the HEC exit, which should be surrounded with police by now. If we use the exit from the other platform, we'll end up on G and 9th Street, which will be less crowded, with less police presence than the 7th Street exits."

"Fair enough. Just let me put the C-4 back into the bag first." From where he stood in the tunnel, Alex mentally placed the C-4 back into the duffle bag where he had found it. He stumbled as he turned to face Amanda again. She reached out and wedged herself under his right arm, while tightening her grip around his waist. They walked over to the opposite platform. As they rode the escalators up to the street level, the Metro attendant from the opposite platform ushered them out of the way, unaware of the role the two had played in the day's activities.

* * *

John Fischer heard the boom and felt the slight tremor underground. Like Amanda, he too was expecting more from the blast. He knew there should be more because he had built the bomb to have a more catastrophic effect. The bomb was his final attempt to purge America of its sinful ways before it could be set down the path to redemption. He had invested considerable time in making the bomb. He had drawn on his past military experience with explosives. He had even spent five years working for that wretched excavation company to get his hands on the right type of explosives.

He waited a moment longer, then he checked his watch. He was certain the bomb should have gone off already. But where was the big boom? Why was the HEC still standing? Where were the cameras for him to beam his message about God's purification process into every home in America? He didn't understand what could have possibly gone wrong. He was certain he'd set the timer. All the detonators were properly inserted into the C-4 blocks.

Suddenly, he heard sirens. John felt his blood boiling with rage. *No, no, no*, he thought. This is not how it's supposed to end. He paced the sidewalk uncontrollably, mumbling to himself. This was supposed to be his big moment. This was his duty as the sole messenger from God. And he had failed. He could not accept this. He would not accept defeat. He had to stick around to learn what had happened to his plan.

John looked on in a daze as an onslaught of emergency vehicles descended on the area, in the midst of frantic civilians running around and abandoned vehicles left idling everywhere. So far, there were at least ten fire trucks, eight squad cars, three bomb squad vans, and six black Suburbans—no doubt filled with G-men. A herd of firemen and members of the bomb squad leaped out of their respective vehicles and funneled through the traffic over to the Metro station entrance by F and 7th Street. G-men from the black Suburbans, two fire chiefs, and several top police officials set up a command post.

John watched as Metro attendants updated the newcomers of the scenario unfolding before them. He couldn't hear what was being said. He had to get closer. He had to be in *the know*. He started to draw closer to the emergency personnel, when a DC police officer told him to move back so they could secure the area. He complied—for the moment. His eyes fixed on the spectacle in front of him, he moved slowly toward 7th Street. He almost walked right into a parked fire truck, when suddenly he had an idea. First, he needed to find either a hazmat or fire-and-rescue truck. He scanned the area and saw a hazmat fire truck along the sidewalk at 7th Street. Slowly, he inched his way toward the truck, trying not to make any drastic movement that would catch the attention of the police officers roaming the area, maintaining control of the growing crowd.

When he got to the truck, he was relieved that the left side was facing away from the Metro. With the truck as his shield, he moved more freely. He found the external compartment, near the rear wheel on the vehicle. He recalled from his military service that certain fire trucks were equipped with extra fire suits. Quickly, he donned the fire suit he found in the compartment, including a hat. Once suited up, he walked confidently toward the Metro.

"Hey you," shouted a fire captain, pointing at John. "Take the entrance on 7th and H Street."

John nodded in compliance and walked around to the other Metro entrance. There, he saw a lone Metro attendant securing the perimeters. Most of the attention was focused on the F Street entrance because of where the bomb was found. He looked behind him and saw that two other firemen and three officers were heading his way. He turned back around to see the Metro attendant, who was now ushering two teenagers out of the station. He watched as a girl acted as a crutch for a boy, who was having trouble with his balance. The boy's face was covered with blood. *Well at least one infidel felt the wrath of God on this miserable day*, he thought, as he walked over to the Metro attendant.

"Can you tell me what happened here?" he asked.

"I wish I knew," the attendant said, out of breath. "My partner from the other side of the station radioed in a few minutes ago that some kid told him that there was a bomb on the platform. He was skeptical at first, because we get a few pranksters down here every now and then. So he went to check it out for himself and saw that it wasn't a joke."

"So who was this kid?"

"I don't know. You'd have to ask the other attendant, Jimmy ... Jimmy Denton."

Just then, the other firemen and police officers approached them. One of the officers asked, "Is there anyone else left down there?" John assumed that this officer must be a sergeant because of the take-charge aura that surrounded him, compared to the other two.

"I don't think so," the attendant responded.

The sergeant relayed the attendant's response via the radio he had clipped to a shoulder strap. To avoid detection, John held his head down and hovered near the escalators with his back to the group.

"Hey," the sergeant said to John, "Stand back from there. We haven't gotten the all-clear yet to enter."

"Well, what are they waiting for—Christmas?" John asked.

"From what the attendant who found the bomb said, there was a small explosion earlier. But according to our bomb experts, the amount of explosives that the attendant saw should have at least torn down half of the HEC."

That was my intention, John thought.

"Maybe the attendant got it wrong," John said. "Maybe the explosion earlier is all there was, and we're just waiting around here for nothing."

"You want to relay your theory to the Command Post —be my guest."

"You know what, I think I will," John said, seizing the opportunity to get away from the real authorities.

"What a jerk," said one of the firemen after John left.

"Have you worked with him before?" the sergeant asked.

"Nah, and I thought I had worked with just about everyone from Engine 2 already," the fireman replied, referring to the number on John's fire hat.

* * *

Alex and Amanda were walking westbound on G Street, past 9th. More police cars and fire trucks were heading toward the Metro entrance next to the HEC. Although the police were trying to push the growing crowd out of harm's way, the spectators were reluctant in their efforts to comply. The crowd would take a few steps back whenever an officer was present, but would eventually make their way back to their original position or beyond as soon as the officer was gone.

"Alex, stop for a minute and let me clean the blood off your face," Amanda said, realizing that people were staring at them as they walked by. She pulled out Wet-Naps from her pocketbook and started wiping his face. "So, you mentioned that you started to get frequent nosebleeds at Camp APRICOT yesterday, but you didn't explain why exactly."

"I get them whenever I overexert my abilities. I also get them whenever I have to make a concerted effort not to use them."

"Okay, you might know what you're talking about, but that doesn't mean we mortals do. Explain."

"In order to suppress the blast from the detonators, it literally took a lot out of me. I don't remember ever exerting so much energy into a force field before, which is probably why there's so much blood this time."

"This time?"

"Whenever I experiment with my abilities, I try to push myself a little bit further each time. On a few occasions, I get a little nosebleed. Nothing like this before, though," he said, looking at his T-shirt. It was a good thing it was black, or else there would be red bloodstains all over the front of the shirt.

"I also get nosebleeds in gym, depending on what we're doing," he added.

"Gym? Why gym?"

"In sports like basketball and football, where you have an opponent coming directly at you, naturally your body goes into self-defense mode. For me, that means my abilities also go into defense mode. So for those games, I have to make an effort not to use my abilities, or else my opponents could spontaneously combust or go flying through the air. The more opponents I have coming at me, the more my nose bleeds, because I have to try to not hurt all of them at the same time and concentrate on playing the game."

"Stop moving your mouth for a minute," she said as she cleaned his lips. He complied.

"There," she said when she was all done. "Looking better already. Where to now, oh fearless leader?"

"Metro Center should be a few more blocks down this way," he said, pointing down the street. "We can get on the Orange train there."

"Your mom is going to freak out when she hears what happened,"

Alex pulled Amanda to a stop by the shoulders. "Amanda, my mom cannot know anything about this."

"Are you kidding me?"

"No, I'm not. No one can know about what really happened today."

"Alex, I swear I don't get you sometimes. Why would you want to keep such cool powers a secret, especially from your mom? Your mom is like the coolest person ever. She's not going to be mad at you."

"I don't want to end up in some laboratory, with people poking me, trying to figure out what makes me tick. And I don't want my mom to know about this because … I don't want her to think that she gave birth to a freak." The words resonated in his head. Finally, he was able to say the words he had thought for almost two years, but never dared to say aloud.

"Okay. We won't say anything to anyone," she said disappointedly. "But I think you're wrong about your mom. She would never think you're a freak."

Deep down, Alex wanted to believe Amanda. But what if she was wrong?

John reached the Metro entrance at the intersection at F and 7th Street. More and more emergency personnel were pouring in. The streets were now visibly blocked off. He was beginning to feel uncomfortable in his surroundings. He avoided eye contact with everyone and stayed clear of their paths. His priority now was to find Jimmy Denton, find out who foiled his plan, and get the hell out of Dodge.

From a safe distance on 7th Street, he watched the commotion in front of him. Suddenly, he spotted the Metro attendant that was manning the booth he passed earlier. *That must be Denton*, he thought. Denton was talking to plain-clothed police officers, G-men, and fire chiefs. Frustrated that he couldn't overhear their conversation, he decided to get closer. With his back turned to the men, John fiddled with the apparatus on a fire truck nearby to avoid detection. All the men standing behind him were relaying their opinions and findings to a special-agent-in-charge by the name of Michael Trace. John assumed the man was with the Federal Bureau of Investigation given his title—SAC. These men must be members of the Washington Joint Terrorism Task Force, which John had read about. He listened as he heard SAC Trace make the decision to send a special unit, comprised of members of the Hazardous Material Response Team, National Capital Response Squad, and bomb technicians, into the station to investigate.

John didn't like the idea of the FBI being here. The mere presence of the Bureau would label his efforts here as those of a domestic terrorist. Although he had grown sympathetic to those who opposed the American ideology after the way the military treated him, he did not consider himself a terrorist. He was an American, of Irish descent. He had served his country by fighting in two of the Iraq wars —the occupation of Iraq and the second Gulf War—before being kicked out with a dishonorable discharge.

His purpose here today was to hold the mirror in which America would be forced to examine itself. John had chosen DC to broadcast his message because it was the seat of the U.S. government, which had allowed the country to deteriorate into its current hedonistic state. The same government that sent so many of its young citizens to die for a cause they didn't entirely believe or understand.

He'd specifically selected the HEC as his target for three reasons. One, security at the national monuments was impenetrable. Two, there was a concert there today, which meant a high body count. It would be impossible for the government to quietly sweep him under the rug if there was a high body count. Three, the pop idol performing there had to be stopped. She was responsible for leading thousands of young people astray by encouraging them to break the Sabbath when she scheduled her concert on a Sunday. From her own lips, she confessed to engaging in every sexually deviant behavior under the sun. It was unfortunate that so many would had to suffer for the sins of one, but the audience had to be punished too, for worshipping this false idol.

For the next hour, John wandered around the cordoned area, keeping an eye on Denton. Sometimes, he pretended to be a part of crowd control and mingled with the spectators and the press. He had heard the official report when the special bomb unit came back about half an hour ago, that it seemed that the bomb itself had not detonated, but the detonators and timer were missing. Everyone was puzzled. From the information that Denton and the passengers gave the task force, there was an explosion of sorts. Plus, there were remnants of an explosion in a small crater the bomb unit saw in the tunnel. Despite the information he'd overheard, John still wanted to talk to Jimmy Denton. He must talk to this man to find out what he had done to his bomb.

Another fifteen minutes went by before John finally saw his opportunity to talk to Denton. Jimmy Denton had just told one of the fire chiefs that he was going to grab a sandwich from a deli three blocks away, since he had forgotten to eat lunch with all the commotion. Jimmy headed down 7th Street, where John was waiting for him.

"Excuse me, Mr. Denton," John called as Jimmy crossed the police barricade.

"Yes, can I help you?"

"My name is Charles Bufford and I'm with Engine 2. I was wondering if I could talk to you about how you were able to detect that bomb."

"Hey, buddy, your captain should be able to fill you in on all the information you need about that. I've given so many statements today, I'm exhausted," Jimmy said, continuing to walk toward the deli.

"Yeah I know, but I heard that it was really a little boy who found the bomb. I just wanted to hear how he was able to tell that it was a bomb." Realizing that Denton was not heeding him, John continued, "See, I volunteer to talk to various schools in the community about what the fire department does. As a part of my presentation, I usually like to include examples of how kids can help us do our jobs better. I remember this one incident where a couple and their two kids were asleep and their house caught on fire.

The kids shared a bedroom and the parents were in their room down the hall. The fire must have started near the parents' bedroom, because they were trapped inside and we had to get them out through the window. The whole time they were screaming that their two boys were still in the house. Little did they know that their six year old son, Stephen, had carried his baby brother out of the burning house and was waiting for us by the door when we arrived. The kids love that one."

"I remember that one. That happened in Southeast, right?"

"Yeah, that's the one," John said, holding the door to the deli open for Jimmy. "It didn't matter how I tried to explain to them how difficult it was for us to put out the fire, or how the fire started; all they wanted to hear about was Stephen and his little brother." John smiled.

"Kids," Jimmy said in agreement as he reached for his wallet.

"No, let me get this for you," John said, offering to pay for Jimmy's lunch.

"You sure, man? Because I think firemen are about the worst-paid civil servants around."

"I'm sure we are, but you just saved me from spending countless hours putting out a fire, and let's not forget about all those lives you saved," he said, buttering up Jimmy.

"Hey man, thanks. You're all right," he said before placing his order. The two men took a seat at a nearby table.

"So what the hell happened man? You are like *the hero* of the day," John said loud enough for the other patrons to hear. He was hoping that Jimmy would loosen up from all the admiring eyes around him.

"I can't take credit for finding the bomb. That kid is the one who really deserves all the credit."

"What kid? I didn't see any kid outside the station just now."

"No, this was earlier. I heard him and his girlfriend yelling bomb and running like hell. Then he came up to me and said there was a bomb on the platform. At first I was like, these kids have to be on something. But the voice in my head said, just go and check it out for yourself because you never know. So I walked down there and there it was."

"Man! Did you shit your pants?"

"I have to admit, I almost did," he laughed.

"So what did you do afterwards?"

"I got on the radio and radioed everyone I could reach, then told everyone to get the hell out of there."

"So what about the boy and his girlfriend? The kids are going to love this story—I can see it now."

"The boy—I don't remember seeing the boy after he took me down to the platform."

"Really?"

"Nah, I didn't see him again. But the girl—I saw the girl upstairs on the street level. In fact, she was asking me for her boyfriend. When I couldn't find him, she wanted to go back downstairs to look for him. Can you believe it? I mean, what part of bomb did she not understand?"

"Kids—go figure. How old do you think they were?"

"They were maybe sixteen or seventeen years old; no older than eighteen though. Heck, it's so hard to tell how old these kids are nowadays. I don't know what they feed them."

"I hear yah. I have a little niece, and I swear she hasn't been little since she was five." That got a good laugh out of

Jimmy, who heard his number being called from behind the deli counter.

After Jimmy retrieved his lunch, he thanked *Charles Bufford* again. "Don't mention it," John said. "Anyway, I have to get back before they send the whole brigade out looking for me. Enjoy your lunch."

"You mean my dinner, don't you?" Jimmy chuckled.

John smiled and headed for the door. When he reached the door, he turned and said to Jimmy, "What did you say our little hero's name was again? I sure could use it for my next school presentation."

Jimmy stopped and thought for a while. Then finally he said, "Alex."

"Just Alex?"

"Just Alex. That's what the girl called him."

"What does he look like?"

"Tall, lean ... long, curly brown hair."

"Thanks man," he said, exiting the deli. Tall, lean, long, curly brown hair—John knew exactly who Denton was referring to. As he walked down 7th Street, he started to unfasten his fire suit.

* * *

The journey back to Virginia was unusually long due to the bomb threat on the Red Line at Gallery Place Chinatown Metro Station. Although the Orange Line to Vienna possessed no similar threat, Metro took extra precautions to safeguard the operation of all its lines, like it did following the crash of two commuter trains in 2009. Nothing gets a bureaucrat to do his job better than an incident that shows he was not doing his job—until complacency sets in again.

The wait for the Orange train was horrendous. As they waited, Alex received a text from his mother, asking whether he and Amanda were caught up in the bomb threat she'd heard about on television. He texted her back and told her no. The two teens traveled to Vienna in welcome silence, partially due to Alex's headache. They didn't seem to mind when the train operator repeatedly announced over the intercom that they were experiencing delays and should be moving shortly. They arrived at Vienna hours later. Once at Vienna, they were the last two to detrain from their car. Alex still felt woozy from his episode with the bomb, so Amanda continued to act as a crutch for him. She let him into the passenger side of her car before making her way to the driver side.

It was dark outside of the Fuller house when Amanda's silver Audi pulled into the driveway. An awkward silence filled the car when Amanda shut off the engine and Alex made no attempt to get out. Unsure of how to proceed, she sat there twiddling her fingers in her lap. A few minutes went by and she looked over at Alex, who wore the same blank expression on his face that he had when he first got into the car.

"Are you okay?" she finally asked.

"Yeah, I'm good," he said after clearing his throat.

"You're not ready to go in?"

He shook his head. "Not yet. Can we just sit here for a while?"

"Sure." She left him to his solitude, then reclined her chair. Once she found a comfortable position, she placed her hands behind her head and closed her eyes. She had almost forgotten how much she liked being around Alex. She could sit here all night like this, with the reassuring thought that he was in the seat next to her.

"Do you mind if I try something?" she heard Alex ask.

"Knock yourself out," she answered without moving.

Amanda exhaled deeply from exhaustion. Not in a million years would she have thought that agreeing to go to the museum with Alex would have turned out like this. Just then, she heard a creaking sound as Alex moved in the leather passenger seat. *Poor Alex*, she thought, *having to live with such a secret and not tell anyone, including his mother.* It must be killing him inside.

Suddenly, she felt a dark image move across her face, followed by a warm, sweet wind that tingled the skin near her mouth. She opened her eyes to see Alex's face less than an inch from hers. He was looking at her inquisitively, as if he was trying to figure out what planet she was from. She was about to ask him what he was doing, when she felt his lips brush against hers. *Am I dreaming?* she asked herself. Before her mind could form a cognitive answer, she felt the warm, moist invasion of his mouth on hers. At that moment, it didn't matter whether she was asleep or awake. Gently, she freed her hands from behind her head, laying the right one on Alex's shoulder and slipping the other into his soft, curly hair. Her heart hastened as she pulled his face into hers and their breathing became more labored. Slowly, she felt Alex retreat.

Her eyes were still closed when she felt him kiss her on her right temple and told her good night. She heard the car door open, but was still unable to move. She wasn't sure how long she was like that, before she opened her eyes and saw Alex waving to her from his front door. Out of habit, she waved back. After he disappeared inside, she sat there staring at the beige garage door in front of her.

What the hell just happened? she thought as she started the engine. Sure she had kissed a few boys before—including Alex—but they were nothing compared to this one. For that brief moment, it felt like it was just her and him alone in their own little world. Then that jittery feeling in her stomach started, followed by a tingly sensation that surged through her body, leaving behind a total feeling of transcendence. *Was this how I was supposed to feel after I kissed Alex yesterday?* she wondered. She would never know because Alex had had control over her mind, which meant she didn't remember any of it. Suddenly, she felt cheated, and she wanted to knock on his door to demand a re-do. She looked at the clock, which said 8:28 p.m., and decided not to. She pulled out of the driveway, content with the thought that she could cash in her kiss coupon some other day.

* * *

Inside the house, Margaret had left the light on in the foyer for her son. Alex turned off the light and listened for a minute. *Mom must be in bed,* he thought, since he didn't hear the familiar sound of her voice calling him from upstairs. Slowly, he climbed the stairs and walked into his room, without incident. He decided against taking a shower, out of fear of waking his mother. He didn't want to run the risk of having her ask him what happened at the museum. He hated lying to her, and that's precisely what he would have to do if she started asking questions.

He sat down on his bed and took off his shoes. As he pulled off his shirt, which still had traces of Amanda's scent on it, his thoughts turned to her. Kissing her just now had yielded the same euphoric feeling he got when he visited the Gardens. *Why is that?* he wondered. He didn't feel woozy anymore. His headache was gone. In fact, his mind was totally at ease now. He recalled that earlier in the train tunnel it was the thought of Amanda being hurt that gave him the extra boost of energy needed to overpower the blast. He knew he liked Amanda and would do anything to protect her. However, he couldn't help wondering why his abilities only reacted to *her* in such a way. The question lingered in his mind until he fell asleep.

8. THE INVESTIGATION

John did not sleep after he arrived at his studio apartment in southeast DC. He rented the place from an elderly woman by the name of Roberta Jackson, who occasionally rented her basement to people who were temporarily down on their luck, or out-of-towners who needed a place to stay longer than a week but couldn't afford a hotel. John had liked Ms. Jackson from the first moment he met her because she had various characteristics he admired. Most importantly, she minded her own business and was partially blind from glaucoma. John needed to be able to come and go as he pleased without being questioned or spied on, and Ms. Jackson provided him with that. He also liked her cooking. John always wondered how Ms. Jackson cooked without the full use of her sight. She reassured him that cooking didn't require the full use of one's sight. The most important senses needed for cooking, she told him, were smell and taste. After tasting her shrimp gumbo for the first time, he never questioned her on that subject again.

Finally, Ms. Jackson was a God-fearing woman, and that had cemented John's admiration of her. Like John, she had grown up in the Baptist faith. John was born on a military installation in Fort Hood, Texas. His mother was a good Christian woman who resorted to her faith whenever her husband, a sergeant in the Army, physically abused her. He didn't remember much about his father, because he'd killed himself when John was only six years old. All John remembered about his father was he got his name from him, and after being deployed four times to Vietnam, his father had killed himself with the handgun he brought back as a souvenir.

After his father's funeral, John's mother moved them to Kansas, her hometown. He grew up normally enough— went to school, played football, hung out with his friends on the weekend, and went to church on Sundays. A month after he graduated from high school, his mother died. He joined the military two days after he buried her and served seventeen years before receiving a dishonorable discharge.

John used to be a member of an elite Black Ops unit, and he was frequently deployed due to his lack of familial ties. During his last deployment to Iraq, his team was sent on two missions that turned out to be based on bad intel. The failed missions resulted in heavy casualties and John lost three of the guys he'd gone to basic training with. There were rumors that John's friends may have been ex-posed to a chemical weapon agent during the second mission, but their chain of command denied the claim. His team was scheduled to embark on its third mission, when John refused to participate until the initial intel could be corroborated and the presence of chemical agents determined. He also started to question the government's interest in this region of the world and how this mission would further that interest.

His commander had called him into his office and told him that the intel they had was as good as it was going to get. He also reminded John that as a Marine, he would do as he was told. When John refused again, his commander gave him a direct order to join his team. John refused and was immediately returned stateside and referred to a general court martial for misbehavior before the enemy. For the seventeen years he had spent in the military, John had nothing to show for it—no pension, no benefits, no college degree. With a dishonorable discharge, he had a hard time finding decent employment.

Month after month, year after year, John's hatred for his government grew because he blamed it for his current predicament. He turned to his religion in search of solace, but found its teaching of peace and forgiveness lacking. It was during this time that the words of several radical extremist groups he found online appealed to him. He drew elements from the radical extremist teachings to fill his perceived voids in his religion to form a new ideology that better suited his needs for a belief system and retribution.

John moved back to Kansas, where he reunited with some of his friends from high school. Some of them were down on their luck like him. It was easy for him to convince them that their country had fallen from grace and was responsible for their inability to find good paying jobs, but lost them when he tried to convince them to bear arms against it. Shortly thereafter, John moved to another town to formulate God's plan to restore grace to America. His plans had led him to Ms. Jackson's basement.

He came in late that night, still confused about what had happened to his divine plan. Although he got dressed for bed, he stayed up all night, going over every detail of what took place the day before. He was convinced that someone had thwarted his plan, and he had to find out who was it. The only suspects he had were the Metro attendant and the kid who saw him leave the bag. He dismissed the attendant as a suspect, because he recalled seeing him outside the station before the bomb went off. He didn't remember seeing the boy, but he seriously doubted that a child had the capacity to foil his plan.

John had spent months studying the Metro system. He selected the Gallery Place Chinatown station because it was located underneath the HEC. For days, he surveyed the station, in search of the perfect spot for the bomb. His plan was to place the bomb where it could cause the most damage to both the train station and the HEC. The Shady Grove platform offered him the most advantageous point. Once he decided where to place the bomb, he made notes of acceptable response time to incidents in the station, video surveillance, staff change, etc.

He had travelled with the components of the bomb from Kansas in his cargo van. Getting the detonators and making the timer was easy, but the C-4 took more effort. Prior to venturing east, John took a job with Pearlman Excavating Corporation, an excavation company in Kansas. The company figured that anyone who served their country for seventeen years deserved a second chance. He worked there for five years, just long enough to gain access to their explosive materials supplies. It was easy for him to get a position with the company, given the expertise in explosives that he'd gained from the military. He left the company three weeks after it was reported that someone had stolen two hundred and fifty pounds of C-4 out of its inventory. No one suspected John because he was such a good Christian, and he had even offered to say a prayer for the culprit to return the material. Plus, according to John, he only left the company to care for his ailing mother in Texas.

Putting the bomb together in Ms. Jackson's basement took no time at all. He had displayed such care in its transportation to the Gallery Place Chinatown Metro station. John thought he had evaded every wondering eye when he entered the Metro. He paid for his fare card weeks ago with cash at one of the ticket vending machines. Once inside the station, he turned on the video signal jammer he had bought off the Internet. He was careful not to turn it on too soon, because he didn't want to alert the attendant of his intentions early in the process. Therefore, he had waited until he saw the camera that covered the end of the Glenmont-bound platform of the Red Line, then turned on the jammer and dropped it in the nearest trash can.

He had tested the jammer several weeks ago when another attendant was manning the booth. He turned on the jammer and saw when the attendant scrambled to figure out what was wrong with the video feed. John ran this test with several other attendants until he found the one who did not notice the feed interruption for several minutes— Jimmy Denton.

Now here he was, on the day of judgment, ready to exact his revenge. Everything had gone perfectly, except for the boy who saw him leave the bag. John brooded over whether the boy had anything to do with the diffusion of his bomb. He sat on the edge of his twin-size bed with his head between his knees. He remained in that position for a while, until he decided to get up and work out, which always soothed his mind. First he started out with pushups, then sit-ups. Afterwards, he retrieved his pull-up bar from the closet and placed it firmly over the bathroom door's threshold. On his third rep of fours, he stopped and released the bar.

Why hadn't he thought about it before? Why hadn't he made the connection? It couldn't be mere coincidence. Besides, he didn't believe in coincidences. He had seen someone run back inside the station after the attendant evacuated everyone. Although he hadn't seen the person's face, he knew it was female, with light-colored hair. Then when the fire chief sent him to secure the other Metro exit, he saw another attendant helping a boy and a girl out of the station. The girl was blonde. Although he was not a hundred percent sure that this girl was the same one he had seen earlier, he was positive it was the same boy from the platform earlier—tall, lean, with long, curly brown hair. Instinctively, John punched a hole in the wall and screamed. Then he remembered, Ms. Jackson was blind, not deaf. So he paced the floor while thinking, until his anger subsided. When he was finally in charge of his faculties, he got dressed.

* * *

At 5:42 a.m. on Monday, Margaret heard the doorbell ring. She automatically rolled over and looked at her alarm clock, which she had set for six.

"Oh come on!" she yelled to herself. "I have eighteen more minutes to go." As the doorbell rang again, she kicked the covers off and grabbed her robe.

Downstairs, she almost yanked the door off its hinges when she opened it. "Who the hell is it?" she demanded.

"FBI, Assistant Special-Agent-in-Charge Maxwell Brody,"

said a handsome gentleman in a dark suit, holding his credentials high enough for her to see.

Margaret was taken aback and immediately fell mute. She looked past Agent Brody and saw several other men standing behind him in her front yard.

"May we come in?" Agent Brody asked.

"Why?" she asked quizzically.

"I have a very sensitive matter to discuss with your son and—"

"My son?"

"Yes, your son, Alex Fuller, and I don't think your front stoop is the best place for this conversation. So again, can we come in?"

Margaret waved him in. Agent Brody was followed by three gentlemen, two of whom were as well-groomed as he was. The third guy looked a bit out of place and uncomfortable in the suit he wore.

"Ms. Fuller, these are Agents Bobby Mitchell and Hector Sanchez with the FBI," he said, pointing to the two well-groomed gentlemen. "This gentleman is Detective Joseph Murray with the Metropolitan Police Department," Agent Brody said of the third gentleman, who was also a bit shorter and thicker in the mid-section than the other men. "Is your son home?" he asked.

"Why do you ask?"

"Ms. Fuller, your son is not in any trouble, I assure you. As we understand it, your son might have valuable information about the bombing that took place yesterday at the Gallery Place Chinatown Metro station."

"The bombing?" Margaret remembered hearing about a bomb threat on the television, when she was waiting for the weather report. As far as she could remember, it was merely a bomb threat, not an actual bombing, and no one was hurt. "My son doesn't know anything about any bombing, as you claim. He wasn't even there."

"Well, we would like to hear that from your son, Ms. Fuller." Noting her hesitation, Agent Brody continued, "Ma'am, this is a matter of national security. We can either do this here or head down to our office. I was hoping we could do this here, so you and Alex can carry on with your day at Stanley & Gable and Prestige Preparatory High School once we're done."

The agent's knowledge of where she worked and where Alex went to school caught Margaret off-guard. She was about to fire back with a feisty reply when she decided against it, especially when the phrase "national security" was being thrown around. If Alex had information that the FBI thought was a matter of national security, there was nothing she could do to prevent them from getting it from him.

"Have a seat in the living room. I'll get him."

* * *

Three minutes later, Margaret reappeared, followed by her disheveled son.

"Honey, these are the gentlemen that need to talk to you," she said, patting him on the back.

"Good morning, Alex," Agent Brody said, smiling and stretching his arm out to the teenager. "I'm Agent Brody of the FBI. I just have a few questions for you about yesterday."

Alex looked at him with a skeptical glare as he shook his hand. "Sure. What do you want to know?"

"Why don't we have a seat over there?" he said, motioning to the table in the dining area. Agent Brody walked over to the table and sat down in the chair with its back to the wall. Once situated, he pulled a small recording device out of his pocket and set it down on the table in front of him. "If you don't mind, I'm going to record our conversation." He then flipped on a switch and a little red light came on.

"Were you at the Gallery Place Metro Station yesterday around 3:30 p.m.?"

Alex debated whether he should lie to the FBI Agent, but decided against it. "Yeah," he answered.

"What can you tell me about what happened at that Metro station?"

"You mean about the bombing?"

"Yes, Alex—the bombing."

Alex looked at his mother, who still had her arm around him. "It's okay, son. I'm right here."

Alex sat in the chair opposite Agent Brody and recounted the day he had spent with Amanda. He described their visit to the museum, their lunch at the restaurant nearby, and finally their unfortunate venture home. During Alex's oratory, Agent Brody tried to move him along through the museum and restaurant scene with obvious impatience, but Alex belabored insubstantial details, just to further irritate the man sitting across from him.

"After the restaurant, we went to the station. Amanda stopped to talk to some friends and I waited by the Metro entrance. I saw this guy carrying a big, black duffle bag down into the station."

"The guy carrying the duffle bag, can you describe him?" Agent Brody asked.

"Ah, he was kind of thin, pale complexion. Horrifying-looking face."

"You saw his face?"

"Yes."

"What did he look like?" Agent Brody asked, snapping his fingers at one of the men standing behind Alex. In a second, Agent Mitchell appeared and sat in the chair next to Agent Brody with a sketch pad.

"He was ... very slender. His cheeks seemed hollowed out, you know ... kind of sunken in. His skin was a bit blotchy. His hair was light brown, and kind of thinning and receding at the same time at the top."

"What about his nose, eyes, ears?" Agent Mitchell asked.

"His nose was straight and small. His ears were a little bit bigger than what I would consider normal for a guy with such a slender face. His lips were small, with a noticeable philtrum, even from where I was standing."

"Philtrum? What's a philtrum?" Agent Brody asked.

"It's that concave curve between your nose and upper lip," Agent Mitchell responded. Agent Brody looked at Alex questioningly.

"I paid attention in biology," Alex said, answering Agent Brody's unasked question. "His eyes," he continued, "were small, dark ... almost black, and beady."

"Anything else about the face?" Agent Mitchell asked, sketching on the pad in his hand.

"No, not really—wait, he had a part in his hair, or should I say a comb-over. On the right side."

"Anything else?"

"Not about his face."

"Does this look like the man you saw, Alex?" Agent

Mitchell asked, turning around his notepad, which displayed a sketched face.

"Wow. That's a very good likeness. Yeah, that looks like him."

"Did you notice anything else unusual about him?" Agent Brody picked up as Agent Mitchell rejoined the men behind Alex.

"Just that duffle bag. Oh, he had a tattoo."

"What kind of tattoo? Where?"

"It was on his back, I think, because parts of it were visible from under his T-shirt on his neck and the back of his arms."

"What was it of?"

"I don't know. All I saw was black, maybe some white or silver ink on his skin."

"What was he wearing?"

"Black T-shirt, dark blue jeans, and a pair of black-and-white canvas sneakers."

"Okay. So you saw this guy walk into the station. What happened afterwards?"

"I waited for Amanda and we went down into the station. Once we got to the Red-Line platform on the second level, I saw the guy again. He was sitting on one of the benches, close to the end of the platform. He had placed the bag to the left of the bench, next to him. It was kind of hidden from where I stood, but I could still see a small part of it due to the size. About a couple of minutes later, he just got up and left the platform, leaving the bag behind." Alex heard his mother let out a sigh next to him. "I thought it was weird that he'd just leave his bag there, so I told him and he just looked at me."

"He looked at you?" Agent Brody asked.

"Yeah, and he looked kinda pissed too."

"He knows what you look like," Margaret interjected. "This is not good. Why the hell didn't you tell me any of this?" She was frantic and about to go into one of her tirades.

"Mom, I didn't want you to worry. And from your reaction now, I was right not to tell you."

"No, you weren't!" she snapped. "This is not—"

"Ms. Fuller," Agent Brody interrupted. "If you're worried about Alex's safety, we can definitely arrange for someone to keep an eye on him until we catch this guy. Your son did a brave thing here. I just wish more people had the guts to do what he did."

"Easy for you to say. He's not *your* son."

"Mom," Alex whined.

"Do you have any children, Agent Brody?" she asked, hovering over the table and looking directly at the FBI Agent.

"Mom!" Alex yelled, gently pushing her away from the table with the back of his hand. "You're not helping. Please, go … make coffee or something." Margaret retreated to his side, pacing the floor.

"What happened after the guy left?" Agent Brody asked, eyeing Margaret a bit uneasily.

"Well I just thought it was weird the way he left and everything, so I walked over to the bag. And that's when I saw the bomb."

"Oh, Jesus, Mary, and Joseph," Margaret said, half to herself.

Agent Brody glanced at Margaret. She was clutching a necklace hanging from her neck and trembling as she paced the floor. "Where was your girlfriend at this time?"

"Girlfriend? What girlfriend?" Alex asked.

"I thought it was you and your girlfriend, Amanda, in—"

"My friend," Alex corrected. Although he didn't object to Amanda being his girlfriend, he wasn't sure she would approve of him calling her his girlfriend without first consulting with her.

"Your friend?" Agent Brody asked with a smirk on his face. Alex frowned at him. "Okay. Your friend Amanda," the agent said, correcting himself after seeing the serious expression on Alex's face. "Where was she?"

"She was right next to me the whole time."

"So she saw the bomb too?"

"Yes."

"What did the bomb look like?"

"It had some beige bricks in it, a lot of wires, and a digital clock that was counting down."

"Are you sure you saw wires and a timer in the bag?"

Alex knew exactly why the FBI agent would be concerned about the detonators and timer. He also knew that the attendant would have already told them about these items. Therefore, he would draw unnecessary attention to himself from a federal agency if he were to contradict the attendant's statement. "Yes," he replied. "In fact, the timer initially had 5:09 minutes on it."

"Okay," Agent Brody said, nodding his head. Then he stopped and his eyebrows furrowed. "Alex, was the bag open or closed when you found it?"

"Open," he lied nonchalantly, hoping that would end the inquiry in that subject.

"What did you do after that?"

Relieved that the agent believed him, Alex continued, "We tried to warn people on the platform that there was a bomb in the station, but they just stared at us. So I told the attendant." Alex smiled coyly and sarcastically added, "You know, in accordance with Homeland Security's 'if you see something, say something' public awareness campaign."

"Oh, you know about that?"

"Yeah, we kept hearing the announcements throughout the stations that day."

"What did the attendant do when you told him?"

"He went to check it out himself. I tried to stop him, given the amount of time that was left on the bomb, but he insisted. So after Amanda left, I followed him back onto the platform and showed him where the bomb was. That's when he evacuated the station and you guys showed up."

"What did you do after the attendant evacuated the station?"

"I evacuated the station," he replied.

"You didn't go back into the station?" Agent Brody asked with a confused look on his face.

"No."

Agent Brody pondered Alex's response for a minute, as he sat back in the chair and rubbed his chin, trying to assess the boy that sat in front of him. His eyes were met by a boy who appeared half-asleep and bored.

"The attendant at the station said your girlfriend, Amanda—"

"My friend," Alex corrected him again.

"I'm sorry, your friend Amanda. She was looking for you after the explosion."

"Explosion?" Margaret exclaimed. "I thought they said the bomb didn't go off? That's what all the news channels reported."

"I'm sorry, Ms. Fuller. That was a poor choice of words

on my part," Agent Brody said, facing her. "The main body of the bomb did not go off as intended, but we have evidence that indicates the detonators did. Which is why I wanted to make sure that Alex was certain he saw wires and a timer in the bag. The wires, a.k.a. detonators, are what would have connected the main bomb to the timer. We discovered the main body of the bomb at the scene, but not the detonators or timer."

Margaret's jaw dropped as she tried to make sense of what Agent Brody had just said to her.

"Where were you when the explosion, for lack of a better term, went off?" Agent Brody asked Alex.

"I think I was across the street."

"Which street?"

"G Street," he lied without blinking.

"Did you feel the tremor from the blast?"

"There was a tremor from the blast?"

"Yes. A few witnesses, who were near the HEC, said they felt a slight tremor."

"I didn't feel any tremor. Maybe I was too far away. The HEC is on the southeastern corner of F and 7th Street, whereas I was on the northwestern corner of G and 9th."

Agent Brody shook his head as he contemplated Alex's answer. "When did you meet up with Amanda?"

"Probably a few minutes later. It took me a while to find her because of the crowd and all."

"Why didn't you wait to give your statement or description of the assailant to the police?"

"Because the attendant told us to evacuate the area. Besides, being blown to smithereens was not on my list of things to do that day."

"Did you see anyone enter the station after the attendant evacuated it?" Agent Brody picked up.

Alex feigned being in deep thought for a while, then he shook his head and said, "No, not that I can remember."

Anxiously, he waited as Agent Brody searched his pockets. His heartbeat increased as he anticipated the worst. *Holy cow, he's going to pull out a piece of evidence that will incriminate me,* Alex thought. He swallowed hard as he awaited his fate.

"Well, if you remember anything else," Agent Brody said, placing a business card on the table, "about what happened yesterday, give me a call. Also, I'll get back to you about that security detail as soon as I get back to the office." He picked up the recorder and tossed it to Agent Sanchez.

"I don't need a security detail," Alex protested.

"Like hell you don't," Margaret snapped crossly to Alex, and then turned her gaze to Agent Brody. "You send that detail over as soon as you get one."

"Will do, ma'am." Agent Brody smiled as he got up from the table. "It was nice meeting you, Alex," he said, extending his hand again. Alex reciprocated the gesture and shook his hand. "Thanks for being so cooperative."

"Sure thing. Can I ask you a question?"

"You just did," he responded with a huge grin on his face.

Very funny, smart ass, Alex thought. "I was just wondering, how did you know I was at that train station yesterday?"

"The attendant at the station," he answered. "He gave us your first name and physical description, but it was your SmarTrip card and the security cameras in the station that gave us the rest."

Up until now, Alex had found his SmarTrip card to be very helpful, but he may have to rethink its usefulness in the future.

"By swiping your card at the station yesterday, we found out that you had created an account for your card when you registered it. You also used your mother's credit card to refill your card. Plus, we were able to retrieve a partial image of you entering the station from the security cameras. Unfortunately, there's no footage of the actual blast or what happened afterwards. It must have knocked out the cameras. Does that answer your question?"

"It does, but it raised another one."

"Shoot."

"You said you have footage of the station prior to the blast, right?"

"Right."

"So why didn't you review the footage to find the guy who planted the bomb and what happened to the detonators?"

Agent Brody looked over at his colleagues, who were already waiting by the front door and on their cell phones. They were already reporting the latest developments in the case to their appropriate chains of command.

"Well, I guess there's no harm in telling you this. But we think our culprit knew exactly which security camera covered the end of the platform where he placed the bomb. When he got to that platform, he turned on a video signal jammer that disabled the camera. We found the jammer in the trash bin on the platform. So there's a blind spot in our video coverage. We saw him enter the station with the bag, but he knew how to angle his head to avoid the cameras from capturing a clear image of his face. We never saw him on the platform. With your help, we can now fill in the blanks."

"Wow. He must have been planning this for a while."

"Seems that way."

"Thanks, Agent Brody."

"Take care, Alex," Agent Brody said, patting him on the back. "Ms. Fuller," he said, extending his hand to her, "it was ... interesting meeting you. Thanks for your cooperation."

"I'll walk you out," Margaret responded curtly, without shaking his hand.

Alex remained at the table, going over the information Agent Brody had just given him about the security cameras. How could he have forgotten about the security cameras? He had to be smarter than that next time. *Next time? There won't be a next time,* he thought. He was never going to use his abilities like that again in public. If it wasn't for that tattooed, thin man, his abilities would have been exposed to the FBI. *The frigging FBI! This cannot—*

"You and I need to talk, young man," Margaret said to her son, interrupting his train of thoughts. "Go get dressed. I'm taking you to school."

"Mom, you're going to be late for work if you drop me off."

"Do I look like I care what time I get to work today, Alex Michael Fuller?"

Oh crap, she had called him by his full name. *This can't be good,* he thought. He looked at his mother and he was right; she didn't look like she had work on her mind right now. Instead, she looked like a banshee, getting ready to pounce on him. Not wanting to irritate her any further, he went upstairs and got ready for school.

* * *

John walked into the Washington, DC Police Department on Indiana Avenue and asked to talk to the desk sergeant. He was wearing a protruding prosthetic nose and a wig and cap that partially hid his face, and had a satchel slung over his shoulder. He had a lanyard around his neck that dangled down by his abdomen with a laminated card that had "Press" written on it. In his hand, he had a notepad and a pencil. He was told to have a seat in the waiting area across from the large bulletproof window. Behind the window were a number of police officers going about their normal daily routine. Soon it would be six o'clock, and they would make their shift change. John waited nineteen minutes when a tall, muscular man impeccably dressed in a police uniform called him up to the window.

"I'm Sergeant Wilson—the desk sergeant," the man said in a deep voice. "Can I help you?"

"Yes," John said. "I'm Chris Connolly, a freelance writer for the Washington Post." He flashed a fake piece of identification in front of the sergeant, who seemed uninterested in anything he had to say so far. "I'm doing a piece on the little boy who found the bomb yesterday in the Metro. I'm trying to get an interview set up with him, but I don't know how to contact him. I was wondering if your office had any information on him that I could use to track him down."

"Whatever information we're going to release to the public will be in the captain's press conference at eight o'clock. Excuse me," Sergeant Wilson said, heading back to the rear of the room.

"Sergeant Wilson!" John yelled.

Sergeant Wilson stopped and faced him.

"The public has a right to know what happened in that tunnel. Now, I'm perfectly willing to pay my sources like any—"

"Are you trying to bribe me, Mr. Connolly?" Sergeant Wilson said, loud enough to get the attention of some of his fellow officers.

"No! It's just that I'm on a tight deadline and need the information pronto."

Sergeant Wilson walked off and grumbled something unpleasant under his breath. John watched as the Sergeant disappeared behind a wall. As he stood there wondering whether the sergeant was coming back, John felt a few of the other officers' eyes on him. Their stares were not welcoming, so he decided to leave.

On his way out of the building, John stopped in the restroom. How else could he get the information? He knew the FBI would have the information he needed, but he wouldn't dare walk into their facility like he just did here. He was certain that in such a case as this, the FBI would be forced to share portions of their investigation with the local authorities. He just had to come up with a more creative way of obtaining the information.

Outside, John walked back toward the bus station where he'd gotten off earlier that morning. He was about two blocks away when a guy walked up to him. The guy was dressed in cargo pants and a polo shirt and had a backpack.

"You the reporter looking for information on the kid from last night's bombing?" the guy asked.

"Yeah. Who are you?"

"No names," the guy said, putting his hand up in protest. "How much are you paying for the information?"

"I only have a thousand dollars."

"Let's see it."

John stopped and pulled an envelope out of his satchel. The envelope contained ten one-hundred-dollar bills, which he showed the guy.

"Okay. The kid's name is Alex Fuller, and he goes to some prep school in Virginia called Prestige."

"Where does he live?"

"Hey man, that's all I could find out. This is a big hush-hush case and the feds are already muscling us out of it. You're lucky I even got that much information. Now hand over the dough." John handed him the envelope. "You're only going to do a piece on the kid, right?"

"Yeah, sure," John said and walked away.

* * *

"Why wouldn't you tell me something like this, Alex?" Margaret asked as she drove her son to school. "Why did I have to find out about this from the FBI? The FBI."

Alex remained silent, staring through the windshield from the passenger seat of his mother's Toyota Corolla. She was upset with him, and had every right to be. She hadn't let up once since Agent Brody left the house. He could hear her from his room while she got dressed in hers. As he waited for her downstairs, he overheard her on the telephone, telling her supervisor she was going to be late because of a family emergency. She'd been ranting now for about twenty minutes as she drove the familiar road to

Prestige. He didn't interrupt her. The occasional "I'm sorry, Mom," was all he could muster up in response.

"You're sorry? You're sorry? Alex, this is not like when you ate the last of my Ben and Jerry's ice cream, or when you forget to take out the trash. This is huge. Do you understand that?"

"Yes, Mom."

"I don't think you do. This isn't even about you getting caught up in this whole fiasco. What kills me, Alex ... what breaks my heart is that you didn't tell me anything." She paused for her comment to sink in. "I thought we had something here. You and I are all we've got. Other than Molly, I don't have anyone else here—and Molly is not family. Do you understand what I'm saying to you?"

"Yes," he replied, as his voice cracked. Alex struggled to contain the lump developing in his throat.

Margaret let out a deep sigh. "My intent is not to upset you," she said as she tousled his hair and allowed her hand to fall on his shoulders. "I just thought our relationship had a stronger trust foundation than this. You should have come to me first. You should have called me as soon as this happened."

"I'm sorry, Mom," he said, more composed. "I just didn't want you to worry."

"Alex, I'm your mother. I'm supposed to worry about you."

"I'm sorry," he repeated as he leaned in to peck her on the cheek.

"I know you are, but damn it, Alex—you have to do better."

"I will. I promise."

Margaret stopped at a red light and turned to face her

son. "You better," she said, then smiled and shook her head.

It was the first time Alex had seen her smile for the day and magically, it lightened his mood. When the light turned green, Margaret slowly accelerated, then asked, "Now, are there any more secrets I need to know about?"

Alex felt his chest tighten. Why couldn't he lie to his mom without the anxieties, like he had to Agent Brody? With the FBI agent, the lies came naturally. It had to, because FBI agents were trained to read a person's body language to detect if they were lying. With his mom, it was different. He always felt physically ill and mentally worn when he lied to her.

"No," he responded to her inquiry.

"Good," she said, pulling into the pick-up/drop-off zone in front of Prestige High School. "Because I don't want another repeat of this morning. Now give me a hug, then tuck and roll."

Alex gave his mom a long hug and said, "I love you, mom."

"I love you too, kiddo."

Alex exited the car and waved to his mother from the sidewalk. He was still staring down the street after she pulled off. He was about to turn around when he heard someone behind him smacking their lips together, emulating the sound of kisses. He turned around to see David with his arms tightly wrapped around himself and his lips puckered, while he shimmied up and down.

"I love you, Mommy. Please don't leave me alone, Mommy."

Timothy and Rafi were standing behind David, and

joined in the laughter. A few students who were getting off the school bus stopped to watch out of curiosity.

"Momma's boy," David spat. "You're so fucking pathetic."

"Well at least I have a mother who cares enough about me to drop me off at school," Alex retorted. "The real question is, where's your mother, David? In bed with the gardener again? Or is it the pool boy's turn today? Oh wait, it's Monday, so that makes it the chauffeur's turn. How does she keep it all straight?"

The passersby erupted in a loud, synchronized "Woooo." Humiliated, David was about to lurch at Alex when he found himself frozen in his tracks—unable to speak or move his legs and arms. No one seemed to notice David's predicament except Alex, whose stare was fixed on the jock.

"Or is it their job to keep it straight for her?" Alex added, as he walked by David and his friends. From behind him, he could hear the crowd laughing. When he was about fifteen yards away from the jock, he released his telekinetic hold on him.

* * *

"What the hell was that all about?" Amanda asked as she stood up to greet Alex under the large maple tree.

"Just David being an idiot."

"How did it go with your mom last night?"

"Last night?"

"Yes, after I left."

"Oh. Nothing. She was asleep when I got in, but she

was rudely awakened this morning by the FBI," he said, walking toward the school building.

"The FBI?" Amanda said in astonishment. "Wait a minute," she added, running behind him on the Quad. "Where are you off to in such a rush? School hasn't even started yet."

"I know, but I'm supposed to meet with the headmaster today, remember?"

"Oh that's right. With everything that happened over the weekend, that kind of pales in comparison."

"To you maybe."

"Alex, stop being a prick," she said, interpreting his comment as a reference to her Novies status. "You know what I meant."

"I know, but I'm still worried about what he's going to decide. If I get kicked out of Prestige, my mother is going to kill me, then flip out—in that order."

"You'll be fine. He won't find anything connecting you to those idiots over there," she said, nodding in the direction of David and his friends. "Now, tell me about the FBI," she added, following him up the stairs to the school's main entrance.

"They showed up this morning and asked me a bunch of questions about yesterday," he said, crossing the threshold into the building.

"And?"

"And … I answered them."

"Alex, this isn't funny," she said, annoyed.

"Why do you let me get under your skin so easily?" he laughed. Amanda rolled her eyes, then smiled at him. "Okay. They wanted to know what happened to the detonators and the timer."

"What did you tell them?"

"I told them I didn't know."

"Did they buy it?"

"I don't know. If they didn't, they didn't let on. Which reminds me," he said, as he stopped to face her in the long hallway that led to the headmaster's office. "They're probably going to get in touch with you also to get a statement. So our account of what happened has to match. Do you understand?"

"Yes. So what did you tell them?"

"I told them that I left you by the turnstile to show the attendant where the bomb was. When the attendant evacuated the station, I left, but was swept up in the group of people that ended up by the G and 9th Street exit. That's where I was until you found me. Got it?"

"We found each other at the G and 9th Street exit after the bombing," she repeated, memorizing what Alex had just said. "Got it."

"Good," he said as he resumed walking. Suddenly, he smiled to himself.

"What's so funny?" she asked.

"Nothing," he said, with an even wider smile on his face.

"Tell me," she demanded.

"Nope."

"Fuller, if you don't tell me, I'm going to run you over with my car, reverse, then run you over again."

"My, aren't we the violent type?" he said, taunting her. She didn't answer him and tried to look uninterested. "Okay. The FBI thinks you're my girlfriend." He waited for her reaction, but there was none. She just kept walking with the same look on her face. "I had to keep correcting them that you weren't." Alex saw when Amanda stopped, but he kept walking and talking, pretending not to have noticed. "And that Agent Brody, I don't know what his problem was. When I told him you weren't my girlfriend, he smirked, like yeah right—like I was lying or something."

Alex stopped outside the door to the headmaster's waiting area, where his secretary sat. He looked down the hallway at Amanda, pretending that he had just noticed she wasn't beside him. "What are you doing back there?" Alex couldn't see her face clearly, because she had it down. He walked over to Amanda and lifted up her chin with his fingers. She had a somber look on her face, as if she was going to cry. In all the years Alex had known Amanda, he had never seen her genuinely cry before, so her expression confused him.

"Are you okay, Mandy?"

"Why would you tell them I'm not your girlfriend? Is the idea of me being your girlfriend such an alien concept to you?" she asked, visibly upset.

Alex was speechless for a moment. He hadn't realized that it was his attempt at humor that had upset Amanda. He scrambled to think of the right thing to say. Unsure of what the right thing was, he went with, "It's not a *total* alien concept, but it is pretty out there. I mean, you're Amanda Bridgewater, and I'm nobody—the total social reject, remember? And let's not forget the unpredictable freaky powers."

She didn't answer him, but kept her head down.

"I mean, you don't want to go out with someone like me ... do you?"

Amanda looked up so her face was about an inch away

from his. "Well, it took you long enough to ask me to be your girlfriend."

"You want to go out with me?" he asked, perplexed.

"Say it a little louder, Fuller. I don't think the entire Quad heard you. And the answer is yes by the way." They both jumped when they heard the school bell ring. When the students started pouring into the hallway, they entered the headmaster's waiting area.

* * *

Inside Headmaster Anderson's office, Alex, Amanda, and Ms. Lucci sat in the leather couch that was in the far right corner. David, Timothy, and Rafi sat in the chairs around the conference table to the left. On the other side of the door, they heard when the headmaster arrived and his secretary told him he had visitors in his office. A moment later, Headmaster Anderson walked in with his briefcase and umbrella.

"Good morning, students—Ms. Lucci."

"Good morning, Headmaster Anderson" was the response in unison.

"Okay, let's get this over with," he said, placing his briefcase on his desk and hanging the umbrella on a coat rack. He walked back over to his chair, sat down, and pulled several documents out of his briefcase. He then retired the briefcase under the desk.

"Mr. Locke, Mr. Fuller—please have a seat," he said, motioning to the two armchairs in front of him. The two students complied.

"Mr. Fuller, Mr. Locke made an accusation against you, whereby he alleged that you assaulted him and his cohorts in the locker room last week, on Thursday. Mr. Locke's co-horts—Timothy Waltz and Rafi al-Sharif—chose not to lodge similar complaints against you." He picked up what appeared to be a textbook and read, "According to the Prestige Preparatory High School Student's Code of Conduct, section 14, subparagraph 2-57, an assault occurs when a student intentionally cause bodily harm or offensive contact to another student. A student found guilty of committing an assault shall be automatically expelled." Both Alex and David jumped when the headmaster slammed the book closed.

"Last week, I interviewed both of you. Mr. Locke, you indicated that Mr. Fuller attacked you in the locker room. Specifically, you stated that Mr. Fuller knocked your legs out from under you, thereby causing you to fall. You did not see Mr. Fuller knock your legs out from under you, because your back was to him at the moment, but he was the only person behind you. Mr. Fuller, you denied having anything to do with Mr. Locke's fall. Specifically, you stated that you never laid a finger on him, and that it was a slippery substance on the floor that caused Mr. Locke's fall.

"During my investigation into Mr. Locke's accusation, I also spoke to Mr. Waltz and Mr. Sharif. Both gentlemen admit to falling in the locker room, but do not recall the specifics of how they fell. However, both gentlemen indicated that Mr. Fuller was at the opposite end of the aisle when they fell. I also spoke to Charlie Smalls, the janitor on duty that day. He recalled the events of that day, and gave me a statement." Headmaster Anderson paused and sat back in his chair. His sour face looked over at the two students in front of him, then at the spectators in the back of the room dismissively. "Now, before I tell you what information I gathered from Mr. Smalls," he said, cleaning his glasses with the end of his tie, "is there anything else you gentlemen would like to share with me?"

The two teens looked at each other with questioning eyes, then back at the headmaster.

"Nothing? Nothing at all?" Headmaster Anderson asked, as he replaced his glasses onto his face and picked up a piece of paper. Both boys shook their heads.

Neither Alex nor David fell for the bait to offer an incriminating statement, so the headmaster continued.

"Very well. I spoke to Mr. Smalls, who informed me that Mr. Fuller came to him and told him that Mr. Locke and his friends fell on a slippery substance on the floor in the locker room. Mr. Smalls stated that he went inside the locker room, where he did indeed find a slippery substance on the floor. He said the substance was all over the area where Mr. Locke and his cohorts fell. In fact, Mr. Smalls said he had to help Mr. Locke and his friends get up off the floor and clean the substance off their clothes and shoes."

Gently, he placed the paper on the desk.

"I have been deliberating about this all weekend. Expelling a student from Prestige High is not something I take lightly; neither do I appreciate students making false accusations against each other. Therefore, based on all the evidence I've gathered, I find that Mr. Fuller did not assault Mr. Locke."

"Yes," Amanda said quietly, as Ms. Lucci grabbed her hand. David looked at Alex with hateful eyes.

"The preponderance of evidence shows," Headmaster Anderson continued, "that Mr. Fuller did not cause Mr. Locke to fall. From his own admission, Mr. Locke said he did not see Mr. Fuller knock his feet out from under him;

he merely suspected that he did. Furthermore, the unbiased statement of Mr. Smalls supports Alex's account of the incident because he too found a slippery substance on the locker room floor, and more importantly, on Mr. Locke's shoes."

Headmaster Anderson pushed the documents aside and took off his glasses. "I don't want my decision to spawn any ill-will between you two gentlemen. The men of Prestige are known for their strong ties of camaraderie and I expect nothing less of you. Now shake hands and put this matter behind you."

The two boys complied. Seeing the disdain in David's eyes, Headmaster Anderson added, "Now a word of caution. The bullying that goes on at other schools will not be tolerated at Prestige. Any sign of retaliation on either of your parts will result in severe consequences. Is that understood?"

"Yes, headmaster," they replied.

"Dismissed."

* * *

It was still early, so John decided to return to his basement apartment. As soon as he opened the door to the apartment, the smell of fried bacon slapped him across the face. John inhaled deeply. *Ms. Jackson must be at it again,* he thought. He walked into the bathroom where he took off the prosthetic nose and wig, before splashing cold water onto his face. He stared at the face that looked back at him. His thoughts were interrupted by a familiar voice from atop the stairs, above his apartment.

"Gabriel," Ms. Jackson cried. "Breakfast's ready."

Gabriel Blackwell was how he had introduced himself to Ms. Jackson when they first met.

"Thank you, Ms. Jackson. I'll be right up," he yelled up the stairs to Ms. Jackson. He then washed his hands and carefully examined himself in the mirror, making sure nothing was out of place that would alarm Ms. Jackson.

Upstairs, the kitchen table was covered with John's favorite breakfast: grits, buttermilk biscuits, gravy, scrambled eggs, bacon, country ham, and a pot of coffee. Before taking a seat, John asked Ms. Jackson if it was okay to turn on the television to see whether the police had any more information on the bombing yesterday. She didn't have any objection.

After saying grace, John asked, "Can you believe it—I was caught up in that whole fiasco yesterday."

"You were? Good Lord. Is that why you came home so late?"

"Yes ma'am. Everything was shut down until they had the situation under control."

"What is this world coming to?"

"I've been asking myself that very same question, and I still have not figured it out," he said, taking a bite out of a biscuit.

"My, my, my—I just hope that no one got hurt."

John did not respond, but kept eating. He was pouring his second cup of coffee when he heard the eight o'clock news theme music and the police chief's face flashed across the television screen.

"Here it is, Ms. Jackson. The news about the bombing is about to start," he said, rushing over to the old television set to turn up the volume. The old television reminded him of the one he grew up watching, which his mother had purchased in the 1970's. It had a wooden frame with legs, buttons to the right of the screen, and an equally antiquated remote. No matter how hard she tried, Ms. Jackson kept losing the universal remote because she wasn't used to it. *Back in my day,* she often said, *if you wanted to change the channel, you got up, walked over to the television and changed the channel.* John had another theory for why she kept losing the remote: she couldn't remember where she last put it. Nevertheless, he was amazed at the fact that the old unit had survived the 2009 congressional mandate for all broadcast stations to transmit in digital only; no longer could they transmit in analog.

The news anchorman, who was sitting behind a desk, reappeared on the television and gave a recap of the latest news. He then turned his attention to what John was waiting for. As he spoke, a small, square insert appeared to his left, depicting the Gallery Place Chinatown Metro Station. He reported:

Police are still hunting for the person, or persons, responsible for leaving a bomb at the Gallery Place Chinatown Metro Station yesterday afternoon. Patricia Simmons reports from Metropolitan Police Department Headquarters. Patricia.

The screen switched to another scene, where a woman dressed in a navy suit was standing in front of a large commercial building, holding a mic. She reported:

Thanks, Donnie. We're standing outside the Metropolitan Police Department Headquarters building in downtown DC, where Police Chief Elaine Berger is set to make an official statement. Let's listen in.

The screen switched again to another scene, where a woman dressed in a police uniform was standing behind a podium, flanked by several men in suits and police uniforms on her left and right. The flickering of cameras could be heard in the background. The woman spoke:

Ladies and gentlemen of the press, thank you for coming out this morning. The Metropolitan Police Department is working feverishly with the FBI to arrest the culprits responsible for yesterday's attempted bombing of the Gallery Place Chinatown Metro Station. As we've indicated last night, the bomb did not detonate and no one was hurt due to the quick thinking of some of our brave citizens. Although I can't give you anything specific about this ongoing investigation, rest assured that we have several viable leads, which we will continue to explore until those responsible are brought to justice. Now, I'll only take a few questions...

Suddenly, several hands flew up in the air from the audience that the woman was addressing.

Chief Berger, Chief Berger...

John turned off the television. He was infuriated by the chief's assessment of the situation. Culprits? Attempted bombing? Brave citizens? Viable leads? *Why the secret coded messages?* he thought. Nowhere did they link the bombing to that pop idol slut who had performed at the HEC or the current hedonistic state of the Union.

"Don't worry," he whispered, consoling himself. "I'll make the link soon enough for them, but for now, I must find the little runt who diffused my bomb."

"Did you say something, Gabriel?" Ms. Jackson asked.

"Ah … I need to go to the library."

"Oh, you're going to do some more research?"

"Yes ma'am."

"Good for you. I like a man who keeps his mind sharp. What is it going to be today?"

"Just a prep school in Virginia."

"Which one, if you don't mind my asking? I used to be a school teacher, you know."

"I know, Ms. Jackson. You've mentioned it a few times." John wondered how much he should tell her. Realizing that the end was near, he decided that it didn't matter. "It's Prestige."

"Oh, the high school over in McLean."

"Mc—what?"

"McLean, over in Virginia. Near Tyson's Corner."

"You know this school?"

"Of course I do. I must have tried about three different times to get a job over there, but kept getting denied."

"Do you know how to get to the school?"

"No. I was never fortunate enough to be granted an interview, so there was no need for me to travel out there. But I know it's in McLean."

"And it's a high school?"

"That's right."

"Is it near the Metro?"

"Schools like that—I doubt it. All those kids are probably chauffeured to school."

John thought for a minute. "You know what, Ms. Jackson—I'm going to need to get into the garage. Are you going to be around later today?"

"Unless the good Lord takes me, I should be right here."

"Okay, I'll be back in about an hour." John exited the house through his basement apartment. He had to find out exactly where Prestige High School was located. *A quick Google search should do the trick,* he thought. The only problem was, he didn't have Internet access in his apartment. The public library was his only option. While he was at it, he would get driving directions to the school also. He was going to make Alex wish he had never been born.

9. SECURITY DETAIL

Ms. Graham was taking attendance when Leslie walked into the classroom. Amanda was already in her seat and heard when Leslie slammed her backpack down on the desk, but chose not to pay her any attention. Spending the weekend with Alex had left Amanda with very little time to get all her homework done. She was finishing up the last two pages of her Computer Science reading assignment when Leslie sighed loudly. Whatever was eating Leslie, Amanda was in no rush to find out.

"Leslie Knolls," Ms. Graham called from behind her spectacles.

"Here."

Amanda kept reading, but could feel Leslie's stare burning into her right cheek.

"What is it, Leslie?" Amanda finally asked after two uncomfortable minutes passed.

"Nothing," Leslie said innocently enough.

"I know you; something's up."

"Well, if you insist," she said, turning around in her chair to dish the latest gossip. "I was just talking to Krista…"

Before Leslie said anything else, Amanda instantly regretted not going with her initial instinct.

"… and she told me the weirdest thing ever. She said that she saw you and Alex in DC this weekend." Leslie paused for dramatic effect, while she pulled out a Blow Pop from her bag.

"So?" Leslie prompted.

"So, what?" Amanda replied.

"So, is it true?"

Amanda sighed and rolled her eyes as she turned to face Leslie.

"Yes it is. And as a matter of fact, Alex and I are now officially dating. Now you're free to Tweet it to the entire school, for all I care," she said, before returning to her book.

* * *

In between bites of her bagel covered with cream cheese and jelly, Margaret dialed the telephone number on the card Agent Brody had left at her house. It was Wednesday, and she did not understand why he hadn't sent over the security detail for Alex. Ever since the bombing, she had spent restless nights worrying about her son. She found herself waking up three, four times a night to check on him and make sure all the doors and windows were locked. She listened as the telephone rang.

"FBI—Washington Field Office."

"Agent Brody, please."

"Speaking."

"Agent Brody, this is Margaret Fuller—Alex Fuller's

mother. You know, the kid that gave you guys all that good intel about the bombing at Gallery Place."

"Yes, Ms. Fuller. How can I help you?"

"I would like to know when you intend to send over the security detail for Alex."

"Did something happen?" he asked, concerned.

"No, nothing happened, but you promised you would get him one."

"I know, Ms. Fuller, and I'm still working on it. But—"

"No buts, Agent Brody. This madman knows what my son looks like. He had no qualms about walking into a crowded train station and leaving a bomb there. I would hate to think what he would do if he knew Alex could identify him."

"Ms. Fuller, I understand your concern, but I won't let anything happen to your son."

"I would really love to believe that, Agent Brody, but here's my dilemma. I'm a single mother and Alex is my only child. At night, we're the only two people in our house and I'm scared out of my mind. What are we supposed to do if this psycho decides to pay us a visit before you send over the detail?"

"Ms. Fuller, I don't think I need to tell you how thin my agency has been stretched since 9/11, but we have. With that said, I did put in a request to have a security detail assigned to Alex, just in case the bomber comes after him. I even contemplated getting one for Miss Bridgewater, but her father declined, stating that his security detail can take care of his daughter."

"You spoke to the Bridgewaters?"

"Yes, we had to get her statement as well. She basically corroborated everything your son said. From what I under-

stand, I don't think the bomber got a good look at her because she herself could not describe him or even recall
coming into direct contact with him."

"Okay, so Amanda is taken care of. What about Alex?"

"I'm still working on it. If I don't hear anything by the
end of the week, I'll personally check in on Alex until a per-
manent detail is assigned."

"Fine." She sighed. "I'll take whatever we can get."

"Fair enough. I'll be in touch."

"Thanks, Agent Brody."

"No problem, Ms. Fuller."

* * *

The next couple of days at Prestige High were very trying
for Alex and Amanda. By then, everyone had heard about
the unlikely pairing. A lot of them were not familiar with
Amanda's and Alex's friendship before Prestige, so they
didn't understand the attraction. Sure they looked great
together, but she was so popular and sociable, and he was
so—not.

Amanda received mixed reviews from both the news
crew and cheerleading squad, although she never asked
them for their opinion. Her girlfriends were more forgiving
because they found Alex's physical attributes, mysterious
nature, and reclusive persona a bit alluring. For Alex, it was
life as usual, except for the constant stares and "hi's" he
now received from the opposite sex. Physically, nothing
had changed about him; but now that everyone knew he
was dating the head cheerleader, it seemed every girl at
Prestige High wanted to see what he looked like or vie for
his attention. Totally baffled by why girls acted this way,

Alex shook off the unwanted attention and went on his way.

By the end of the week, the rumor mills had started to subside. *High school students can be so fickle*, Amanda thought as she walked down the hallway to Gymnasium 2. You never know what will interest them, or how long you can keep their attention. These were the words of wisdom Eddie had imparted to her during her first week on the school newspaper. She waited for Alex by the acrobatics room, where her cheerleading squad practiced. For the past week, Alex met her here before heading to his gym class on the other end of Gymnasium 2.

From her left, she saw Alex walking toward her in his matching Prestige High gym shirt and shorts. Today was the first day she saw him wearing shorts to gym; normally he wore sweat pants.

"Nice legs." She giggled.

"Right back at you," he said, tugging at the skimpy shorts he had become accustomed to seeing the cheerleaders practice in.

"So, what are we doing this weekend?" she asked.

"You tell me—I'm not the one with the social calendar."

"Ha ha." Amanda feigned amusement. "Other than an away game on Saturday at one o'clock, I'm free."

"Are you going to study with me today in Ms. Lucci's office?"

"No can do. I actually have to stop by the newsroom after practice. Katt is going ballistic again over a piece she wrote on the growing debt of the country and how future generations—i.e. us—will be crippled by it. Eddie is trying to get her to tone it down, or else he'll have to run it as an op-ed piece. Needless to say, Katt is not happy. So I have to play the voice of reason."

"Katt can be … pretty intense," he said, recalling that Katt was the girl who gave him the finger when he and Amanda were on the outs.

"You think?" she replied, as they both laughed. "I've got an idea. Why don't we rent a couple of movies and watch them at your house tonight?"

"That sounds fine, since there's nothing good on TV. But I should warn you, our television is not as awesome as your dad's home theater system."

She sighed deeply, and then rolled her eyes. "Well, I'm not taking visitors now anyway. My parents have not been on their best behavior of late, so I would prefer not to have you around them right now."

"Does this have anything to do with us going out?"

"No. They've been having problems—marital problems —for a while."

"Oh, I didn't know that. When did it start?"

"A little over two years ago now."

"Two years? Wow," Alex said, suddenly feeling even guiltier for not staying in touch with her. "I'm sorry," was all he could muster up.

"Don't be," she said, trying to perk herself up. "Que sera sera, no?"

"Amanda, that's not—"

"What kind of movie do you want to see?" she said, reverting the conversation back to its original subject. "Action? Drama? Classical? Romantic comedy?"

"Mandy," he said, with a look of concern on his face.

"Alex, don't let their problem become ours. They're

adults. If they can't sort out their own mess, I doubt we can."

"So you're not bummed about this?"

"Absolutely not," she lied.

Alex didn't believe her, but decided to let it go for now since they didn't have much time to discuss it before the bell would ring. "Okay then."

"So, what type of movie do you want to see?"

"Surprise me," he said, kissing her on the cheek before leaving for his gym class.

"I'll get the movies and meet you at your house tonight around six," she yelled after him.

"Works for me."

* * *

It was fairly easy for John to gain access to Prestige High's school grounds. After printing the school's address from the Internet at the local library, he retrieved his white panel van from Ms. Jackson's garage. The vehicle had a grill push guard bar across the front bumper. He had not driven it since his arrival to DC five months ago. Carefully, he outfitted the van with the logo of a local utility company in Virginia, and then drove from DC to McLean. At the entrance to the high school, he told the guards that someone had called to report that some of the lights on the lacrosse field weren't working and he was there to check them out. He was waved in without any hassle.

Once on school grounds, he observed a few mainten-ance workers sprinkled around the campus. At lunch time, he struck up a conversation with one of the workers, who went by the name Rocky. He learned from Rocky that as long as they performed their work, the head of maintenance pretty much left them alone. The only time they normally came in contact with the head of maintenance was Monday mornings, to learn what their area of responsibility would be for the week, and Friday afternoons, when they got paid. Before heading back to his van, John swiped Rocky's badge.

Later that day, John saw Alex exit the school building. Before Alex boarded the school bus, a blonde girl ran up to him in a cheerleader uniform and kissed him goodbye. John wondered if this was the same girl he saw Alex with at the train station. To make sure, he stuck around after Alex left and followed the girl to the lacrosse field. He later found out that the blonde was Amanda Bridgewater, Alex's new girlfriend and head of the cheerleading squad. He stuck around for the game, and then decided to follow her home afterwards. He was disappointed to learn that she lived in an affluent neighborhood, which would make his movements easily detectable.

That night when John got home, he created a maintenance worker badge to resemble the one he stole from Rocky. For the rest of the week, he posed as a maintenance worker to gain access to Prestige. No one ever questioned his assertions, because John had the innate ability to blend into his surroundings. John didn't mind caring for the beautiful grounds of Prestige High, because he loved working with his hands. Throughout the day, he worked in isolated areas around the campus, which were abundant. The only exception was before school started and after it ended. In those two instances, John worked primarily in the front of the school, where there was a lot of traffic, so he could study the comings and goings of Amanda and Alex.

By the end of week, he thought he had Alex's schedule figured out. Alex caught Prestige High's school bus, number sixty-two, at 07:15, a block away from his house. He arrived at Prestige by 07:50. Amanda was usually already there by that time, waiting for him under a large maple tree in front of the school. At 08:00 when the school bell rang, they would hurry off to homeroom. Prestige High's last class for the day ended at 15:15, but Alex would consistently leave after 17:20. He later learned that Alex spent two hours every day studying after school. On Tuesday and Thursday, when he followed Alex home, the teen usually arrived by 18:00. For the next few hours, Alex was home alone, until his mother arrived between 20:30 and 21:00.

Amanda's schedule, however, was a little more erratic. She left home between 07:00 and 07:30. Depending on her mood, she either drove straight to school or stopped by the neighborhood Starbucks or the French bakery on Main Street. She always made sure she was under the maple tree before Alex. After school, she never left at the same time. Monday, she cheered at a game after school and didn't leave until 19:00. Tuesday, she met with the newspaper crew for an hour, and then left in a hurry. Wednesday, she joined Alex at his study session and took him home afterwards. She stayed with him until his mother got home. Thursday, he learned that she met with the news crew again for three hours.

Friday, John exited Prestige High's school grounds at 15:00, before the other workers finished working and collected their pay checks. He parked along Lewinsville Road and waited. Today was the day he had decided to confront Alex about his interference in his plans on Sunday. He knew it wouldn't be long before the FBI started to close in on him. He assumed that they had already contacted Alex by now, who would have given them an accurate description of him from their encounter in the Metro station.

At 17:15, he saw Amanda exit the school grounds. He sat back in his van as she sped past him in her fancy car. At 17:27, school bus sixty-two drove by him and he started his engine. John followed the bus down Lewinsville Road, until he ascertained that Alex was the kid seated in the last row on the right. He then drove past the bus and made his way to Alex's stop at Pleasant Street and Stratford Avenue.

On Stratford Avenue, John parked his van a few yards ahead of the bus stop. From underneath the passenger seat, he pulled out a black leather bag. He looked inside the bag at the small brown glass bottle he had filled last night with chloroform—the clear, colorless liquid, which he had made from pure acetone, bleach, and ice. He also made sure he still had the pieces of cloth he'd taken from the cleaning supply closet today at Prestige. He placed the bag behind the passenger seat, near the side sliding door. Then, he waited.

As John waited, he scanned the block for passersby—there were none. From his surveillance earlier this week, it would take fifteen minutes for the bus to get from Lewinsville Road to Chain Bridge Road, where the bus would start unloading students. From there, he knew, the bus would make five stops before it got to Alex's stop, where he would dismount, along with another boy and a girl. Alex would need to walk past his van to get to his house, while the other students went in the opposite direction.

In his rearview mirror, John saw school bus sixty-two turn onto Stratford Avenue. He exited the van through the side door and stood there, rummaging through the black

bag—pretending to look for something. He heard the
school bus brakes shriek to a halt. The doors swung open.
John opened the small brown bottle. Two eager feet
hopped off the bus as John picked up a piece of cloth. Another set of feet jumped off the bus and John placed the
cloth over the open mouth of the bottle. As a third set of
sluggish feet exited the bus, John tilted the bottle over onto
the cloth and let the clear liquid saturate it. Slowly, sluggish
footsteps walked toward him. John recapped the bottle and
slowly begun to turn to his left.

"Alex," a voice echoed from John's right.

The sluggish set of footsteps stopped. So did John.

"Agent Brody?" John heard Alex ask.

Agent? John wondered. Slowly, he turned back to his
van and leaned over into the side door.

"What are you doing here?" he heard Alex ask, walking
by him. With his head inside the van, John looked through
the windshield and saw a man dressed in a dark blue suit,
with sunglasses. He was walking from the intersection at
the end of the block toward them. Everything about the
man screamed *fed*. John turned his attention back to the bag
in front of him.

"I'm here to see you," Agent Brody said.

"Me? Why?" Alex said, as he and Agent Brody walked
toward Pleasant Street.

"I'm filling in until your security detail is assigned." The
words 'security detail' resonated in John's head.

"You?" was the last thing John heard Alex say, as he
and Agent Brody made a right onto the street where Alex
lived.

John was furious when his prey disappeared around the
corner. He dare not follow them and risk being discovered

before he confronted the boy. So, he decided to wait until the fed left. He looked at the brown bottle and saw that most of its contents were still intact. With the fed guarding the kid, he wished he had carried more ammunition than the one fifteen-round magazine he had in his 9-mm handgun. John contemplated whether he'd have to go back to his apartment for more firepower. He didn't like the idea of letting Alex out of his sight without knowing for sure he'd still be there when he returned. Come what may, he was going to finish this tonight, even if he had to break into the house.

John was still evaluating his options as he closed the side door and walked to the driver side of the van. He opened the van door just as Amanda's car drove by him. With a scowl on his face, he watched as the car turned right at the end of the block. Then he thought—*maybe I don't need to go back home after all.*

10. MOVIE NIGHT

On their way to the Fuller house, Agent Brody explained to Alex the phone conversation he'd had with Margaret earlier that week. He also mentioned stopping by Prestige to pick him up today, but he was informed by Ms. Lucci that he had already left. Agent Brody reached the Fuller house just a split second before school bus sixty-two reached Alex's stop. He had to scramble to find parking before rushing back to Stratford Avenue in time to meet Alex as he got off the bus. Alex found all this fuss over him totally unnecessary, but it seemed Agent Brody and his mother were now in agreement about his safety.

Outside the Fuller house, Agent Brody got back into his car, where he intended to conduct his surveillance. He gave Alex another one of his cards and told him to keep it handy. Although Alex hated the idea of having a 'suit' watching over him, he hated the idea of Agent Brody sitting alone in an uncomfortable car for hours. So, he invited the agent to wait inside the house.

As they walked into the foyer, Alex told Agent Brody to make himself at home. Agent Brody asked if it was okay to set up his equipment on the dining room table, which Alex said was fine as he disappeared upstairs.

In his room, Alex changed out of his school uniform and into cargo shorts and a T-shirt. The picture of Amanda on his nightstand caught his attention, which reminded him of a surprise he had for her. With Amanda coming over, this would be the perfect time for him to give it to her. After opening the drawer to his nightstand to reassure himself it was still there, he ran back downstairs.

Agent Brody was standing in the dining area. Alex walked over to the sofa and turned on the television.

"Just so you know, Amanda is coming over today. We're going to watch some movies."

"I meant to ask you about that." Agent Brody smiled.

"Meant to ask me what?"

"Well, on Monday when I spoke to you, you told me that Amanda was not your girlfriend."

"Uh huh."

"And on Tuesday, when I spoke to Amanda, she told me she *was* your girlfriend. Care to elaborate on that?"

"Yeah, about that," Alex said, collecting himself. "Well, when I went to school Monday, we sort of decided to start dating."

Agent Brody shook his head as a huge smile spread across his face.

"Please don't say anything about it when she gets here," Alex begged. "The kids at school have been giving her a hard enough time already. And it's kinda, sorta all your fault."

"My fault? How is that?" he asked, taking a seat in the armchair adjacent to Alex.

"Well, you were the one who kept calling her my girlfriend, when in fact she was not at the time. When I told Amanda that I had to keep correcting you, she got upset, thinking I didn't want to date her or something. Anyway, it led to us DTRing right then and there. So now she's getting grief for it."

Agent Brody laughed. "Okay, I won't say anything to her about it. But what about you? Aren't the kids giving you a hard time, too?"

"Not really. The kids at school pretty much leave me alone, except for a few stares—but I'm used to that."

"Why is that?

"I don't have a lot of friends, Agent Brody, and I tend to keep to myself; a combination that sentenced me to social damnation in the world of high school."

"Does it bother you?"

"No, not really. The only person whose friendship I ever wanted was Amanda's; now she's back."

A knock at the door interrupted their conversation. Alex got up to answer it, but Agent Brody told him to stay put while he got the door. Agent Brody opened the door for a jovial Amanda, whose expression turned sullen when she saw the FBI agent.

"Amanda," he said, trying to put her at ease. "Alex has been waiting for you. Come in."

"Thanks," Amanda said, stepping into the house and eyeing the agent uneasily. She made her way over to the sofa and shot nervous glances at Alex. "Hi, Alex."

"Hey. You've met Agent Brody?"

"Of course. It's not every day the FBI shows up at my house and wants to talk to me instead of my father."

"Well, he'll be checking in on me until my security detail is assigned or until they catch the bomber, whichever comes first... at my mother's insistence of course."

"Oh," she said with enlightened eyes, sitting next to

Alex on the sofa. Agent Brody returned to the dining room area and rifled through his equipment.

"What did you get?"

"Get what?" she said, looking lost. Alex raised his eyebrows in confusion, as he cocked his head to the side. "Oh," she finally blurted out. "The movies. I got an action, a classic, and one scary movie."

"Let's see them," he said. Amanda retrieved the three movies from her bag and handed them to Alex. He examined the movies, and then looked at Amanda.

"What?" she asked.

"I'm assuming this is the action flick," he said holding up one of the movies. Amanda nodded. "And I'm assuming this is the thriller." He held up another movie. Again, Amanda nodded. "Then what is this?" he asked holding up the third movie, entitled *Clueless*.

"That's the classic," she retorted.

"*Clueless* is not a classic."

"Says who?"

"Says me. Says the entire movie-going population."

Just then, they both heard a chuckle coming from the dining room.

"Amanda, *The Godfather* is a classic. *Psycho* is a classic. *Airplane* is a classic. This," he said, holding up the movie *Clueless* again, "is not a classic."

"I disagree. And so would *Entertainment Weekly*, which listed *Clueless* as number forty-two on its list of 'new classics' back in 2008."

"It is scary that you actually committed that sort of information to memory."

"Whatever," she said, forming the letter "W" with her fingers like the character Amber in *Clueless*. "I don't care what you say. *Clueless* is funny, engaging, and clever. It did an amazing job of retelling Jane Austen's *Emma*, a classic novel of teen angst—"

"I know what it—"

"—into something totally relatable to us millennials."

Alex looked at a spirited Amanda, content with his decision to finally start dating her. The thought of dating someone without her esprit would not have been an option. "I guess if you put it that way, one *could* think of *Clueless* as a classic."

"Don't pacify me, Fuller," she said. More snickers came from the dining room.

Alex joined in the laughter before asking, "Which one would you like to see first?"

"Let's go with the action flick first."

"Alex, before you get too absorbed with your movies," Agent Brody interjected, "Can you tell me which room in the house has the best view of the street?"

"Sure, but why do you need to know that?"

"I just need to take some pictures."

"Why?" Amanda pressed.

"Well, if this guy is really out to get Alex, it's not improbable to think that he would be watching your house or other places you hang out. I wanted to take some pictures of the vehicles up and down your street and see if any of their license plates turn up anything."

"Okay," Alex responded. "The window over by the foyer is okay to get some street-level shots. But the best view would be from my bedroom, above the garage. You could also get some good shots of Stratford Avenue from my Mom's room."

"Do you mind if I go upstairs and take some shots?"

"No, go ahead."

Agent Brody snapped the telescopic zoom lens onto his camera, and then headed upstairs.

"Wow, I never thought about that psychopath actually going through the trouble of finding out where you live," Amanda said.

"Yeah, weird, isn't it?"

"Aren't you scared?"

Alex thought for a moment. "Not really. Ever since I came into my abilities, I've never really been afraid of anything ... except being discovered, of course."

"Abilities or not, just promise me you'll take some precautions until he's caught."

"I will."

"Are we going to watch these down here, or in your room?" she asked, turning her attention back to the movies.

"Upstairs. I have something for you up there anyway."

"You got me something?" Amanda said, clapping her hands together and bouncing up and down on the couch. "What is it? Tell me, tell me, please."

"Not a chance. You'll just have to wait the whole two minutes it takes us to get to my room."

Amanda gathered up the movies, stood up and slung her bag over her shoulder. "Okay, let's go."

"Patience, Amanda. We haven't even popped any popcorn or made any slushy drinks."

"Popcorn? Slushies?"

"Yes, popcorn and slushies. We're going to make this a real movie night," he said, heading into the kitchen with Amanda shadowing him.

"Alex, why do you insist on torturing me?"

"You call this torture?" he said, tossing her a bag of un-

222

popped popcorn. "Put this in the microwave. I'll make the slushies." Amanda placed the bag in the microwave while Alex searched the cupboards for the blender.

"When did you learn to make slushies?"

"When I started spending most of my summers at the Gardens. After the Camp APRICOT incident, I asked my mom to sign me up for all their summer programs. It gets hot up there, so I used to make slushies and carry them with me. What flavor would you like?"

"What do you have?"

"Just about everything. We have fruit-flavored juices, as well as fresh fruits."

"Can I have a smoothie instead?"

"Sure. I can make that too. Soy or regular milk?"

"Soy."

"Fruits?"

"Strawberry and banana."

"One strawberry-banana smoothie coming up."

When the timer went off, Amanda pulled the scorching hot bag out of the microwave. "I think we're going to need another bag of popcorn. I don't think this one will make it through the first movie," she said, holding up the bag.

"There's more in the cupboard over your head," Alex said as he powered on the blender.

The two teens busied themselves for the next few minutes as they created their own movie snacks. A moment later, Agent Brody returned to the dining room, content with the photos he had taken. Alex saw when the agent made a note of their security system, then pulled out his phone from his pocket and made a call.

With their full menu of tasty treats, Amanda and Alex

retired to his bedroom upstairs, while Agent Brody continued with his telephone conversation.

* * *

Amanda created a picnic area at the foot of Alex's bed while he got the movie ready. As she was finishing her task, Amanda spotted her Braemar Academy graduation photo on Alex's night stand.

"We so have to get you an updated picture of me," she said, taking up the frame and examining her photo. "I don't want anyone to know my cheeks were ever that fat."

"Give me that," Alex said, pulling the frame out of her hands. "Your cheeks were not fat—they were rosy and plump."

"'Plump' is another word for fat."

"No it's not. Your cheeks were fine. I liked your cheeks," he admitted with a slight hint of embarrassment.

Amanda's eyes twinkled from the broad smile that covered her face. Nervously, she leaned over and kissed Alex on his cheek. "I like your cheeks too. Now, where's my gift?"

"It's right here," he said, pulling out the drawer in his nightstand. His hand emerged holding a small jewelry box. Amanda looked on with great anticipation. "Do you remember the earrings your mother gave you when you graduated from Braemar?"

"How can I forget? I got an ear-full from her when I lost one of them on the day of graduation."

"They were heart-shaped, with half the heart made of yellow gold with an intricate design, and—"

"The other half of the heart was filled with diamonds

set in white gold," Amanda added, finishing his sentence. "I loved those earrings. I thought they made me look so grown up."

"Yeah, I know. You thought you lost it at Chelsea Ashby's graduation party."

"What does that have to do with my gift?"

"You didn't lose your earring at Chelsea's. That night when you had your driver drop me off at my old apartment building, I hugged you so tight because you were leaving for England the next morning."

"Oh that's right. It was going to be the first summer we spent apart since you moved to Virginia. You were so sad," she said faintly. "We both were." Suddenly, she perked up. "Well, if it's any consolation, it turned out to be one of the worst summers of my life. I loved the lush, green English countryside, but the food and weather that year were awful. Good thing we were so close to the Continent so I could hop over to France, or I would have just died. And my cousin, Victoria, what a little biatch she turned out to be."

"I remember. You relived every painstaking moment for me over the phone when you got back."

"I'm sorry we didn't get to hang out much after that summer, but that's when things started going haywire with my parents."

"Don't apologize. I had some issues of my own that contributed to the demise of our friendship." He smiled. "Anyway, the day after you left for England, I found your earring outside my apartment building. I probably knocked it out of your ear when I hugged you goodbye. I kept it, meaning to give it back to you when you returned, but totally forgot about it."

"Don't worry about it. I got rid of the other one a while ago anyway."

"I came across it again when I discovered my abilities, and decided to test out my jewelry-making abilities," he said, lifting the lid off the box. "Tell me if I should keep looking for another job."

Amanda looked at the box with her mouth opened wide. She lifted the piece of jewelry out of the box, examining it carefully. It was her old earring, but Alex had turned it into a pendant. The heart was exactly the same as she remembered it, but he had turned the post into a loop, through which a new white-gold chain necklace now hung.

"Oh my God," she whispered.

"Do you like it?"

"It's perfect. It actually looks better as a pendant than it did as an earring." She looked up at Alex, a bit misty-eyed, and said, "Thank you. It's beautiful."

"Good. Now let's see what it looks like on," he said, fastening the necklace around her neck.

* * *

When Margaret got home that night, she found Agent Brody seated at her dining room table, working on his laptop while talking on his cell phone. When he saw her, he stood up.

"Well, let me get back to you on that," he said, talking into the receiver. "I'm going to drop by the office after I'm done here. Will you still be around? Okay, thanks."

"Ms. Fuller," he said after he hung up.

"Agent Brody, you came."

"Yes. I don't think you left me with much of a choice."

"Sorry about that. I thought you were only going to stop by to make sure Alex got home safely. I hope we didn't keep you from your work."

"You didn't. In fact, I've been working the whole time since I've been here. I walked around your home, securing the perimeters. I finally got a chance to read through a couple of preliminary reports on the bombing—a task that could've taken days to complete if I were in the office with all the distractions. I've made a few calls. In fact, I just got some good news for you a few minutes ago."

"You found Alex a security detail?"

"You've guessed it. His name is Tom Paxton. He'll start Sunday after he finishes up another case."

"Thank you, Agent Brody. That is great news. Did you tell Alex?"

"No ma'am. Like I said, I just found out myself about five minutes ago."

"Okay good, I'll tell him. I know he hates the idea of having someone follow him around, so I don't want him to take out his frustration on you. Teenagers—they love their privacy," she said, heading toward the stairs.

"I'm fully aware."

As she reached the foot of the stairs, she turned back around. "Oh, where are my manners? Can I offer you something to eat or drink?

"Don't worry about it. Alex had that covered. He checked in on me in between movies. So I'm good. Besides, I have to be heading out in a little while anyway."

"Movies?"

"Yes. He's upstairs watching movies with Amanda."

"Oh, Amanda is here. So that was her car parked across

the street," she deduced. "Okay, I'll be right back," she said, as she hopped up the stairs.

As she neared Alex's bedroom door, Margaret heard laughter that instantly filled the hallway with life. It had been so long since she'd heard her son laugh out loud. Instead of interrupting, she stood next to the door, relishing in the whimsical outburst of laughter that continued. She waited a few more minutes until the laughter subsided, and then knocked on the door.

"Come in, Mom," she heard Alex say.

"Hi, Ms. Fuller." Amanda waved from the floor at the foot of the bed.

"Hi, Amanda," she replied, walking over to them. "Nice little bash you guys have going on here," she said, taking stock of the empty containers on the floor around them.

"Yeah, we're having a movie night, with all the trimmings," Amanda replied.

"Are you staying over?"

"No. I have an away game tomorrow, so I have to go home tonight."

"Alex, I don't want you to keep Amanda here too late. It's already after ten. When does this movie end?" she said, motioning to the television.

"Maybe another twenty or thirty minutes," Alex said.

"Well, as soon as it ends, make sure Amanda is on her way home." She then turned to Amanda and said, "It's not that I don't love having you here, Amanda, but if you are going home tonight, I don't want you driving around too late by yourself. Of course, you're free to stay over, if you'd like."

"Thanks, Ms. Fuller, but I do have to get home."

Turning her attention back to Alex, Margaret said, "I just got some great news from Agent Brody."

"What kind of news?" he asked.

"He found you a security det—"

"Oh, Mom," he whined.

"Don't 'oh Mom' me. This is for your protection. He starts Sunday. His name is Tom Paxton. And it will only be until they catch the bomber." She knew he was rolling his eyes, although she couldn't see his face from the way he shook his head.

"You know, I'm fully capable of taking care of myself. I don't need a babysitter. You already had Agent Brody waste his evening babysitting me. Must we waste more tax dollars on another babysitter?"

Margaret walked over to him and said, "Did I ever tell you how cute you are when you're mad?" When she was standing in front of him, she leaned over and squeezed his cheek.

"Mom," he said, brushing her hand away.

"Okay, okay. Not in front of company—I get it," she said, retreating. Amanda giggled as Alex's cheeks became flushed. She heard Amanda burst out laughing after she closed the door behind her.

* * *

After a quick shower, Margaret headed downstairs. She walked past Alex and Amanda, who were standing in the foyer. He was helping her with her bag. She headed over to the kitchen, where she saw Agent Brody standing by the dining room table, packing up his equipment.

"Need a hand with that?" she asked.

"No ma'am, I'm all done," he said, sliding his laptop into its case.

"Good night, Ms. Fuller. Agent Brody," Amanda called from the front door, which Alex had open for her.

"Good night, Amanda," Margaret said.

"Hold on a sec, Amanda," Agent Brody said, walking toward them. "I'll walk you out."

"Ah, no," Alex said, intercepting him. "That's my job."

"Not tonight. You need to stay indoors as much as possible until we catch this guy, or ascertain that he's no longer in the area."

"Do you see what you've started?" he said to his mother, who was trying to find something to eat in the kitchen.

"And yet, I remain unmoved," she answered. Everyone erupted in laughter, except Alex.

Agent Brody looked away as Amanda kissed Alex good night, then he walked her to her car outside. After she pulled off, he walked back to the house.

"I need to be heading out too," Agent Brody said. "You okay, Alex?"

"I'm good," he said, looking bummed.

"Listen, it won't be that bad. Tom is a really cool guy. You probably won't even notice he's around."

That's what I'm afraid of, he thought. "I guess it will be all right," he said before turning toward his mother. "You need me for anything?"

"No. Just clean up that mess you guys created in your room."

"Okay," he said, heading upstairs.

"Oh, before I forget," Agent Brody said, which caused Alex to stop in his tracks. "I took the liberty of contacting your home security provider and asked that my office be notified if there's an alarm here—in addition to your local law enforcement."

"Oh thank you, Agent Brody. That was very thoughtful," she said, as she stuck her head out of the kitchen, so Alex could see her from the staircase. "Did you hear that, Alex?"

Alex rolled his eyes and continued his ascent. After Agent Brody got his equipment, Margaret walked him to the door and they exchanged good nights. After he left, she locked the door and armed the alarm system.

11. KIDNAPPED

Amanda was still thinking about Alex after she left his house. He had not said much to her after his mother left his room. To comply with his mother's wishes about getting her home at a decent time, they decided not to watch the third movie. They agreed that they would watch it tomorrow night, after Amanda's lacrosse game in Maryland. She would call him after the game, just in case he had errands to run. Slowly, she brought her car to a halt at a stop light.

Not for the life of her could she understand why Alex had gotten so wigged out about having a security detail. She'd reminded him that she used to have one too back at Braemar, before having just a chauffeur. All he had to do was not use his powers while the agent was around, which shouldn't be hard since he said he had better control over them now.

WHAM!!!

A powerful and violent force ripped through Amanda's car from behind, throwing her forward. Without the protection of her airbags in a rear-end collision, her head slammed into the steering wheel, then bounced backward, crashing against the head restraint. Her vision went dark and she became lightheaded as pain shot through her head, neck, and back. Suddenly, she heard her car door open.

Oh thank God, a good Samaritan, she thought.

She felt her body being lifted out of the car, and then set down on the hard tarmac. No matter how hard she tried, she could not get her head to stop spinning or hurting. She faintly heard the OnStar representative's voice saying something in the distance, and then felt herself being lifted again.

"Where are you taking me?" she whispered in a stupor.

She heard a vehicle door slide open, and then she was placed on a cold metallic surface. She struggled to force her eyes open, only catching a glint of light here and there. Suddenly, an arm came down forcefully on her face. With arms flailing, she fought to break free, but she was so disoriented, she couldn't tell which way was the path to freedom. Just then, she realized that the arm held a cloth against her face. She inhaled a sweet-smelling fragrance.

Could this be the paramedics? she wondered. Here? Already? Impossible!

Realizing her dilemma, she struggled harder to escape, but the arm held her more securely. She sank her nails into the arm, which caused another arm to pin hers to the floor, where a knee held them still. Instinctively, she kicked her legs exuberantly, striking an object or two, but failing to expose any weakness in her attacker's fortress. She felt herself becoming dizzier. Soon her body was overcome by an unbelievable feeling of fatigue, and her struggle waned to nothing more than a gentle pat. A moment later, she was perfectly still.

John did not plan to kidnap Amanda, but faith had placed her in his midst after Agent Brody foiled his plans for Alex. It would be an arduous task for him to even approach Alex with an FBI agent nearby. His alternative options were to either initiate an aggressive assault on the house with the agent inside or separate the boy from his protector. Amanda had provided him with the means to achieve the latter. He was certain he could convince the cheerleader to get her boyfriend to meet them alone. So, he waited for her outside the Fullers' house for over five hours.

After Amanda first passed him on Stratford Avenue that evening, he had waited for her to reemerge. As the hours ticked by, he decided to park his van a block away from Alex's house on Pleasant Street to avoid detection. He was careful not to park too far away, where his view of the house would be obstructed. He also made sure his van was parked snuggly behind an SUV, so no one from the house could read his license place.

When he saw the cheerleader emerge hours later, he followed her, waiting for the right moment to strike. He seized the opportunity when she finally stopped at a red light on a poorly lit, secluded street, where he crashed his van into the back of her car. After extracting her from her vehicle and securing her in his van, John returned to Amanda's car. He got into the driver's seat. The car was still on and operational. He listened as the OnStar operator asked how she could assist. Slowly, he steered the car off onto the soft shoulder of the road, before returning to his van.

Alex was in a fantastic mood the following morning when he woke up. He thought about calling Amanda, but remembered that they had agreed she'd call him after her game today. If he didn't hear from her by then, then he'd feel justified in playing the why-didn't-you-call-me card without sounding desperate. He hopped down the stairs and ran into the kitchen. Pulling out pots and pans, he decided to make his mother breakfast.

The scent of the coffee brewing and the bacon frying saturated the house. A few minutes later, Margaret came walking down the stairs.

"Morning," she said, stretching as she reached the kitchen.

"Hi, Mom."

"What are you doing up so early on a Saturday?"

"Making you breakfast."

"Have I told you lately that you are my absolute favorite person in the world?" she said, kissing him on his temple as he took the pan off the stove.

"Yeah, yeah. Tell me anything while I'm holding a pan filled with fried bacon."

Margaret smiled. "But seriously, why are you up so early?" she said, pouring coffee.

"Well, it's my last day without a suit shadowing me," he said, referring to his new security detail. "So I'd like to go to the Gardens."

"I don't think that's a good idea."

"Why not?"

"Because you heard what Agent Brody said last night about you being outdoors until they capture this guy."

"So I'm under house arrest?"

"Afraid so, kiddo."

"You've got to be shi—I mean kidding me. But it's my last day—"

"Alex," she said, holding up her left hand. "I'm sorry. You're not leaving this house unless you're being escorted by your new security detail, or until the FBI catches this guy."

"But I've been doing just fine all week without some suit following me."

"That was different. During the week, you left the house, went to school—which is on secured grounds—then you came home. But now you're talking about the Gardens, which doesn't have any security and is open to the public."

"This blows," he said, sighing heavily.

"Sorry sweetie," she said, putting her hand on his shoulder. "It won't be for too long."

"It won't be long? You are aware that the FBI has a list of most-wanted criminals that they've been trying to capture *for years* now, right?

"Alex, must you be so pessimistic?"

"I'm a realist. I just hope Amanda really doesn't mind having a suit around all the time."

"Why would Amanda be concerned about you having a security detail?

"You haven't heard?"

"Heard what?"

Oh," Alex said, relishing in his mother's ignorance.

"What is it?

Alex got two plates from the cupboard and started fixing hers.

"Alex?"

He started whistling as he finished fixing her plate and started on his.

"What is going on? What haven't I heard?"

"Amanda and I are dating now."

"Shut the front door!" she said with her eyes bulging out of her head.

* * *

"Wake up, sleeping beauty," John said, waving a small bottle of smelling salt under Amanda's nose. Amanda's head, which had been nestled against her chest for the past few hours, jerked backwards as the scent burned through her nostrils and down into her throat. She tried to cough, but her mouth was muffled by a gag tied securely around her head.

"We don't have all day, and we have a lot to cover in a very short time frame," John said.

Amanda's head continued to swim, a combination of the chloroform wearing off, her head slamming into her steering wheel, and the introduction of the smelling salt. At first her vision was blurry. As she concentrated on the voice in the background, glints of light slowly formed objects.

"Welcome back," John said when he saw Amanda open her eyes.

Instinctively, Amanda jumped away from the grisly face that looked back at her. She suddenly felt herself falling backwards, but was unable to move any of her limbs to break her fall. She landed with a great thud on the floor, as pain shot through her head, neck, and back. She screamed out in anguish, but her voice was muted by the gag.

"Oh careful little one, we don't want you to hurt your-self before we're done."

Amanda's brain scrambled to figure out what was happening to her. She was on her back, but she could see her thighs in the air. She struggled to move her hands, but could not. Slowly, she realized she was tied to an armchair that had capsized. Each foot was securely tied to one of the chair's legs. Her hands were bound to each arm of the chair. The more she struggled, the more her restraints cut into her hands and feet, so she stopped moving.

John walked over to her and stooped down near her head. He looked at her as if he was contemplating his next move in a chess game. Then, slowly, he lifted the chair with her in it, back to its original upright position, with much ease. Once he had her facing him again, he leaned against the chair, holding the back. Amanda closed her eyes, trying to get the image of John's face out of her mind.

"Amanda," his icy monotone voice said. She shuddered at the sound of her name coming from his mouth. "Do you know who I am?"

Amanda closed her eyes tighter, fighting back tears.

"ANSWER ME!"

Amanda jolted backwards from his monstrous roar. Lucky for her, John's large hands kept the chair from falling over again. She started to cry. John stood up with a smug look on his face.

"This is why women should not be allowed in combat," he spat as he walked away from her.

Sensing that her captor was no longer near her, Amanda blinked away tears from her eyes. Up until now, she was not fully aware of her surroundings. She looked around and saw that she was in a dirty, musky room. The only source of lighting was a bulb that dangled from wires, protruding from an unfinished ceiling. To her left, she could see three small windows that hung unusually high on the wall, but no light was coming through them. She couldn't tell if the windows were just filthy, or the sun wasn't up yet. Other than the chair she was sitting on, the only other furniture was a large, old, industrial worktable in the middle of the room, and another chair by a wooden staircase, which led up to a door. Her captor was standing by the table, with his back to her, rummaging through something she couldn't see. There were several work tools on the table, along with a black duffle bag. The floor was covered with a thick layer of dust, and bits and pieces of debris from home improvements gone wrong—such as uneven planks of wood, a broken toilet bowl, scraps of carpets, rolls of padding, paint cans, etc. From the looks of things, she concluded that she was in an unfinished basement.

She returned her gaze to her captor, who was still preoccupied with something on the table. *What is he doing?* she wondered. Her mind suddenly started to think of worst-case scenarios. Was he looking for a gun or saw? No, those would be too noisy. A knife ... tweezers, maybe? She felt tears welling up in her eyes again. Suddenly, she shook her head to regain her composure. *This is not me*, she thought. She wasn't a sniffling crybaby. *I have to be brave if I want to live through this*, she told herself.

Still, her curiosity was piqued by whatever her captor was doing. She felt a sharp pain in her neck as she stretched to see. Suddenly, she had an idea. Maybe if she talked to him, he would find her lovable and adorable like everybody else. She was a great orator and could definitely talk herself out of this situation ... hopefully.

Here goes.

Suddenly, Amanda started screaming into the gag and jumping up and down on the chair. The commotion caught the attention of her captor, who turned around. On the table she saw what he was rummaging through. It was her pocketbook. In his hand, he held her cell phone.

"Found it," he said, holding up the phone triumphantly. "How do you find anything in that bag of yours? It's like journeying to the center of the earth in there." Slowly, he started to walk back toward her. Amanda started to mumble against the cloth in her mouth and sway her head. "Oh, so you're ready to talk now, I see."

He stopped in front of her, and then stooped down, so he was eye-level with her. A chill ran down Amanda's back as she looked into John's grotesque face. She saw immediately that it would be pointless to try to reason with him, because his face was so devoid of anything human.

"I'm going to take your gag off now," he said. "You could scream if you want to, but it will do you no good, because … no one will hear you. The only thing you will achieve, however, is pissing me off. So, if I were you," he added, brandishing a large hunting knife, "I would try my best not to piss me off."

With rough, sturdy hands, he reached behind Amanda's head and untied the knot. She spat out the rag that was lodged in her mouth.

"Now," he continued, "back to my original question. Do you know who I am?"

"You're—" Surprised at the hoarseness of her voice, Amanda cleared her throat. "You're the guy who tried to blow up the Metro station," she said nervously.

"Very good, Amanda."

"H-how do you know my name?"

"Oh, I know a lot about you, Amanda," he said cockily. "I know where you live. I know most of your friends by name—Leslie, Krista, David, Eddie, et cetera, et cetera. I know you like the Starbucks White Chocolate Mocha Frappuccino. I also know you were hanging out with your boyfriend, Alex Fuller, right before our little ... run-in," he said slyly.

Amanda gawked at him with her mouth slightly open.

"Close your mouth, Amanda," he said, pushing her lower jaw upwards until it snapped shut. "I know all of this because I've been watching you, ever since you and your boyfriend interfered with my plans on Sunday," he said, standing upright. "My intention was to have this conversation with your boyfriend, but then that FBI maggot showed up and ruined that plan as well. So now, I'm on my Plan C. You are my Plan C."

"Me?" Amanda asked, befuddled. "What do I have to do with anything?"

"I know you didn't have anything to do with my"—he searched for the right word to described the bomb—"*package* not unraveling as planned. I know this because I saw you in front of the station when the package was scheduled to unfold. But your boyfriend, he was still in the tunnel, wasn't he, Amanda?"

Amanda was silent as the grave.

"You don't have to answer that. I know how loyal you are to your friends, especially Alex. Nevertheless, your silence is confirmation enough. So," he continued, "what was he doing in the tunnel after the attendant ordered its evacuation?" he asked rhetorically. "Correct me if I'm wrong, but the only thing I came up with was, he must have been tampering with my package." He paused, waiting for a response, but expected none. "Then later on, I saw you helping him flee the scene. You were helping him because he was injured. He got injured when he meddled with my package. Isn't that right?"

Amanda felt sick as she squirmed uneasily in the chair.

"You see, Amanda," he said, squeezing her cheeks in one of his enormous hands until her lips puckered, "I went through a lot of trouble to put that package together. That package had a very specific purpose. That package was supposed to be the start of America's purification process. Then your snot-nosed boyfriend—the little Babylonian heathen—derailed the entire operation!" John shouted as he released her face to regain his composure. Amanda opened and closed her mouth repeatedly to alleviate the pain in her cheeks. "You asked me earlier what you had to do with this? Well my dear, you have everything to do with my plan now. *You*," he said, poking her in the chest with the point of the knife, "are going to help me get Alex away from his bodyguard."

"What do you want with Alex?"

"Alex stuck his nose where it didn't belong. All those years of planning and precious resources, down the drain because of that … that … hedonistic heathen. And like all heathens, Alex must be cast out and punished."

"Punished?" she exclaimed. "Punished for what?"

"Haven't you been listening to a word I said?" he said, tapping her on the head with the flat side of the knife's blade. "He interfered with God's divine plan for this country."

"What divine plan?"

John looked at her with assessing eyes as he circled

around her, like a vulture homing in on its prey. Finally, he stopped and said, "The plan to restore God's good grace upon this land. For years I was tasked with designing and implementing his plan. Years where I couldn't divulge a single word about it to anyone. It was the greatest honor that could have been bestowed on a mere mortal. But instead of executing the plan as intended, here I am discussing what should have been with the likes of you," he said with a look of disappointment. "I can tell the end is near, so it doesn't really matter who knows what anymore. What matters now is to get the message out there."

"What message?"

"Have you ever heard of the archangel Gabriel?" he asked.

Amanda scanned through her limited knowledge of the Bible, and then responded, "No."

"Don't you go to church?" John asked, teetering on the brink of being annoyed with the teenager.

"No, not really," she said, trying to figure out where he was going with this line of questioning.

John sighed and shook his head. "You see—*this* is what I'm talking about," he said, visibly upset. "America has lost its way, and now it's up to me to set it back on the right path. My righteous brothers from the Internet were right—America can never win this war against them. At least they believe in something, Amanda – a cause, whether it's religion or an ideology. They believe so strongly, they're willing to die for it. But us, we believe in nothing, except the dollar. That's all we worship now—the almighty dollar."

Amanda's eyebrows furrowed as she tried to figure out what her captor was saying. Seeing her confused expression, John spoke.

"I don't blame you, Amanda. You're a child and don't know any better. Instead, I blame your parents. I blame the church. And I blame our ever-compromising government. If they had done their job—if they had *trained up the child in the way he should go, then when he got old, he would not depart from it*—then you would know that Gabriel is God's messenger," he said as he tapped her nose with the point of his knife.

"Instead, our society teaches us that everyone is free to do whatever abominable thing they can conjure up. There's no more accountability, because no one believes in heaven or hell anymore. But I was sent here to remind America that there is a heaven, there is a hell, and there are consequences for every sinful act committed."

Gently, he lifted her chin up, so he could see her eyes. "I ... am Gabriel and I have been sent here to deliver a message to this once-great nation. Repent or be destroyed."

12. DISCOMBOBULATED

By ten o'clock, the Fullers were enjoying a quiet day at home after Alex's big reveal at breakfast. Outside his bedroom door, Alex could hear his mother cleaning his bathroom. He set aside his algebra textbook and went to ask her if there was anything he could do to help. When he finally convinced her that it wasn't a trick question, Alex had the option of either doing the laundry or vacuuming the house. Unsure of what temperature water went with what colors or how to separate the loads, and always forgetting to add the fabric softener, which his mother insisted on, Alex decided to go with vacuuming.

He had just finished the second floor and was about to go downstairs when his cell phone rang. Other than his mother, Amanda, and a few select businesses, Alex didn't recall giving his number to anyone else. He hesitated before answering his phone because he wasn't expecting Amanda to call him before her game was over, but he welcomed hearing her voice at any time.

"Hey, Mandy," he said without checking the caller ID.

"Mandy?" an unfamiliar female voice said. "She actually lets *you* call her Mandy and I can't."

"Who is this?"

"It's Leslie ... Leslie Knolls."

"What do you want and how did you get my number?"

"Relax, this is not a social call. I got your number from the school directory."

"Okay, and you're calling me because…"

"I'm looking for Amanda."

"Amanda?"

"Yes, that's what I said," she said condescendingly.

"Amanda's not here. She has a game today."

"I know that, Alex; I'm on the cheerleading squad with her, remember?" she said impatiently. "Anyway, we were supposed to meet this morning at school before riding up to Maryland together on the bus, but she's not here."

"Isn't the game at one? It's only after ten now."

Leslie sighed in annoyance. "Oh thank you for reminding me of what time the game starts, because I would have never figured that out," she said.

"Leslie, just stop with the dramatics and get to the point already, you're wasting my—"

"Well, excuse me for wasting your precious time. Do you think I wanted to call—"

Alex removed the phone from his ear as Leslie ranted and raved in a shrill voice. Gingerly, he tapped the phone against his head a few times before returning it to his ear. Leslie was still ranting on about how rude he was and that's why he didn't have any friends.

"Leslie," he said, interrupting her monologue, "I'm sorry. Now, can you please tell me what this has to do with Amanda?"

Leslie exhaled heavily into the phone. "Like I was saying earlier, before I was so rudely interrupted"—Alex resisted the urge to tell her to move it along—"normally the squad meets at school, then we go to wherever the game is being played. We always arrive at our destination a few hours early so we can go over our routines and make adjustments as needed. Amanda should have been here at ten a.m. When she didn't show up, I called her cell phone. It rang a couple of times, and then went to voicemail—which was weird. So then I called her house, but her mother said she can't be sure if Amanda came home last night because she went to bed early and when she woke up, the house was empty and Amanda's bed was made—which was even weirder. Then I remembered that Amanda said she was going to your house last night. So naturally, I thought that if Amanda did not go home last night, then she might be at your house."

"Amanda's not here," Alex said, befuddled. "She left here last night around eleven. Is her mother sure she didn't come home last night?"

"I don't think she's a hundred percent sure, but regardless, Amanda's not there now."

"Where could she be?" Alex whispered, half to himself.

"I don't know, but it's weird, right? Anyway, I'll try her cell again."

"I'll try calling her too. And Leslie…"

"Yeah."

"Thanks. And sorry about earlier."

"Don't worry about it."

Alex was still in a daze when he hung up. If Amanda had trouble getting home last night, she would have called him. Why didn't she call? Maybe something had prevented her from calling. Maybe her phone battery had died, but Leslie said it rang then went to voicemail when she called. Maybe Amanda had left her phone somewhere, or maybe she had lost it. Yeah, that had to be it. Alex refused to believe that something sinister could have happened to Amanda. Anxiously, he dialed her number. The line was busy. *Leslie must be calling her again*, he thought. Hesitantly, he dialed Amanda's home number.

Mrs. Bridgewater answered the phone. She was hysterical. After Alex reminded her of who he was, she calmed down a little.

"Alex, I don't know what's going on," she sobbed into the phone. "The police just left. They said OnStar called them last night to report that Amanda's car was involved in a crash. When they reported to the scene, there was no sign of Amanda—just her car on the shoulder of some deserted street, with the back smashed in. According to her GPS, she was heading home and the address before that was somewhere in Vienna. They think she's been kidnapped. Or she may have had an accident and fled the scene because she's a young driver; but I know my daughter and she would never do that. Then they said they've been calling me since midnight, but ... I didn't hear the phone, Alex. I couldn't hear the phone," she said as she started sobbing again.

"It's okay, Mrs. Bridgewater. These things happen. Did they say anything else?"

"No ... oh, her bag is missing too. They also kept saying that they're not ruling out the possibility that she might have run away from home. Alex, Amanda wouldn't run away from me, would she?"

"No, Mrs. Bridgewater. Amanda loves you."

"Does she?" she said, sniffling. "I know things around here have been a little strained lately, and we may have exchanged words about my occasional use of alcohol, but she wouldn't run away from me for that, would she? I mean, I only had one drink last night before I went to bed. How was I supposed to know the police were going to call so late?"

Alex was certain it would take more than one drink for someone to not hear a ringing telephone, but he didn't want to further upset her.

"Mrs. Bridgewater, it's going to be okay. Amanda did not run away from you."

"Are you sure?"

"I'm pretty sure."

"Pretty sure?" she said, as she burst into tears. "Oh, Alex, you think I'm a bad mother too?"

"Mrs. Bridgewater, you're not a bad mother ... j-just look at Amanda. Amanda is awesome, and ... and I know that you had everything to do with that, because you are an awesome mom," Alex said, carefully selecting his words. "I'm sure they'll find her. As a matter of fact, I'm going to call a friend of mine at the FBI who would love to help."

Mrs. Bridgewater listened as Alex explained Agent Brody's involvement in the case thus far, which seemed to calm her down a bit. Afterwards, she thanked him before hanging up.

Can you say awkward? Alex thought to himself, after ending their conversation. He didn't realize that things at the Bridgewater's house had gotten so bad Mrs. Bridgewater thought Amanda would run away. He definitely had to follow up with Amanda on that subject—when he found her. He was searching his room feverishly for Agent Brody's card when Margaret walked by.

"Hey, can I join in the scavenger hunt?" she said on her way to the laundry room with a clothes hamper in her hands.

"I'm looking for Agent Brody's number because Amanda's missing," he said without looking up from his search.

"What?" Margaret asked, dropping the hamper and walking into his room.

"Last night her car was involved in a crash and now no one can find her. Where the hell did I put that card?"

"Alex, slow down a minute."

"Mom, I don't have a minute. I'm trying to find Agent Brody's num—" he stopped suddenly as he examined a card he found in his backpack. "Got it." He then turned his attention back to his mother and said, "I'm calling Agent Brody to see if he can help me find her." He picked up the house phone and dialed the number. Margaret walked over to Alex, so she could listen in on the conversation also.

"Put it on speaker," Margaret directed.

Alex complied as the phone rang.

"FBI Washington Field Office. Agent Brody speaking."

"Agent Brody, it's Alex."

"And Margaret," she interjected.

"Hey guys, how are you doing?"

"We're fine," Alex said, "but Amanda's missing."

"Oh, you guys heard about that too."

"What? You knew about this?" Alex asked accusatorily.

"Calm down, Alex, I just found out when I stopped by the office this morning. Apparently, the local authorities found her car just after midnight and thought it was just your run-of-the-mill kidnapping. They didn't make the connection between her and the bombing until an hour ago. That's when they contacted us."

"So, do you know where she is?"

"No. And," he sighed, "I have some more bad news for you."

"What is it?" Alex and Margaret said simultaneously.

"Yesterday when I was taking pictures of the vehicles around your block, I saw a van through your mother's bedroom window. I took pictures of it, but didn't think much of it because it wasn't there when I secured the perimeters around the house later in the evening. I just thought it was a delivery van. Anyway, we ran checks on all the vehicles' license plates I shot yesterday. Turned out the van belonged to a guy by the name of John Fischer from Texas, ex-military with Special Ops training. The photo on his driver's license matched the sketch of the guy you saw in the train station."

Alex felt his heart sink as his knees gave out and he collapsed to the floor.

"Alex!" Margaret screamed as she tried to catch her falling son. She set him down on the floor and picked up the phone that fell out of his hand. She sat next to him with the phone between their ears so he could hear the rest of the conversation. "Max, I'm sorry. Alex just had a fainting spell. Please tell us what else you found out."

"One of the agents here had an idea that if Fischer was the bomber, he may have stuck around at the Metro station to figure out why the bomb didn't go off. So he ran Fischer's face through our facial image recognition database against Metropolitan Police Department's closed circuit television system, trying to get a match."

"Did he find anything?" Margaret asked.

"Not on CCTV, but he got a match from news footage."

"News footage?"

"Yeah, after CCTV didn't reveal anything, he started running Fischer's face against images he found on news footage from that night of the bombing. Sure enough, one of the local news crew caught Fischer on camera, as he was walking around in the background, dressed as a firefighter."

"So now what?"

"We're trying to figure out where he's staying in town. He must have stayed local, because he would need to stay close by to run the kind of surveillance he did on the Metro system. We also have an agent trying to track Amanda's cell phone, but don't have anything definitive yet. I'll call you back when I hear something. Tell Alex I'm sorry about his girlfriend, but we are going to catch this guy before anything happens to her."

"I will."

"I also want you to keep an eye on Alex until I get back there with reinforcement."

"Reinforcement?"

"We are almost certain that Fischer is the one who took Amanda. He probably took her hoping that she could lure Alex to them. If that's the case, then we need to be there when they try to contact Alex. Meanwhile, you stay put until I get there"."

Alex stared blankly in front of him, trying to soothe his mind. He heard his mother thank the agent and promise to keep an eye on him.

Margaret hung up the phone and looked at Alex. He was visibly upset and shocked at the same time.

"Honey, she's going to be fine."

"It's all my fault," he said, gently massaging his temples.

"Sweetie, don't blame yourself for this."

"In through the nose, out through the mouth," he whispered, as he inhaled and exhaled deeply.

Margaret looked at Alex, who was breathing deeply

with his eyes closed, while massaging his temples and whispering to himself.

"This is my fault," he said, whispering again.

"No, it's not. There's no way you could have known that this Fischer person would have kidnapped Amanda."

"Just breathe," he said as he began to rock back and forth.

"Alex?" she called. He was still absorbed by his self-soothing ritual. He never had to self soothe whenever he was around his mother before. Even when they had their little spats, he was still able to remain calm.

"Are you okay?" she asked as she raised her arm and swung it over his head, and started to wrap it around him. As her arm drew closer to his skin, the hair on his body stood up. The sensation cause him to cease all self-soothing activities as his eyes flew open.

"Mom, don't," he begged, but it was too late. When her arm made contact with him, he felt the sensation invoke his abilities, which erupted and overpowered his futile attempts to suppress them. A strong, warm gush of air swept across his room, throwing everything in its path against the wall in front of them. The force pulled several of the loose leaves of paper from Alex's desk, then set them ablaze, trickling down to the floor.

"Alex!" Margaret shouted as she shot up from the floor and ran over to where some of the fiery particles started to land. Feverishly, she stomped at them.

Alex stood up and the fiery particles started to converge to form one large, round mass. Margaret watched as the particles she had just trampled floated to join the others in what appeared to be a circle. When they were all assembled, the round mass collapsed, putting out the fiery particles within the confines of the circle. It then floated over to the wastebasket and fell in.

Alex watched his mother, whose eyes were still glued to the trash bin. She was standing in the middle of his room, where his bed had been a moment ago. Slowly, she turned her head around to look at him. He could see that her brain was still trying to interpret what her eyes had seen. He gave her another minute to see how she'd react to discovering his abilities. To his surprise, she didn't run or back away. She just looked at him, waiting for an explanation. So, he explained—everything.

* * *

OMG, this guy is nuts, Amanda thought. If she laughed at the absurdity that her captor was a messenger sent by God, she knew it would piss him off. So she decided to play along. She swallowed hard, and then asked, "How do I know for sure that you are who you say you are?"

"Oh Doubting Thomas," he said, smiling at her. "You want proof of my divinity." He walked over to the table, where he put down the knife and her cell phone. No sooner had he set down the cell phone than it started vibrating. John picked up the phone and looked at it.

"It's only Leslie," he said, as if he was referring to a mutual friend of theirs. "She's probably trying to figure out why you haven't shown up yet for today's game. Oh well," he said dismissively. "I'm about to show you irrefutable proof that I am the archangel Gabriel." Slowly, John started to take off his T-shirt.

Holy crap, what is he doing? Amanda wondered, as the man started to take his clothes off. She writhed in discomfort as she scanned the room again for a possible escape route. To her surprise, John's strip-tease ended with just his shirt. He looked at her ecstatically and said, "I have never showed anyone what I'm about to show you, which goes to show how much I trust you, Amanda."

Pompously, John turned around, so his back was facing Amanda. "Do you see it, Amanda?" he asked excitedly.

Amanda sat speechless in the chair as she gazed at the spectacle in front of her. On her captor's back was a large tattoo of what appeared to be a pair of retracted *wings*. The tattoo extended from the nape of his neck all the way down his back, and disappeared underneath his trousers. Edges of the wings could also be seen on the backside of his arms. The tattoo was outlined in black ink, but filled in with silver and white. Suddenly, the wings started to move as John flexed the muscles in his back, like a body builder at the Olympics. This was just too much for her. She wasn't sure how much more of this she could put up with until help arrived. Would help ever come? She wasn't sure.

"Now do you believe me?" John asked, smiling with her as he put back on his shirt.

"Yeah, you're a messenger all right," Amanda said sarcastically, which John failed to detect.

"It's unfortunate that it had to come to this. If Alex had just left the package alone," he tried to explain to her, "America would have heard the message of God and be on its way back to redemption."

"What message? What are you talking about?" Amanda asked, allowing her annoyance to seep into her tone just a little.

"To fully understand the message, we have to go back in time to when our ancestors inherited this great land called America," John said, pulling up the other chair that was by the staircase and placing it in front of Amanda.

"Long before you were born," he continued as he sat down, "this country served as a refuge for those who were persecuted for their religious beliefs. People from all over the world would come here to practice their religion—that was the principle America was founded on. As a result, religion became a part of our government, a part of our community, and a part of who we were. And God smiled upon America and blessed it, because he was pleased. But over time, America started to push religion into the background. They took prayers out of the schools. Some want to get rid of the phrase 'In God We Trust' from our currency. People started replacing 'Christmas' with 'X-mas.' Nowadays, you can't even wish someone Merry Christmas anymore. Instead, you have to say happy holidays to be politically correct. And now, with gays having the right to marry, what's next? Churches losing their tax-exempted status because they won't officiate a gay marriage in their sanctuary? Or God-fearing citizens being jailed or fined because they disagree with the nine vultures who sit on high issuing false judgments? And don't get me started on the transgender issue. When will these debates over sexual deviance end?"

"But, in school, I was always thought that debate was good, because you at least get to hear the other side of—" she started.

"No, no, no!!!" John cried. "There's only one right way, and that's God's way. In your math class, when your teacher asks what is two plus two, do you debate with him and say, the answer should be six or twenty-two? No, there's only one right answer and that's four. The same principle applies here. God is the only answer."

"But not everyone believes in God." Before she could continue, John sprung from his chair and lunged at her, striking her hard on the cheek. Immediately, tears welled up in her eyes from the burning, stinging sensation where John struck her.

"That's the same kind of thinking that got us in this mess in the first place!" John said hysterically. "Haven't you been listening to a word I said? We've let all these ungodly people and ungodly thoughts creep into our minds and pollute our souls."

Amanda bit her lips as she tried to suppress her tears. She watched as John started to pace the floor in front of her.

"How do I explain this to you?" he continued, trying to be cajoling. "The Bible says that our God is a jealous god, and we shall have no other god but him. So the idea of there being some other god out there somewhere is ludicrous; and the idea that there is no god is likewise nonsensical."

Both of their heads turned toward the table when Amanda's phone started to vibrate again. John walked over to the table and looked at the name displayed in the small screen. "It's your mother," he sighed. He set the phone back down on the table, staring at it with a troubled look.

"Are you waiting for a call on my phone?" Amanda asked, finally mustering up enough courage to talk again.

"Actually, I am."

"Why? And from whom?" she said in one breath.

"Your boyfriend," he said, matter-of-factly. "It's only a

matter of time before he calls. Then you'll invite him over to join our little party."

"I'm not going to lure Alex over here so you can hurt him," she said, but then wondered if someone like her captor could actually hurt Alex. Either way, she was not going to willingly play the pawn in his psychotic scheme.

John's body shook as he laughed hysterically. "You say that as if you have a choice."

* * *

Margaret listened attentively to her son's incredible explanation of all his psychic abilities, when he first became aware of them, and how he used them to diffuse the bomb in the Metro station.

When he was all done, he said, "I'm sorry for not telling you about them before. But after Justin died, I just couldn't bear the thought of anyone else getting hurt because they knew what I am."

After a long pause, she asked, "So, all of this started happening at Camp APRICOT?"

"Yes."

"Before that, you never had any indication that your mind could do these things?"

"No."

"Are you sure? Maybe you missed some subtle hint, dismissing it as being impossible."

"I don't think so, Mom. I think I would remember if an object suddenly moved or burst into flames just because I thought about it."

"And you have no idea how it happened?'

"Nope. I mulled over that question for months after it

happened, but nothing seemed to make the link between my near-death experience and all these phenomena.

"Alex, do you remember why we left California?"

"Yeah, our apartment burnt down."

"Yes, but remember that government-funded research lab I use to talk about?"

"Oh yeah. You were mad about leaving my grandmother in Boron and moving to San Diego to be a lab rat—your words, not mine. You used to blame yourself for not being there when she died."

Memories of her mother surfaced in her mind. Intent on not dwelling on them, she said, "Well, there was a little more to that story,"

"Like what?"

"For starters, that laboratory I worked for—Allied Research Institute, or ARI—they were experimenting with psychic phenomena to gather intelligence for the government."

"You mean like my psychic phenomena?' he asked excitedly.

"No sweetheart. Nothing as advanced or sophisticated as yours. Your abilities are not even on the same realm as what they were doing."

"So what type of psychic phenomena were they experimenting with?"

"Mostly just remote viewing."

"You mean like the Stargate Project, where psychics tried to see things or people in real time, but from a faraway distance?"

"Yes. So you've heard of it?"

"Yeah," he said disappointedly. "I came across the information when I was looking for answers to why I was like this. But Mom, I can't remote view."

"Have you tried?"

"Yeah. I've tried replicating every psychic phenomena I read about during my research, trying to see which ones and how many I had. But the only ones that stuck were telepathy, telekinesis, pyrokinesis, and out-of-body experience." He stopped as a thought occurred to him. "What exactly did you do at ARI?"

"I was one of their remote viewers. Well, they thought they could train me to become a remote viewer."

"So you're a psychic?" he asked excitedly again.

"Not really. Well not a good one anyway. I was barely able to predict anything accurately without help."

"Wait. How could you have participated in the Stargate Project? I thought it ended in the nineteen-nineties or something. And you've told me you moved to San Diego two years before I was born."

"Yes, but ARI carried on with its experiments long after the CIA shut down the program in 1995. ARI thought they were on the verge of making a breakthrough in remote viewing that would've enticed the government back into funding the project. But year after year, when their big gamble didn't pay off, they ended their experiments—the year after you were born."

Alex sighed heavily and looked through his bedroom window.

"What's the matter?" she asked.

"I thought," he started, but shrugged his shoulders and shook his head. "I don't know what I thought." He continued to stare through the window. "I just thought that maybe you were going to help me finally figure out why I am the way I am."

"But I think I can."

Alex looked at his mother in total disbelief. "But you said ARI only did remote viewing and I can't do that," he said, his mind totally discombobulated.

"You have to understand, this is not how I wanted you to learn the complete story about your father an—"

"My father?" he spat. "What does he have to do with this?"

"Everything, I think."

"You think? Did he do this to me?"

"Not intentionally, I don't think."

"Okay, now I'm totally confused."

"Maybe I should start from the beginning."

13. PREDICTIONS

"I was eighteen when I left Boron and moved to San Diego. ARI was looking for psychics in the California area and had heard about your grandmother."

"My grandmother was a psychic?" he asked. Alex's sole memory of his grandmother was seeing her face in old family photographs, since she died when he was only two years old.

"Yes, she was a real psychic. Originally, ARI wanted her for the project, but she turned them down. So they turned their attention to me, assuming that maybe she passed down some psychic genes to me. I mean, they were willing to explore every aspect of psychic phenomena to get the government to fund the project again.

"So I moved to California. That's where I met your father."

"In California?" Alex asked.

"Yes, but specifically at ARI."

Alex scanned his memory of the few conversations he'd had with his mother about his father. "But I thought you said my father was in the military."

"No. I said he worked for the military. He was a civilian who worked with the Defense Intelligence Agency at Fort

Meade. He was on detail to ARI to oversee certain aspects of the program."

"Oh, I must have misunderstood then."

"It's okay, and perfectly understandable. So anyway, I met him about a year after I got to ARI. And like I said before, I was not a psychic. And I told ARI that when they first approached me. But they said they wanted to experiment on someone who didn't exhibit any psychic abilities, but who was a good candidate to develop them if given the proper training. I was considered a good candidate because I was the child of a psychic. They had hoped that someday, they would be able to teach anyone to remote view." She thought for a moment, then asked, "Do you know how remote viewing works?"

"Ah, not really—just what I told you earlier."

"Well the type of remote viewing they subjected me to involved testers asking me to visualize a target that was far away. During the initial testing, they would have another individual I'd never met at the same location as the target. The testers would tell me to clear my mind of everything and just focus on that one particular object, trying to visualize where it was. They believed that if you focused hard enough on the target, you would develop some psychic link with it and that you'd be able to find it. Once I found the target, they would ask me to describe and sketch my impression of the target and its surroundings. At the end of each test, the results were given to two scientists, who would interpret the sketches and record the data. That's how they would test to see how accurate your impressions or predictions were. Once you convinced them of the accuracy of your predictions, then you'd be asked to visualize targets without the aid of another person being at the target site.

"My initial testing accuracy ratings were the highest they had ever been. But once I actually joined the project, my ratings started to decline. I was at ARI for about a year with very little success of improving my remote viewing abilities. That's when your father showed up. He was a parapsychologist with DIA. His name is Karl Vaughan. He asked to be detailed to ARI because he still believed the Stargate Project had probative value that would be beneficial to the military someday. He was quite handsome, like you. Tall, slender, but blonde—"

"Okay, okay—I get it. You had the hots for him. Can we skip the ogling part and get back to what he did to make me this way?"

"Sorry. So anyway, he came to ARI and saw my poor test results. At the time, I didn't know that that was why he befriended me. With my poor results, he figured I was easy prey that would jump at the opportunity to be a part of his plan. And he was right.

"One night, he took me to dinner and told me that he knew a way I could increase the accuracy of my predictions again. He explained that he had been working on a serum, designed to enhance the extrasensory and nonphysical mental processes via sensory stimulation. He also claimed that he wasn't aware of any side effect to the drug. The government wasn't aware of the serum, he explained, because he wanted to perfect it before approaching them. The whole thing sounded sketchy, but you have to understand something. One, I was young and impressionable, and I thought I was in love with this man. Two, when I left Boron, I had told myself that I was never going back there."

"But what about my grandmother?"

"She remained in Boron. I didn't leave on good terms with her."

"Is that why you get mad at yourself whenever you talk about her?"

Margaret nodded. "She didn't want me to leave. She warned me that my involvement in that project wouldn't end well. I was so upset with her for saying that," she said, with her eyes filled with tears. "I thought maybe she only said that to make me stay. Then she died before I got a chance to go back," she said, sobbing.

Alex reached over and placed his hand on his mother's knee as she tried to compose herself. After a few sniffles, and after wiping her eyes, she continued.

"Anyway, a week after your father—"

"Can we just refer to him as my sperm donor?"

Margaret smiled. "It's not going to change the fact that he is your father."

"Fine," he sighed.

"So a week after we went to dinner, I agreed to let *Dr. Vaughan* secretly inject me with his extrasensory serum. The serum had a psychedelic effect, which was short-lived. I saw some improvement in my accuracy rating. Although my ratings were not as high as when I first tested to join ARI, it was better than nothing. Because of the short duration of the serum's effect on me, I insisted on Dr. Vaughan administering it to me on a daily basis. To avoid detection, I kept my distance from the other psychics. Dr. Vaughan also kept his distance from the other viewers by not administering the tests, but he chose instead to analyze the test data and draft after-action reports.

"We worked closely together in secret for the next

couple of months to continue with the daily injections and to record his findings. One thing led to another, and I became pregnant with you. I was already two months pregnant before I even noticed. At first, I didn't want to tell Dr. Vaughan because I didn't know how he'd react, but Molly convinced me I should tell him. So I told him about the pregnancy, but was still undecided about what I was going to do about it. Before I got a chance to tell him about my decision, the military ended his detail at ARI and recalled him to Fort Meade. He left without saying goodbye, or before I could ask him what effects the serum might have on a fetus."

"So he just left us there?"

Margaret stared past him into oblivion and whispered, "Yes."

"Did you ever tell him about me?"

"Yes."

"When?"

"About a month after he left, I wrote to him at Fort Meade just to let him know that I intended to keep the ... you. But I never received any reply."

Alex sat motionless as he mulled over her response. He had lived his life not knowing much about his father. He'd believed that his father was a member of the military who was not ready for the responsibilities of parenthood. He was content with that explanation. But what his mother was telling him now was downright disturbing. Although he understood why she had never told him before now and appreciated the fact that she finally did, Alex had heard enough about his sperm donor. He cemented his decision to have nothing to do with him. He quickly changed the subject.

"So, this serum—do you think it's the reason why I'm like this?"

"I think so. Although I never said anything to anyone at the time, the serum gave me a tingling sensation in my abdomen whenever I took it. Without any external symptoms to point to, I kept my thoughts to myself. After you were born, I watched you so carefully for any signs out of the ordinary. When I didn't see anything, I was convinced that the serum had no effect on you.

"You know," she continued, "your grandmother wanted to come visit you when you were born, but I told her no because I was still upset with her. The last time I spoke to her, she told me that she could sense a great source of psychic energy in the San Diego area. By this time, ARI had ended their remote viewing project. I was unemployed with a new baby to feed. And I had had enough psychic babble to last me a lifetime, so I stopped taking her calls. I never gave any thought to our last conversation, until today."

They sat in silence as they processed the information they had just exchanged. They were both startled when the phone rang. Alex, who was closer to the phone, picked it up. It was Agent Brody. He placed the call on speaker and laid it on the floor between them.

"Good news," he said. "We showed the sketch of the bomber around southwest DC, not too far from a library where we found some unusual research activity involving the Metro system."

"Define unusual," Margaret pressed.

"Just odd Internet searches from the library's computer, books about the Metro train system being checked out by someone not in school, and so on."

"What did you find out?" Alex asked.

"It seemed that John Fischer lived with an elderly woman named Roberta Jackson, who lives several blocks away from the library. We have a unit heading to her house as I speak. Hold on a minute." They listened as Agent Brody conducted a brief conversation with one of his colleagues in the background.

"I'm back," he announced when he returned to the phone. "I have to run because I think we're getting some intel from the field. Hang in there, Alex. This should be over real soon."

Margaret hung up the phone and got up to place it back on the base. She sat back down on the floor, rubbing her temples. Her eyes were closed as she thought about her past life in San Diego. Suddenly she felt something. She opened her eyes to see Alex looking at her expectantly. Her forehead furrowed as she tried to figure out what had come over him.

"What?" she asked after failing to understand why he was so excited.

"You were a remote viewer, right?"

"Yes, with the help of the serum."

"But the serum became a part of you, which is how it became a part of me, right?"

"I suppose, but where are you going with this?"

"Have you tried to remote view after leaving ARI?"

"No. In fact, I didn't do much remote viewing after I had you. Since ARI was gearing up to scrap the project, we didn't do much testing. Why?"

"I bet, if this serum did this to me, it must have done something to you to cause your remote viewing ratings to go up."

"That's an interesting theory. So, let's say what you're suggesting is true, what's your sudden interest in my remote viewing ability?"

"You could tell me where Amanda is," he blurted out.

"Oh no," she said, getting up and walking out of his room. "First of all, I have not done any of that stuff since I left ARI. Second, the FBI is already handling this."

"Mom, but you could help me find Amanda."

"There goes that word *me* again. Alex, no—you're going to stay here with me and wait. The FBI will find Amanda. You heard Agent Brody. They're on their way to that woman's house and she will tell them where the bomber is."

"But what if she doesn't know? And what if they don't find Amanda in time?

"What if, what if? You're speculating."

"But Mom, what if something happens to Amanda while the FBI is looking for her? I know you won't be able to forgive yourself."

"Alex, I know you want to find Amanda, and so do I. But I'm not going to give you information—information I doubt I'd be able to access—that would put you at risk of getting hurt."

"Mom, do you honestly think that guy could hurt me?"

Margaret opened her mouth to rebut his claim, but she had to admit he had a point.

"If you're able to tell me where Amanda is, I promise to be extra careful and I'll use my powers so that I won't even have to interact with this guy," Alex said, trying to appease her.

"Alex, I can't just flip a switch in my brain and tell it to remote view after all these years of not practicing."

"Why not? You had never remote viewed before you

moved to San Diego and look how well you did. You even said that your test scores were the highest they've ever been when you tested to join ARI," he said, running out of breath. "All I want you to do is try."

Why did he pick now to start listening to me? Margaret wondered. Why hadn't this selective hearing of his worked in her favor when she repeatedly told him not to put his cup down on her coffee table without a coaster under it? She stood in the hallway outside their bedrooms, contemplating his request. Finally she sighed and said, "I'll do it under one condition."

Alex instantly grabbed her in a bear hug, lifting her off the ground. She screamed excitedly as he swung her back and forth.

"Put me down," she chuckled. Alex complied.

"I'm going with you," Margaret said.

"Okay."

"And at the first sign of trouble, we're calling Agent Brody."

"Deal," Alex exclaimed.

* * *

John watched as the icon for the battery on Amanda's cell phone started to flash.

"Where's your charger?" he asked her.

"Why?"

"Your battery is about to die."

"Well, my charger is at home, but someone kidnapped me before I got there."

John dismissed her presence as he tried his charger with her phone. It didn't fit. He was obviously annoyed as he walked over to her. "Okay, I need you to call Alex now, before your battery dies," he said, holding the phone in front of her face.

"No," she said defiantly.

"Come on, I don't have much time," he said through gritted teeth.

"Which part of no don't you understand, the 'N' or the 'O'?"

John tried to access Amanda's phone book in search of Alex's number, but the phone was locked. "What's your password?"

Amanda rolled her eyes and fixed her stare on the ceiling.

"What's the fucking password?" he barked in her face. Amanda could feel his breath on her face, and smelled it too. *Eww!*

Amanda continued to stare at the ceiling, and then smiled deviously when she heard her phone shutting down.

"Shit!" John screamed.

Next, his right arm came crashing down on Amanda's cheek again, toppling her and the chair to the floor. She fell to the side, which aggravated the pain in her head, neck, and back. Amanda felt blood in her mouth as she tried to reorient herself from her new point of view on the ground. Suddenly she saw her phone smash into pieces after John threw it into the wall. She watched as he paced the floor, trying to think of something.

Suddenly his phone rang. He fished it out of his pocket and inspected the number.

"Hello," he said, changing his voice slightly.

"Joh—G-Gabriel," said a frail voice on the other line.

"It's Roberta, Roberta Jackson. I hope I didn't catch you at a bad time."

Instantly, John knew something was wrong. He'd never told Ms. Jackson his real name, so she always referred to him as Gabriel. She had slipped up and was about to call him John when she spoke just now. Plus, there was something absent from her voice. He was certain the FBI was there and listening to their conversation. Regardless, he decided to play along.

"No, this is as good a time as any. Did you need something Ms. Jackson?"

"I-I think the boiler is on the fritz again, Gabriel. Would you mind coming and taking a look at it for me?"

"Sure, Ms. Jackson, as soon as I'm done here."

There was a pause. "Do you mind coming to look at it now? I think Old Man Winter might be making a reappearance this spring, because it feels a little drafty in here today."

"Ms. Jackson, I'll come look at it as soon as I'm done here," he said firmly, determined not to prolong the call long enough for it to be traced.

"Okay, okay, Gabby," she said feebly.

John bit into his bottom lip hard. No one else in the world called him Gabby except for her. She always managed to say it so maternally. Then it dawned on him; that was what was missing from her voice earlier—the maternal intonation. Now it was back.

"Ms. Jackson," he said hesitantly.

"Yes, Gabriel."

John squeezed his eyes shut. He let out a heavy sigh as he opened them again. "You may want to go over to Ms.

Olson's as soon as you hang up the phone and see if her son can help you with the boiler."

"Gabby, I don't understand."

"As soon as you hang up, go over to Ms. Olson," he said, then hung up.

Amanda watched as John adjusted the watch on his arm, so he could see the face. A few minutes passed, and his face was still glued to the watch. *What was he waiting for?* she wondered from her skewed position. A minute later, he made a call from his cell phone. Amanda saw him put the phone against his ear and listen. A second later, he punched in a code and hung up. *What the hell was that about?* she thought.

* * *

"Where do you want to do this?" Alex asked his mother.

"Do what?"

"Your remote viewing," he said impatiently.

"Oh, that," she said, clearly intent on winding up her son, who was already on edge. He gave her a disapproving look. "Okay, okay. Lighten up."

"Lighten up? Mom, do you need me to remind you that this is Amanda we're talking about?"

"You're right," she said, looking around her surroundings. "What about in my room?"

"You tell me," Alex said.

"At ARI, they got so technical. We would always remote view in dark rooms with soothing sounds..."

"Would white noise help?" Alex interjected.

"I guess."

"Let's go back to my room then."

Alex explained to his mother that he had painted the mural on his bedroom walls to help him relax. He also mentioned that the other day when he asked her for money to buy a new alarm-clock radio, he had purchased one that had a white-noise machine built in, which he used as a sleep aid.

The furniture in Alex's room was still flush against the wall, to the right when they walked in.

"Just give me a minute," he said. Within seconds, the pieces of furniture returned to their original positions. Alex mentally closed his blinds and pulled his light-blocking curtains. Margaret shook her head and smiled. He then had his mother lie on his bed, on her back, as he turned on the white-noise function on his radio.

"Now, just clear your mind," Alex said in a steady, soothing voice. "Take very deep breaths. Feel your limbs go limp as you relax your muscles. Try to hear your heart beating."

Margaret thoughtlessly followed her son's instruction, then jolted forward as she recognized the similarities between what Alex had just instructed her to do and what Dr. Vaughan used to tell her so many years ago.

"Mom, this is not going to work if you don't chillax," Alex said.

"I'm sorry," Margaret said, a bit panic-stricken. Slowly, she allowed herself to relax again as Alex turned up the volume on his radio and the white noise filled her head.

"Are you relaxed now?" he asked.

Bothered again by the similarities in his voice and Dr. Vaughan's, especially in this particular setting, she said, "Alex, could you be quiet while I do this ... please?"

Alex complied as he sat and watched his mother from

across the room. Ten minutes passed and Margaret was still lying there motionless. Twenty minutes passed, and Alex looked around his room and wondered how long this was supposed to take. He resisted the urge to sigh audibly as thirty minutes went by. His eyes then roamed back over to his mother, whose eyelids seemed to be fluttering, although they were closed. He crept closer to the bed to get a better look. She was definitely displaying rapid eye movement, which, he concluded, meant she was seeing something. He waited anxiously for a few more minutes. Suddenly, Margaret started to talk and Alex quietly rushed to get a piece of paper to write on.

"She's in a room…" she said, "…it's dusty, smells musty."

There was a pause for a couple of minutes.

"It's dark, but there's light … from somewhere?" Margaret's face crinkled, and then she added, "She's hurt." Alex's hand flinched as he wrote. Margaret gasped. "He's there. He's upset."

Unable to control himself, Alex quietly asked, "Where? Where are they?"

Margaret's face relaxed again as she breathed evenly. "It's a barn. Painted … no—it's a house. Large, wooden-framed house, painted black and white."

"Go out to the street. What does the street sign say?" Alex booted up his desktop as Margaret tried to get a location on the house. He went to Google's home page and waited for his mother to give him the address.

"2-7 … 1-0-9…" she finally said, as Alex typed. "13th Road."

"13th Street?"

"No," she said, sitting up on the bed. "13th Road."

"Mom, it has to be 13th Street. There's no 13th Road, not in this part of the country at least."

"I know what I saw," she said, getting up a bit unsteadily from the bed. She walked over to Alex and looked down at the computer screen. "Will you type it in and hit enter? You're beginning to sound and act like some of those skeptics who used to visit us at ARI."

Alex complied. "Well, what do you know?" he said, as the computer displayed a map containing the address he typed in. "There's a 13th Road right here in Arlington."

"Who's the woman?" Margaret joked.

"You're the woman," Alex smiled and high-fived her. He sent the directions to his cell phone while Margaret got her purse. Alex had a fleeting thought of putting his mother in a deep sleep while he went to the address and rescued Amanda. But then he remembered, he had promised to let her come along.

"Ready?" Margaret called from his door.

"Yeah," he said, grabbing his cell phone.

* * *

As Margaret backed out of the driveway, the house phone rang. It was Agent Brody. He wanted to inform them of his latest findings. After five rings, he concluded they weren't home.

It wasn't too long ago that an agent from the field had called to give him an update on the situation in Southeast DC. Agents had infiltrated Roberta Jackson's house. She was at home and shocked at the accusations they made about her Gabby. However, after being shown his sketch and still photos from a news broadcast, she started to doubt her own resolve. Reluctantly, she agreed to call John, in hopes of luring him back to the house. However, the agents thought that John may have been onto them after the old woman almost called him by his real name, which she had no way of knowing, except from them.

They doubted that John would have returned to the house anyway, irrespective of the slip-up. What they never anticipated was that John cared for this woman. John had rigged his basement apartment with a bomb, designed to go off by calling a cell phone hidden in the apartment, then entering the correct code. However, before blowing up the house, he had told Ms. Jackson to get out of the house and even gave her three minutes to evacuate. Three minutes was generous, but apparently John knew about Ms. Jackson's bad hip and was providing her with enough time to make it safely out of the house.

The agents picked up on the tip and evacuated the premises before the bomb destroyed John's apartment, along with any evidence he may have left there. Eighty-six-year-old Roberta Jackson was in shock as she watched the house she and her husband had bought in 1954, and finally paid off thirty years later, burn down to ashes.

Despite her grief-stricken state, Ms. Jackson was able to tell the agents that John was an active member of her church. He accompanied her to church every Sunday, helped with food and coat drives, and even filled in as a Boy Scout leader. Occasionally, John did odd jobs for members of the church at their homes, or housesat while they were on vacation. She recalled last Sunday after church, Brother Mosley had asked John to keep an eye on his house while he and his wife went to visit their new granddaughter in Tallahassee, Florida. The Mosleys lived in

Northern Virginia and had a large variety of unique and rare plants, which required a lot of care and attention. John eagerly accepted the task of watching over the Mosleys' home, but refused to take any compensation from them.

After informing the agents that the Mosley home was the only other place she thought John could be, Ms. Jackson asked to be left alone. The agents complied, as the old woman stared blankly at the crackling inferno in front of her.

The field agents relayed the information to Agent Brody, who was now on his way to the Mosleys' house. He placed his cell phone back in the pouch on his hip, after receiving no answer from the Fuller house. He then piled into a large black Suburban with five other agents.

* * *

"Now, you listen to me, Cheerleader Barbie. I don't have much time," John said, as he picked up Amanda's chair from off the floor. "There's no doubt that the FBI will be on their way here right now. I, on the other hand, would like to be somewhere else, but I need your boyfriend."

"Why..."

"Quiet!" John barked, and then struggled to regain control of himself. "Now, I would appreciate it if you didn't force me to kill you. Or your little cheerleading buddies," he added.

"What?" Amanda asked, baffled.

John shrugged his shoulders and opened his arms with palms turned upwards, as if to declare his ignorance of the matter. After a momentary pause, he spoke. "Just some insurance I took out under my original plan when Alex was my target. I figured he wouldn't go along willingly with my plans, so I planted a little something special underneath the back seat in the bus that was supposed to take you and your fellow cheerleaders to the game today. If he didn't cooperate with me, I would have blown you and your friends all over I-495."

"How could you be so heartless and think you're God's messenger?" she asked, genuinely trying to understand the person standing before her. "This is wrong. No god would want you to hurt innocent people."

"You know, it's funny how people have this image of God—all loving, cute, and cuddly. Just rub his belly like a genie in a bottle and he'll give you all the desires of your heart. But everyone seems to forget about the God who destroyed the entire earth's population with a flood. Or the God who killed all the firstborns in Egypt and overthrew Pharaoh and his men to free his people. Or the God who destroyed Sodom and Gomorrah with fire and brimstone. No one wants to know this God. Well guess what, Cheerleader Barbie. They are one and the same. My God, Amanda, is a vengeful God."

Amanda shook her head as she pictured the bus filled with her friends. Tears ran down her cheeks as she remembered all the trips they'd taken on that bus. The bus driver and their coach would always tell them to pipe down because they would get so pumped up before and after a game. They would make funny faces or engage in chit-chat via sign language with the other drivers on the road. The thought that someone would want to hurt them had never crossed her mind.

"So what is it going to be, Amanda?" John said, reeling her back in. "You can call Alex and tell him to meet us here and I'll take him for a little ride. In exchange, I'll leave you here for the FBI to rescue and your friends will all return home safely. Eventually someone will find the bomb on their bus and neutralize it—it's not all that complicated. I was in a rush when I made that one."

"You should be careful what you wish for," Amanda whispered.

"What the hell is that supposed to mean?"

"It means, you should be thankful that Alex is not here."

"If you don't call Alex," he barked, clearly on edge and not heeding her warning, "I'll detonate the bomb, instantly killing all your friends. Afterwards, I will kill you, and then I'll find Alex myself and kill him too."

Amanda brooded over the options before her. A part of her wanted to believe this was all just a bad dream, but she knew it wasn't. Another part of her wanted to believe that her captor was bluffing, but the stern expression on his face said otherwise. Then she thought of Alex again. With his abilities, she was fairly certain he could rescue her. But what if something went wrong? What if this psycho had other weapons—like a gun? This was Virginia, after all—home of the National Rifle Association. How would Alex's powers fare against a flying bullet? Undecided, she shook her head, and said, "Why Alex?"

"Alex has to die, Amanda, it's just that simple. No one interferes with God's plan unscathed. If you want to, you could think of Alex as a sacrificial lamb. And as the sacrificial lamb, Alex must be slaughtered to make atonement for not only his sin, but America's too."

Amanda shot him a devilish look. If only her hands were free, she would slap that smirk right off his face.

"I mean, if it helps, you could think of it that way," he added. "Makes no difference to me."

14. THE RESCUE

"Do you want me to drive?" Alex asked his mother.

"Are you trying to say something about my driving?" Margaret retorted defensively.

"No." He smiled. "I just thought you would be more relaxed if you weren't driving. Then you could focus more on guiding us to this house."

Margaret thought for a minute.

"You're right," she said as she pulled off the road. "Remote viewing can be a little tricky, so the more relaxed I am, the better."

"Tricky how?" Alex asked, as he switched places with his mother without either of them exiting the vehicle.

"Like, I could be off by a street or number. Maybe even a zip code," she said, half to herself.

Alex continued down the highway, trying not to think of his mother's last statement about being wrong about where Amanda was being held captive. He didn't understand this whole remote viewing thing. He thought that people were just born psychic, like his grandmother. Who would have thought it could be taught or learned? Leave it to the U.S. military to dabble in things it shouldn't in its race to arms with Russia during the Cold War era. If Russia had psychic spies, the U.S. had to have them too. If Russia trained chipmunks to be combat warriors with Uzis in hand and rocket-propelled grenades strapped to their backs, the U.S. would be right behind them. The mental image of a chipmunk outfitted in combat gear made Alex laugh.

"What's so funny?" Margaret asked.

"Nothing."

"Exit at the next right. We shouldn't be too far now."

For the next few turns, Alex followed his mother's instructions. Soon they were in a quiet residential neighborhood. With all the flags that protruded from decks and porches, it wasn't hard to figure out that a lot of military, or former military, personnel lived in this area.

"Make a right here!" Margaret yelled as Alex made a sharp turn in compliance.

"A little warning next time would be nice."

"Sorry, there's usually not a ... lot ... of..." Margaret started to say, as she stared out her window in a trance-like state.

"Yeah, but try. I don't want to lose my license less than a year after I got it," he said, oblivious to his mother's preoccupation. "We're on 13th Street now, so 13th Road should be one over to the right." Alex proceeded down the street, stopped at the intersection, then signaled to go right. As he started to turn right, Margaret grabbed his hand.

"No, go left."

"But 13th Road is to the right," he protested.

"I know, but something is telling me to go left."

"But at the house, you said..."

"Alex, I know what I said earlier, but now, I'm telling you to go left."

Alex looked at her in obvious confusion. He felt compelled to maintain his current course, but knew that would only result in an argument. The one thing in the world he hated was arguing with his mother. Reluctantly, he complied. As he drove down the street, he started counting the blocks to determine how far away from 13th Road they were going. After the fourth block, he became visibly agitated. He looked at his mother. She had her eyes closed, but they were moving rapidly.

"Make a right ... now!" she yelled. Alex slammed on the brakes.

"What are you talking about? The next right is about 300 yards away."

"Back up!" she ordered.

"What?"

"Back up the car, Alex. Or are you going to second guess everything I tell you?" Suddenly, Alex wasn't the only agitated person in the car. "I swear you're like one of those debunkers of the RV project, always second guessing everything we did."

"Sorry, but earlier you said the address was on 13th Road. God only knows where we are now," he said, as he threw the car in reverse.

"Well, that's how remote viewing works sometimes. We can be off a bit, but we're usually in the general vicinity of where our target is. You just have to know how to interpret the information. Something at 13th Road must have distracted my view."

As Alex reversed the car, a tiny one-way street appeared. It was almost hidden from view by the overgrown trees that hid its entrance. Had they not been looking for it, they would have never known it was there.

"Well, what do you know," Margaret said, astonished.

"The old girl's still got it." She turned and smiled at Alex, who was equally shocked at this point. "Go down this street, and make another right at the end." Alex complied.

The tiny street emptied into a two-way street and Alex could see the Potomac River from the car. Margaret instructed him to slow his roll as they drove down the street, because Amanda was close by. Suddenly, a large white house appeared, with black shutters and roofing.

"There it is. That's where she is," Margaret announced.

Alex parked the car and examined the large, square, symmetrically shaped house in front of him. It was a Georgian-styled colonial house that boasted a paneled front door in the center, with decorative crown molding at the top and flattened columns on either side. It also had five windows across the front and paired chimneys on a medium-pitched roof, with minimal overhang. The grounds surrounding the large structure were equally impressive, with the manicured lawn, multiple gardens, and strategically placed privacy trees. For some reason, the house looked more suited to be a museum than a home to Alex.

"It doesn't look like anyone's home," he said.

"She's in there with him all right," Margaret reassured him.

"Where?"

"Well, I saw her in a dark, musty room, but this house should have light flooding into every room, except…"

"The basement," they said jointly.

Carefully, they exited the car and casually walked toward the trees at the side of the house. Once hidden from view by the tree branches, they ran toward the backyard, which boasted an even more beautiful garden than the front yard. The garden was just beyond the slated stone patio the Mosleys had had John build earlier that spring.

From the rear of the house, they discovered a look-out basement with several small ground-level windows. Margaret immediately recognized the windows as the ones she saw in her vision. Other than the windows, there was no additional outlet from the basement. On the floor above the basement, there was a set of French glass doors atop three stairs that opened up to the main level of the house.

"This door is our only way into the house from back here," Alex deduced.

"Right, but we're not going inside," she said. "Instead, we're going to call Agent Brody."

"Mom, we don't have time for that. We have to get Amanda."

"Alex, we had a deal. I would take you here, but we'd call Agent Brody if things got out of hand."

"Mom, nothing has gotten out of hand. We'll go inside, surprise this psycho, and get Amanda," he said, heading for the door.

"Hold on," she persisted as she dialed Agent Brody's telephone number. The phone rang as Alex continued to walk away from his mother. "Alex, we are not going inside this house," she said, grabbing his arm.

"Why not?"

"One, you will be breaking and entering into someone's home. Two, we don't know what this guy will do if someone tries to interfere with his plans again."

"So what? Amanda is in there. What are we supposed to do—just stand here and wait until he perfects his plan?"

"No, I'm calling Agent Brody," she said, holding up her cell phone.

"You call Agent Brody, but I'm going in," he said. Before she knew it, Alex had freed himself from her grasp and was standing on the steps in front of the French doors. Margaret ran after him, but tripped over a large tin watering can. The loud clunking sound caught them both by surprise.

Startled by the commotion, Alex turned around and gave his mother a scolding stare. Margaret stood frozen and bewildered, with her hands clasped over her agape mouth. Alex sighed heavily, and then looked inside the house to see if anyone had heard the commotion. Luckily no one had, or so he hoped. Margaret picked up her phone, which had fallen out of her hand when she tripped, and then carefully tiptoed over to him.

"Alex, what are you doing?" she whispered.

I'm opening the door, he projected to her.

"You have to show me how you do that someday," she said, slipping her phone in her pocket without realizing it was still on.

Alex shook his head as he focused on the locked door in front of him. He spotted the two bolts that extended from the lock body on the right door panel into the holes in the strike plates on the left door panel. Slowly, he mentally pulled out the locking bolt at the bottom of the lock body, then the spring latch at the top. With his hand on the door handle, he carefully turned it downwards and the door gave way. He stepped into the house and Margaret followed closely behind.

"Okay, so we're going to get Amanda, then leave, right?" she added, as she followed him further into the house.

Right, he projected.

When they got to a long hallway that separated the kitchen from the formal sitting room, she asked, "How do we get to the basement?"

I don't know, but the entrance has to be here somewhere. Why don't you go that way? he added, pointing to his right. *I'll go this way. If I find the entrance, I'll let you know—telepathically. If you find it, call me on my cell.* Just then, he switched his phone to vibrate mode.

"Ok," she whispered.

Only if it's safe to do so, Mom, Alex cautioned.

"Okay, got it," she said and took off down the hallway, away from her son.

* * *

On his way to the Mosleys' house, Agent Brody's phone rang. He picked it up and answered it, but got no response. He looked at his phone and saw that the number on the screen belonged to Margaret, and the call was still connected. He listened as he heard chatter in the background.

"Ms. Fuller, is that you?" he asked, but got no response.

He put the phone back to his ears and listened as Margaret argued with someone about going somewhere. The person she was arguing with sounded like Alex, but he couldn't be sure. He listened attentively, and then determined it was Alex. He also caught the name Amanda. Suddenly, the voices got muffled, but the connection was still there.

"Ms. Fuller. Margaret," he yelled into the phone, but still received no answer. He then turned to the other agents in the van, and asked, "Hey, can I get a trace on this call?"

"Does this have anything to do with the bomber?" the agent closest to him asked.

"Yeah, I think so." The agent took Max's phone and initiated a trace.

A few minutes went by, then the agent announced that the trace was complete and he had an address on Passersby Lane.

"Is that the same address as the Mosleys' house?" Agent Brody asked.

"The very same," the agent responded.

Agent Brody turned to the driver and told him to step on it, because the bomber may have more hostages than they originally thought.

* * *

"Shh!" John said, as Amanda protested over the options he gave her. She ignored his orders and ranted on. "I said be quiet!" he shouted, as he stood up and listened attentively. His behavior made Amanda pause.

"Did you hear that?" he asked her.

Amanda listened intently for a moment. "Hear what?"

"You didn't hear that?"

"Obviously not. Maybe if you tell me what it is that I'm supposed to be listening out for, then maybe I'll hear it."

John slowly walked over to the staircase and stood perfectly still as he listened. A moment later, he rushed back over to Amanda and stuffed the rag back into her mouth, which she fought fervently. With his hand clasped over her mouth to keep her from spitting out the rag, he slid another piece of cloth around her head and tied it. He looked her in the eyes, and then slowly raised his outstretched index finger to his lips. Hurriedly, he walked over to the table and picked up a pistol, which he slid into a holster under his pant leg. Then he picked up his hunting knife and quietly climbed the stairs.

Amanda watched as John disappeared through the door at the top of the stairs. She couldn't figure out what had startled him. He had always seemed so in control, but now he appeared worried. But why? She listened earnestly as she waited in silence.

Suddenly, she heard something, but she couldn't figure out what it was. She looked up at the door, but no one was there. She scanned her surroundings, looking for affirmation, but none appeared. There it goes again. *Am I imaging things?* she thought, because the sound seemed to have been inside her head.

Amanda.

Alex, she thought. *Could it really be him? What is he doing here? How did he know I was here?*

Amanda, where are you?

"I'm here," she tried to scream, but the sound got muffled by the gag in her mouth. *Oh crap, he can't hear me,* she thought. She looked around for something she could use to create a sound. *The table,* she thought. There must be something over there that could make noise. She started dragging herself over to the table on the chair. She stopped abruptly when she heard a sharp, high-pitched sound coming from underneath her. It was the chair, scraping the floor. She looked down at the lines in the dust on the floor that the chair legs had made, exposing tiled flooring.

Amanda, was that you?

Amanda looked up at the door, and then dragged herself a few more inches across the floor.

Keep making that sound. I think I'm near you, she heard Alex project inside her head.

A moment later, Alex appeared in the doorway at the top of the stairs.

Oh thank God, Amanda thought as she let out a sigh of relief. In a split second, Alex was down the stairs and by her side, untying the rope around her arms, which were covered in red welts. She had a large black-and-blue knot in the middle of her forehead. There was dried-up blood at the left corner of her mouth and bruises on both cheeks.

Suddenly, he heard Amanda screaming into the gag in her mouth. He looked at her, and saw that something behind him had her attention.

"Alex," his mother said in a frightened, gargled voice.

He turned around and saw his mother with a large, hunting knife held at her throat and an arm wrapped tightly around her chest.

"Mom," he shouted as he headed toward her.

"Stay where you are," a voice said from the shadows behind Margaret. Alex watched as his mother was pushed forward a few feet and a man appeared behind her. It was John Fischer.

"Hello, Alex," John said in his flat monotone voice, as he slowly descended the stairs with Margaret. "I'm glad you were finally able to make it."

"I doubt that," Alex replied.

"It's true. I am very happy to see you again. And you even brought your mommy with you. Isn't that sweet?" He smiled.

"Why don't you get your filthy hands off my mom and I may consider letting you live?"

"What did you say to me?" John retorted.

"You heard me."

"I don't think I did. In case you missed it, you little brat, I'm the one in control here."

"Guess again," Alex replied, as he mentally entered John's cerebellum and shut down his motor skills. Instantly, John's body jerked upright and stiffened like a board. Next, his hunting knife fell to the ground as his fingers loosened their grip. John's eyeballs danced around in his head as he tried to figure out what was happening to him.

"Mom, get the knife and come over here and finish untying Amanda," Alex said. He noticed the confused look on her face, and then added, "Just move his hands out of the way. He can't do anything to you in this state."

Margaret effortlessly moved John's arms from around her chest and away from her neck. John watched helplessly as his prey escaped his clutches. His eyes found Alex, and asked in a gargled tone, "What are you doing to me?"

"Just keeping you out of the way, so we can get out of here safely," he replied.

"You're... the antichrist?" he asked.

"No. I'm just your ordinary teenager—trying to figure out who I am, why I'm the way I am, and where the hell I fit into this world, if at all. You know, the ordinary meaning-of-life bullshit."

"No, you're evil. Evil incarnate!!!" he shouted, as he fought to free himself.

Just then, Alex felt John struggling to take back control of his brain.

Well, this is new, Alex thought, as John tried to eject him from his head. Usually when he took control of someone's mind, the person was not aware of it, so there'd never really been much of a resistance. But this guy was well aware of it, and didn't like being the backseat driver in his own body. As John continued to fight to regain control of his mind, Alex found it hard to maintain his hold. As Alex felt his grip over John's cerebellum slipping, he instinctively thought about grabbing hold of the other parts of his brain. However, without the benefit of time to carefully think about which bodily function he should target, he dismissed the idea as being too risky. If he thoughtlessly grabbed a hold of another part of John's brain without targeting a specific function, he could end up shutting down the whole thing, which could be fatal.

"Alex, your nose," he heard his mother say as she took the gag out of Amanda's mouth.

"You're bleeding again, Alex," Amanda said. "You have to stop."

Alex released John's brain, which caught the latter by surprise. They were both out of breath. Despite his mentally drained state, John charged at Alex. He had only taken a few steps when he found himself airborne. With a wave of his hand, Alex mentally threw John into the wall to his left. It did little to stop the ex-Marine, who was back on his feet in a second, ready to attack again. This time Alex mentally raised John's body up to the ceiling, then slammed him down hard onto the floor. They all felt the ground shake and the table jump as John's body hit the floor. Alex watched as John squirmed around on the ground in pain. He then turned his attention to Amanda and his mother.

"Are you okay?" he asked.

"We're fine," Margaret said.

"Mandy?" Alex asked as he watched her looking around frantically.

"Yeah, I'm fine too."

"Okay, let's get out of—"

"Alex, he has a gun!" Amanda shouted as she motioned for them to take cover.

Alex turned around and saw John, who was on his feet again, release the safety off his pistol and fire. He got the first round off before Alex could deflect it. The bullet flew by Alex, ricocheted off the floor, and struck the opposite wall. Realizing that the bullets packed quite a punch in such a confined space, and that they were being fired in quick succession, Alex mentally aimed John's gun away from him and toward the tiny windows on the adjacent wall. John struggled to redirect his aim at Alex, but could not escape the mental grasp Alex had over the muscles in his arms. Although he could not fire at his intended target, John continued to pull the trigger on his gun. Bullets smashed through the tiny windows that led to the backyard; some got lodged in the wall while others ricocheted off the metal debris that was nearby. Alex heard his mother and Amanda scream.

Suddenly, the lights went out and the door at the top of the stairs burst open, followed closely behind by men wearing protective FBI gear. One of the men fired two rounds into John's head, killing him instantly. Alex watched as John's lifeless body fell face-up a few inches away from him. John's eyes were open. All of a sudden, an image of Justin's eyes as he fell into the gorge at Camp APRICOT flashed through Alex's mind. A pool of blood started to form on the floor from John's gunshot wounds. Alex watched as the pool grew larger and larger, stretching across the floor, trying to reach the tip of his sneakers. He moved his feet backwards a few inches. Then the floor started moving. Alex tried to fix his gaze on one spot on the floor, but could not. He raised his gaze to the wall, but it was moving too. He felt dizzy, but could hear voices in the distance. He tried to move, but lost his balance. The voices started to echo in his head again before a bright light appeared and engulfed his mind.

15. NINE HOURS

It was dark and quiet, when Alex opened his eyes. He waited a few seconds for his eyes to adjust to the dark. Where was he? And why did he feel so tired? He tried to move his arm, only to find that it was restrained. Alex panicked and fought to free himself, but was caught off-guard at how easily his restraint gave way. He looked down at his body and saw his favorite blanket tightly tucked around him. Only his mother was capable of creating such an ironclad tuck. His eyes searched the rest of his surroundings for confirmation that he was in his room. Satisfied, he sat up in his bed.

Although his blinds and curtains were shut, he could sense that it was nighttime outside. Effortlessly, his feet swung over the side of the bed. His mind recalled the events at the colonial house. He was certain it had been daytime when he was there, but it was night now. How long had he been asleep? Was it even the same day? Panicked again, he rushed to the door, then to his mother's room. She wasn't there.

He turned around and exited her room, when he heard noise coming from downstairs. He rushed down the stairs, taking them two and three at a time. On the sofa, he saw Amanda. She had her back turned to him, facing the kitchen and talking with someone. He walked over and saw his mother and Agent Brody in the kitchen, packing the dishwasher. Alex took a seat next to Amanda, but she didn't move.

"So how long was I out for?" he asked.

Amanda ignored his question and continued her conversation with Margaret and Agent Brody, both of whom were also oblivious to Alex's attempt to capture their attention.

"What am I, invisible now?" he asked.

She didn't respond.

"Amanda, I'm talking to you," he said, reaching to touch her shoulder, but instead his hand went right through her. "Oh shit," he said, as he realized he was having an out-of-body experience and his body was still upstairs in his bed. He levitated up to the ceiling, through the walls, and back into his body.

Back in his room, Alex's body was still tightly tucked in bed, with his blanket all the way up to his chin. How did he not notice that he had left his body behind? Out-of-body experience usually required serious concentration and relaxation. Why was he able to separate from his body with such ease? Just then, he noticed the white noise playing in the background. He looked at the shut blinds and curtains. The absence of light and the low, humming white noise—someone wanted him relaxed. The only person he could think of was his mother. But why would she do that?

Slowly, he pulled the blanket from around his body and got up from the bed. This time, he made sure he had everything with him. He was climbing down the stairs, one at a time, when he heard Amanda shout, "Alex is awake!"

Before he reached the bottom of the stairs, Amanda

was already there with her welted arms wide open, which she threw around him as he descended the last stairs. Although her face was covered with bruises, she was still the most beautiful girl he'd ever seen. Margaret and Agent Brody joined them by the stairs.

"See, Agent Brody," Margaret said. "All he needed was time to rest and he would be fine. Nosebleeds are a common occurrence in our family," she lied.

"I stand corrected," Agent Brody replied.

"And you wanted to take him to the hospital for a little nosebleed," Amanda said, snuggling up to Alex's chest.

"Okay, okay," Agent Brody said, giving in. "But what did you expect me to do? He was unconscious and bleeding at a crime scene. You guys are lucky my SAC—"

"SAC? What's an SAC?" Amanda asked.

"SAC means Special Agent in Charge. Every FBI field office is headed by an SAC," Agent Brody explained. "As I was saying, you're lucky my SAC didn't arrive at the scene until after you took Alex away."

Alex tried to follow the conversation as best as he could, but didn't say anything to throw Margaret or Amanda off their game.

"How are you feeling, Alex?" Agent Brody asked.

"I'm fine," he said meekly. "It's like they said, I just needed some rest."

"Well, I've taken a lot of heat for allowing you guys to come back here, instead of being taken in for questioning. So first thing in the morning, I need you all to come in and give your official statements. Okay?"

"I thought we just gave you our statements over dinner," Amanda said.

"Yes, you gave me your account of what happened

today, which I'll put in my report. But, you still need to give an official statement to one of our agents in a more formal setting. And he or she will not be as warm and fuzzy as I am, so be prepared to get your feathers ruffled a bit tomorrow."

"No problem, Agent Brody," Margaret said. "We'll be there first thing in the morning."

"Okay then," he said, schlepping over to the front door. "Alex, good to see you back on your feet. Ms. Fuller, thanks again for dinner. Amanda … Amanda, you stay out of trouble."

They all laughed, except Alex. Margaret walked Agent Brody out onto the stoop. When they were out of view, Alex asked Amanda, "Why is Agent Brody here?"

"He's here checking on you, after he saved your hind from being tossed into a hospital, where you undoubtedly would have been poked and prodded until your little secret came to light. Your Mom asked him to join us for dinner to keep him distracted while you slept, or whatever you were doing."

Alex was mulling over Amanda's explanation when his mother stepped back inside and closed the door. She grabbed him and threw her arms tightly around him, kissing every inch of his head.

"Mom, please," Alex pleaded, "not in front of Amanda."

"Don't you ever scare me like that again, do you hear me?" she said, with genuine fear in her voice. Apparently her nonchalant attitude earlier had just been a ploy to get Agent Brody to believe that Alex was fine.

Alex took a seat on the stairs, and Amanda joined him.

"Now, what the hell happened to you earlier?" Margaret demanded.

"I don't know," Alex replied.

"Don't lie to me, Alex."

"Mom, I'm not lying."

"You lost consciousness for almost nine hours and you want me to believe you know nothing about it? Or that this has never happened to you before?"

"Mom, nothing like this has ever happened."

"Except for that one time at the Metro station," Amanda interjected.

Margaret looked at her son and his girlfriend, puzzled. "What one time at the Metro is she talking about Alex?"

"Oh yeah, I almost forgot about that *one* time," he said holding up his index finger. Then he shot Amanda an accusatory look, then added, "Thanks for reminding me about that."

"Hey, hey," Margaret said, trying to get his attention. "Don't put this on her. Tell me what happened in the Metro station."

Alex explained how he blacked out after he caused the bomb to implode. "It was only for a few minutes though, Mom, I swear. Isn't that right, Amanda?"

Amanda confirmed his story and added that Alex regained consciousness as soon as she woke him up.

"So, why didn't you wake up earlier today?" Margaret asked.

"I don't know."

"Do you remember anything after you lost consciousness?"

Alex thought for a while, and then shook his head no. "I only remember a bright light, then waking up in my bedroom." He purposely left out the part about his involuntary out-of-body experience.

"What bright light?"

"I don't know."

Margaret thought for a minute, and then spoke. "You listen to me, Alex Michael Fuller. You are not, and I repeat not, to use any of your abilities until we get some help and try to figure out how these abilities work and how they're affecting your health. Do you understand me?"

"Where are we going to get that kind of help from? It's not like being a mind freak is a typical medical condition."

"Your father. Your father will—"

"Absolutely not," Alex said as he stood up. "I don't want anything to do with him. And you're definitely not telling him anything about my abilities," he said as he headed back to his room.

Amanda sat dumbfounded on the stairs, trying to make sense of what had just been said. She had always thought that Alex's father was some Air Force pilot who got shot down during the Gulf War. At least that's what he'd told her. But just now, both Alex and his mother had confirmed that his father was alive. Why would he lie to her about something like that?

"Amanda, your mom will be here soon," Margaret said. "You should get your stuff together."

Amanda recognized the dejected look on Margaret's face, the same expression her mother had been wearing more and more these days.

"Don't worry, Ms. Fuller. Alex can be a little melodramatic sometimes," she said, trying to console Margaret. "Just give him some time and he'll come around."

"I hope so, Amanda. For his sake, I certainly hope so."

Amanda didn't quite get the last part of Margaret's statement, but decided not to inquire further. Instead she got up and suggested that she go talk to him.

"Thanks, Amanda. You've always been a good friend to us."

Amanda turned to go up the stairs, then Margaret added, "By the way, thanks for telling Agent Brody that you were the one who called Alex to tell him where you were. I would have had a lot of explaining to do if you hadn't thought of that."

"It's no problem, Ms. Fuller."

* * *

Back in his room, Alex turned off the white noise and opened his curtains and blinds. He looked out across his neighborhood, which was either asleep or settling in for the night. Ms. Osaka's lights were still on. Was she still up or did she forget to turn off her lights again? He didn't have the luxury to be worried about Ms. Osaka right now, because he was tired and wanted to sleep.

He walked back over to his bed and lay down on his back, legs crossed with his hands behind his head. He tried to drown out his mother's voice, but her earlier question kept hounding him. Why was he unconscious for nine whole hours? Was he just resting? He needed answers, but where could he get them? Just then, he heard a knock at his door.

"Can I come in?" Amanda asked from the other side of his door.

Alex was contemplating the request when Amanda

walked into his room. "You know, you're supposed to wait for a response when you ask that question," he teased.

"What question?" she asked, not catching the sarcasm in his voice.

"Forget it," he said, as he slumped back down into his bed. He watched as Amanda aimlessly walked around his room, making small talk while trying to conceal her real motive for being there.

After a few minutes of indulging her, Alex got tired of the charade and said, "Okay, Bridgewater, spill it."

Apparently Alex wasn't the only one who was tired of the charade, because Amanda quickly got to the point.

"Why did you tell me your father was dead?" she blurted.

Alex had not anticipated this question, so he didn't know how to respond to it. "I don't know," he said, hoping that the inquiry would end there.

"You're *lying* to me again."

"What do you want from me, Amanda?" he said, sitting up in the middle of the bed.

"How about the truth? You told me your father was dead. And I believed you. Now I find out that not only is your father not dead, but he may know why you're like this."

"There's nothing wrong with me," he snarled.

"I didn't say anything was wrong with you, Alex. But how long are you going to keep lying to yourself? Sitting there pretending that you're normal. The fact is, you are not normal. You are different. And the sooner you grasp that, the better off we'll all be."

"You think I don't know what I am? I know I'm a freak. I just didn't think that you would think I am too."

"Alex, I didn't say you were a freak. I said you're different—huge difference. And what's your big obsession with being normal anyway?"

"What do you mean?"

"Alex, being normal is so boring. I'm normal and I'm boring. So is everybody else I know. Do you think a *normal* person could have saved me and your mom from that psycho today?"

Alex thought for minute. "I guess not. But if I were a normal person, you wouldn't have been in that position in the first place."

"Alex, if you were normal, we would be dead, along with hundreds of others from the Metro bombing," she said. "Do you honestly have to see the glass half empty all the time? You've been like this ever since I've known you. Can you, for once, see the glass half full?"

"I could try, but it wouldn't be natural for me to think that way."

"Okay, fine," she said, sitting at the foot of his bed, "then just be yourself."

"You—" he started to say, then paused. "You wanted to know why I lied to you about my father."

"That's not important," she said unconvincingly.

"Yes it is," he replied. "Up until this morning, I thought my father was some deadbeat military guy who knocked up my mom and bailed on us. Turned out he was a deadbeat mad scientist who experimented on my mom, knocked her up, then bailed on us."

"A scientist?"

"Well, psychologist. Dr. Karl Vaughan to be exact." He then recounted the highlights of Margaret's story for

Amanda, who listened intently about the Stargate Project and its exploration of the human mind.

After hearing his explanation, Amanda couldn't hide her confusion between what she had just heard and what Alex had told her years ago when they went to Braemar Academy together. So she asked, "But how does that tie into what you told me before when we were at Braemar about your dad?"

"It doesn't. I just made that up," he confessed, avoiding the burning gaze of her eyes. "The lie all began when I was supposed to write a report on someone who I thought was a hero for my school back in California. I was researching modern-day heroes when I came across this Navy pilot who got shot down at the beginning of the first Gulf War. This was even before I was born. Anyway, I thought about how brave this pilot must have been, shot down over enemy territory. I remember thinking how awesome it would be to have a dad like that, rather than the loser that left us. So I changed a few facts around and started telling people that he was my dad."

"But what are people going to say now that your dad's alive?"

"First of all, I don't care what people think of me. Well, at least not outside of the two people inside this house right now. Second, since I don't have a lot of friends, the composition of my family never really came up in conversation. Third, I don't see the need to tell anyone about this Vaughan guy. My father is dead to me and that's the way he's going to stay."

He looked at her face and realized that she disapproved of his decision.

"Look," he said, touching the tips of her fingers, which

were sprawled out on his bed, "I don't know anything about this Vaughan guy. My gut feeling is that if he knew my mom was pregnant with me and decided to have nothing to do with us anyway, then he can't be trusted. Promise me you won't tell anyone about him."

Reluctantly, she agreed.

"On a lighter note," he said, changing the subject, "what exactly happened earlier after I fainted?"

"Oh yeah, you do need to know this for your statement tomorrow," she said, climbing further into his bed and finding a cozy spot next to him. "Okay, so when the paramedics arrived, your mother refused you medical service. She told them that you usually got these faintly spells with your nosebleed and it's nothing to worry about as long as you got some rest. I also convinced the paramedics that my injuries were only superficial and I'd rather follow up with my own doctor. Agent Brody then helped us load you into your mom's car and we drove you home. At dinner, we told Agent Brody that you woke up during the drive home, but in reality, you didn't."

"I didn't wake up even for a second?" he asked.

"No, you didn't. Alex, you never woke up even after your mom and I pinched you, bitch-slapped you, and yelled at you."

"I didn't even budge."

"Not even an inch. But we told Agent Brody you did."

"Okay," he said, urging her to continue.

"So we told him that once you got home, you started complaining of how tired you were because of all the excitement. We also told him that you were kind of freaked out about the dead body and all, which he totally bought."

"But what about how we found you? Did my mom tell him about her remote viewing abilities?"

"She told me about it, but not Agent Brody. I told Agent Brody that John forced me to call you, and instructed me to tell you where I was and warned you not to tell the police or FBI, or else he would kill me, right before he smashed my phone."

"Okay, so that's how my mom and I got to the house," he reaffirmed. "How did we hold him off until the FBI showed up?"

"Well, you and your mom were able to calm John down until the FBI showed up. Once the feds arrived, John went berserk and started shooting up the place, which they could hear outside the Mosleys' house."

"Okay, and how were we able to hold off John when he went on his shooting rampage?"

"You held him off."

Alex shot her a puzzling glance. "They're not going to buy that for a second," he said.

"Why not?"

"Because I never touched the guy."

"But you were close enough to him. In fact, the FBI agent who shot John said that he saw you struggling with John, trying to get the gun out of his hand. From the angle that this agent entered the room, especially with them cutting the power to the house and all that protective gear they had on, it looked like you were wrestling with John."

"Okay, so I fainted, then woke up in the car. I got home and felt tired. Then what?"

"You went to sleep and didn't wake up until just now when you came downstairs."

"And he bought that?" he asked skeptically.

"I think so."

"Well, I guess we'll find out tomorrow when we have a more objective person doing the questioning."

Amanda put her arm around Alex, and teasingly asked, "Did I ever tell you how comforted your glass-half-empty perspective on life makes me feel?"

"Well I knew it had to be more than just my dashing good looks that made you stick around," he joked.

Amanda chuckled at first, but then her face became somber.

"What's the matter?" Alex asked.

"It's my dad."

"What happened to your father?"

"Nothing happened to him. But while you were unconscious, I stopped by my house to check in with my mother. She called my dad this morning in Argentina and told him I went missing after watching movies over here with you."

"And?" he urged her on.

"He called his contacts in the FBI and got the real scoop that John had kidnapped me after we saw him planting the bomb in the Metro station. After everything was over, Dad tracked me down here, and laid down some new rules."

"Why do I get the feeling this gets worst?"

"Well, he suspended my driving privileges, so I'm back to being chauffeured around again. I'm supposed to go to school, then directly home afterwards. *No malingering*, he said. I'm also supposed to cut back on extra-curricular activities that cannot be adequately supervised, whatever that means."

"Man, that's harsh," he said. Realizing that the somber expression was still on her face, Alex tried to cheer her up.

"Well, look on the bright side, we still have the weekends to hang out together and being chauffeured around isn't all that bad. I mean, you did it before, so you can certainly do it again, right?"

"Alex," she said turning toward him, but not realizing how close his face was to hers. Her hair filled his nostrils with the smell of fresh berries.

"There's one more thing I'm not supposed to do," she said, as the warm air from her breath washed across Alex's face.

"Tell me later," he said as his hand found the nape of her neck and he pulled her close to him. Softly, he kissed her, and she kissed him back.

* * *

A few minutes later, Alex and Amanda were interrupted by a knock on the door. Startled, they both jumped off the bed and each landed on opposite sides of the room. Margaret opened the door and stuck her head in.

"Amanda, your mother is downstairs," she announced.

"Thanks, Ms. Fuller," she replied as she headed toward the door.

"You may want to take a few minutes and straighten up a bit," Margaret suggested.

Amanda caught a glance of her disheveled reflection in the mirror. "Yes, I think I should," she said, adjusting her shirt.

"Alex, why don't we give Amanda some privacy," she said, as she marched him out of the room in front of her.

Downstairs, Alex saw Melanie Bridgewater standing outside on the stoop.

"Hi, Mrs. Bridgewater," he said.

"Alex?" Melanie said from behind a large pair of designer sunglasses. "Oh goodness, what a handsome young man you've turned out to be. Come over here and give me a hug."

Alex complied while Margaret passed them and made her way into the kitchen.

"I hardly recognized your voice this morning. And now I hardly recognized you in person. I could have easily passed you on the streets and had no idea it was you," she said as they both laughed.

"Listen, Alex," Melanie continued on. "I hope you know that it wasn't my idea to—"

"To come get me," Amanda said, finishing Melanie's sentence, as she appeared on the stairs behind Alex. "It must have been my dad's idea for you to come get me, isn't that right, Mother?"

Melanie looked perplexed, as if she had no idea what her daughter was talking about. "Amanda, what are—"

"Can you wait in the car and give us a few minutes?" Amanda interjected again.

"But Amanda—" Melanie tried to protest.

"Just wait in the car. I would like to say goodbye to Alex in private."

"Very well. Goodbye, Alex."

"Good night, Mrs. Bridgewater," he said.

"Goodbye, Margaret," she yelled before heading to the Lincoln Town Car that was parked in front of the Fullers' house.

"Good night, Melanie. Thanks for stopping by," Margaret yelled back from the kitchen.

Alex had his eyes fixed on Amanda, unsure of what had

just transpired between her and her mother. Apparently, a secret war was just waged between them right in front of his eyes, but he had no idea why.

"Okay. So are you going to tell me what that was all about?" he asked.

"It's nothing," Amanda said, shaking her head. "Just some unresolved issues I have to take care of when I get home."

"Well, if you need any help, you know where to find me."

Amanda thought about Alex's suggestion for a while before saying, "I think I may hold you to that someday."

"Fair enough."

"See you tomorrow then."

"Tomorrow," he agreed, and kissed her goodbye.

Alex walked her out to the front stoop and watched as she got in the back of the car with her mother, and the chauffeur drove them away. Alex stepped back inside once Amanda's car disappeared.

"What a day this has been," Margaret said as she emerged from the kitchen holding two cups filled with hot chocolate. She handed one to him and they sat in the living room reflecting on their day. She asked him if he was at all bothered by John's death, and he assured her he was not.

"There is one thing about him though that I've been wondering about."

"What's that?"

"Do you think he was right, when he said I was evil?"

"Do you think you're evil?"

"Not really, but—"

"No buts, Alex. You are not evil. I don't care what that lunatic said back there. You are a good person; always have been and always will be. Who helps Mommy around the house and never complains about doing his chores?"

When Alex didn't respond, Margaret turned his face to look at her, and asked her question again.

"I do," Alex finally replied.

"Who helps Ms. Osaka find her dog whenever the little bitch gets lost?"

"I do," he chuckled.

"Who saved all those people in the Metro station that day from the bomb?"

"I did," he sighed.

"And who just saved Amanda from that psycho?"

Alex was about to answer, but stopped.

"You did," Margaret said, answering for him. "We may not be perfect, baby, but that doesn't make us evil. It just makes us human. Now go upstairs and get ready for bed."

16. IMMINENT END

The next day, Margaret was up early. She had her day all planned out. She would hit the FBI office first, where she and Alex would give their statements. Afterwards, she'd drop him off at the house before heading to the office for exactly two hours, and hopefully she'd be back on her way home by noon. That way, she'd still have the entire Sunday afternoon to unwind before starting her vicious work cycle again on Monday.

Her first task proved to be an easy feat. She and Alex arrived at the FBI's Washington Field Office, or WFO, around seven o'clock. Agent Brody was there. Although he didn't conduct the interviews, he sat in on Alex's while Margaret was interviewed by two other agents in a separate room. At a quarter to nine, they were done and ready to go home.

As Agent Brody escorted them through the building toward the exit, Alex kept looking around the facility.

"Looking for something?" Agent Brody finally asked.

"Someone," he corrected. "I thought Amanda was going to be here today."

"Oh, they should be here soon," Agent Brody said. "They called earlier to say they were on their way."

"Mom, do you mind if we wait a few minutes until they get here?"

Margaret looked at her watch. "Well, only a few minutes. I want to stop by the office today to help Molly with a large print job of some disclosure documents for a security offering we have scheduled for tomorrow."

"Yes!" Alex said.

"You guys can wait here in—" Agent Brody started to say.

"Amanda!" Alex said, running toward the girl who had just walked through the large glass entrance of the lobby. "You're here. We were just talking about you," he added, lifting her up as he hugged her and swayed with her. He set her down as soon as his eyes met Geoffrey Bridgewater's, who appeared behind Amanda. Melanie Bridgewater was standing next to her husband.

"Hello, Alex," Geoffrey said, in a deep, crisp British accent.

"Good morning, Mr. Bridgewater, Mrs. Bridgewater," Alex replied.

"Good morning, Alex," Melanie responded. Alex turned his attention back to Amanda as their parents exchanged pleasantries. He noticed that the large knot on Amanda's forehead was now purplish in color, and puffier. For a person who had gone several rounds with a psychopath, she looked remarkably well, physically. But her eyes hinted at something altogether different. Alex brushed it off as a by-product of her parents' presence.

"You should totally comb that out," he said.

"Screw you, Fuller. It's nine o'clock on a Sunday morning. You're lucky I even had time to wash my hair."

"No. I'm not talking about your hair. I'm talking about your shiner. On your forehead."

"Oh," she said, touching her forehead.

"It would help to disperse the dead veins that caused your bruise, while helping to stimulate blood circulation to the area, making it heal and disappear faster. The same holds true for your other bruises too."

"Oh, I've never tried that. I'll remember that the next time I take a fall in cheerleading."

They laughed.

"You still look pretty hot with it though."

"Oh yeah?"

"Yeah, but more badass."

They laughed again.

"Amanda, we should get going. You don't want to keep your father for too long. He has a meeting in DC at eleven," Melanie said.

Alex and Amanda turned around and saw their parents, Agent Brody, and two other agents.

"Amanda, these are Agents Stewart and Jimenez," Agent Brody said. "They'll be conducting your interview."

"Well, I guess this is goodbye," Alex said to Amanda. "Call me later when you're done."

"Sure," she said, following behind the agents, with her mother in tow. "Dad, are you coming?" she added, when she looked back and saw him standing next to Alex.

"In a minute, love," Geoffrey replied.

"But, Dad—" she started to plead.

"I said, I'll be there in a minute. I need to have a word with Alex first."

Amanda looked scared and worried as she walked toward the elevators. She kept her eyes on Alex and her father until she disappeared in one of the elevators.

"Alex, would you mind if we had a word over there?" Geoffrey said, motioning in the direction of a semi-secluded area in the lobby.

"Sure thing, Mr. Bridgewater," Alex said as he followed the impeccably dressed gentleman.

"I should be heading upstairs to listen in on Amanda's interview," Agent Brody said to Margaret.

"Yes, of course," she said. "Since this is probably the last time I'll see you again, I wanted to say thank you very much, for everything. You can't imagine what a relief it's been knowing that this guy isn't out there anymore. I can certainly sleep better ... I think we all can sleep better knowing that you guys are out there keeping us safe from the bad guys,"

"It's all a part of the job, ma'am."

"Margaret, please," she insisted. "I think we're past the formalities now."

"Good day, Margaret," Geoffrey interjected as he waved to her from behind Agent Brody and walked toward the elevators. Alex headed straight for the exit.

"It was nice meeting you and your son, Margaret," Agent Brody said, handing her one of his cards. "Don't hesitate to call me if you need anything," he added, before chasing after Geoffrey to accompany him upstairs.

Outside, Margaret found Alex standing next to the car, waiting for her.

"What's wrong?" she asked, noticing the troubled look on his face.

"Nothing," he said, forcing a smile across his face to hide the lie.

It was exam week at Prestige High. Underclassmen were stressed out and could be found aimlessly roaming the campus, going over their class notes and quizzing each other. Seniors were giddy and they frolicked across the Quad, bragging to each other about who they were taking to prom and which colleges had accepted them. Alex watched from under his favorite tree as the school year waned down to its imminent end. Like all the other underclassmen, Alex would be subjected to final examinations in all his classes this week. In addition, he would have to contend with the Scholastic Aptitude Test next week. He was not looking forward to that.

"Hi Alex," said a group of girls as they went out of their way to walk by him.

"Hi," was his normal response. It'd been like that ever since everyone heard about him rescuing Amanda from her psychopath kidnapper. How they found out about the incident was beyond him. He didn't like the attention. And he certainly didn't like the fact that the bell was about to ring and Amanda wasn't at school yet.

She'd called him yesterday after her interview at the WFO. She wanted to talk to him about the conversation he had with her father. Alex insisted that he'd talk to her about it the next time he saw her.

Alex had his eyes fixed on the faculty parking lot where Amanda usually parked her car, hoping that she would magically appear. The bell rang, but Amanda never showed.

As he walked the hallways of Prestige High, Alex found himself outside Amanda's homeroom. Her seat was empty.

"Hi, Alex," said a familiar voice behind him. Alex turned around and saw Leslie, standing a little too close to him.

"Hey, Leslie," he replied, stepping back.

"What are you doing here?"

"I'm looking for Amanda. Have you seen her?"

"No. I tried calling her yesterday after everything died down, but got no answer," she replied. "I can't believe that psycho placed a bomb on our bus; can you believe it? I mean, what the hell—"

Alex looked at her, puzzled. "What bomb? After what died down?"

"Saturday, silly," she said, playfully touching his arm.

Alex recalled his encounter with John Fischer on Saturday, and now the entire school knew about it. How they found out, he had no clue. But something told him that Leslie was not referring to what happened in the Mosleys' basement.

"What happened Saturday?" he finally asked.

Leslie smiled coyly, as she usually did whenever she was about to dish the dirt on a particular subject.

"Well, while you were out fighting crime, in your tights and cape in Metropolis," she teased, "we—meaning the cheerleading squad—were on our way up to Maryland for the big game, when our bus got pulled over by the FBI. I mean, right there on the highway, can you believe it? It was so weird. I mean, there they were with lights flashing and sirens wailing—"

Alex rubbed his temple as he secretly wished she would just tell him what happened without the dramatic flair, but then that wouldn't be Leslie's style. His interest in what she had to say greatly outweighed his annoyance with her, so he listened impatiently.

Leslie talked of how they were escorted off the bus and how the bomb squad disarmed the bomb they found underneath the back seat of the bus. Apparently, Amanda told one of the agents back at the Mosleys' residence what Fischer said—about placing a bomb on the cheerleaders' bus. Each cheerleader was questioned about what they knew of the mysterious groundsman who worked at their school. None of them seemed to know anything about Fischer. As they waited for their parents to retrieve them from the FBI office, they overheard bits and pieces of what had happened at the Mosleys' house that morning. Leslie got the full scoop from her mother, who demanded that the FBI tell her why John Fischer had targeted the cheerleading squad in the first place. Once Leslie knew the details of what happened, it didn't take much time for the story to go viral.

"Thanks, Leslie," Alex said, when she finally came up for air at the end of her story.

"No biggie," she said proudly, assuming that Alex was thanking her for the recount of the story and not that it was his sarcastic way of thanking her for blabbing the story to everyone.

As he started to walk away, he turned and said, "If you see Amanda, could you tell her I'm looking for her?"

"Sure," she shrugged, entering her homeroom.

* * *

By Wednesday, no one had seen or heard from Amanda. Alex was on his way to Ms. Lucci's office, where he'd spent most of his afternoons studying for his final exams—which had wrapped up earlier that morning—and the SAT, which was next weekend. Ms. Lucci had run into him before his last exam this morning, and told him she had great news to share with him later that day. Unless she knew the whereabouts of Amanda, Alex doubted she had anything of importance to tell him. Nevertheless, he agreed to meet with her.

At 3:30 p.m., Ms. Lucci heard someone fumbling about outside her office. "Alex, is that you?" she asked.

"Yes, Ms. Lucci."

"Get in here," she said excitedly. "I have something to tell you." A few seconds passed before the six-foot high school junior filled the threshold to her office. "Sit, sit, sit," she said, motioning to the chairs in front of her desk.

Alex plopped himself down in the chair closest to him.

Ms. Lucci, who was busy rearranging the papers on her desk and peering over at her computer screen, didn't notice the look of indifference on Alex's face.

"I called in a huge favor from your professors this week, to have them submit your final grades for the semester ahead of their other students," she said. "As a matter of fact, I just got your grade from English Literature—the last exam you took this morning."

"Why did you do that?"

"So I could have your grades in before the semester ended, to see if you met your academic obligation and finally get off probation."

"Oh."

"Oh," she mimicked him. "Is that all you have to say for yourself, young man? These professors busted their butts to get your grades in so soon, especially given their workload. Aren't you the least bit interested in how you did this semester?"

Alex was about to give an honest reply, but decided against it, not wanting to sound ungrateful or dampen Ms. Lucci's spirit.

"Why don't you take a look for yourself?" she said, turning her computer screen to face him.

Alex haphazardly slid to the edge of the chair to take a closer look at her computer. The screen depicted his current course load at Prestige and the grades he received in each class. With the exception of Phys-Ed, he had gotten all A's or A-'s.

"The P in Phys-Ed signifies that you passed, but wasn't factored into your grades, because I convinced the grading committee to consider your nosebleeds a disability," she said.

Alex exhaled deeply and looked over at Ms. Lucci, who had a grin from ear to ear on her face. He was unsure of how to react in this situation, because it wasn't the first time he had received all A's. He had been a straight-A student most of his life. However, he knew what a personal triumph this must be for Ms. Lucci, so he feigned a smile for her.

"Three point five—you did it," she exclaimed. "Do you see what you can achieve if only you apply yourself?

"I am so proud of you," she continued, not waiting for him to answer. "Do you know what this means?"

"I'm off probation."

"Precisely. But it also means that you can be placed back into AP classes next year. Once back in AP classes, you stand a better chance of getting into a good college—hopefully on a full scholarship. Isn't that great?" she smiled.

"Thrilling," he managed to cough up. "Does that mean I don't have to study here anymore?"

"No. At your mother's request, you still have to come here and study until you take the SATs. Now that your classes and final exams are over, you can choose any three hours of the day you feel like to study here."

"It's up to three hours now?"

"Yes, that was your mother's idea too. Speaking of which, she is going to be so proud of you. Just wait until I tell her," she said, reaching for her phone. Anxiously, she dialed Margaret's number. As the phone rang, she sat back in her chair and looked at Alex, who sat emotionless in front of her. Suddenly, she leaned forward and placed her finger on the receiver, hanging up the phone before the call went through.

"What's the matter?" she asked. "And don't say nothing," she warned, anticipating his usual response.

Alex swallowed hard, and then asked, "Have you heard from the Bridgewaters?"

"The Bridgewaters?" she asked. "Oh, Amanda. I didn't have direct contact with them, but I know she'll be in tomorrow and Friday to take her final exams."

"Tomorrow? Are you sure?" he asked, with a sense of urgency in his voice for the first time during their conversation. Alex was almost certain that most juniors' final exams were scheduled for the beginning of the week.

"Yes, I'm quite sure. It was at her parents' request."

"Thanks, Ms. Lucci," Alex said as he got up. "Do you mind if I study at home today?"

"With grades like these, I think I could excuse you for one afternoon."

"Thanks again," he said as he walked out of the room.

"You're welcome, but you have to study here tomorrow," she yelled after him.

Tap. Tap. Tap. Alex listened as his pencil drummed on the SAT Prep book in front of him on the dining room table that night. It was almost nine o'clock and he had spent more time trying to figure out why Amanda was avoiding him than he had spent studying for the SAT.

The noise from the garage door closing interrupted Alex's train of thought as his mother appeared in the living room.

"Alex, you're still up," she said, a bit surprised, but pleased at the same time.

"Yeah, just getting ready for the big exam next week," he replied, gathering his books.

"Well, I know you'll do fine, especially since you received all A's this semester and are off academic probation," she boasted.

"I see that Ms. Lucci called you."

"Yes, she did," she said, tossing her bags on the couch. "Best news I've heard all day, possibly all year, come to think of it."

"Well don't forget that some of those were A-minuses, and a P in gym," he said.

"Are you deliberately trying to rain on my parade?" she said, walking over to the dining area.

"No, ma'am," he said.

"Good, because an A is an A, regardless of whether there is a plus or minus at the end."

"I sure hope the colleges see it that way."

"Oh, so now you're worried about what colleges think."

"Perish the thought," he said, getting up from the table.

"Are you off to bed already?" Margaret asked, sounding a bit disappointed.

"Yeah. It's after nine already and I have to be at school tomorrow. Thanks for that, by the way. Although classes are over, I still have to travel all the way to Prestige to study for *three* hours outside Ms. Lucci's office."

"Oh, that's right," she recollected.

"What's the matter, Mom?" he asked, sensing her disappointment.

"No, it's just that we haven't really had a chance to talk since Sunday," she answered.

"What do you want to talk about?"

Margaret sighed as she looked at Alex with a smile. Although it wasn't possible, it seemed like he had aged since the incident at the Mosleys' house. Maybe 'aged' is not quite the right word. Changed, maybe? Yes, that seemed more appropriate. Alex had changed somehow after the incident. But was it the incident with Fischer that accounted for the change? Maybe it had to do with him not being able to see Amanda?

"Nothing that can't wait until after your exam," she said.

"Thanks, Mom," he said as he planted a kiss on her forehead.

"And for the love of God, will you please get a haircut?" she added as a curly lock of his hair tickled her right cheek.

"Good night, Mother," he yelled over his shoulder as he headed upstairs.

* * *

Thursday morning, Alex hopped on to Prestige High's school bus number sixty-two. The girls all smiled and said hi while the boys opted for fist bumps and the sporadic outburst of "my man." He made his way to Ms. Lucci's office when he got off the bus and stayed there until lunchtime. When the bell rang, he gathered his belongings and told Ms. Lucci he was heading home.

He walked into the cafeteria in search of Amanda, but she wasn't there. Next, he tried the Brewery, but had no luck there either. He was walking toward the media center when he looked across the Quad and saw someone sitting under Acer. As he drew closer, he noticed it was Amanda.

"Hey," he said when he reached her.

She was startled and almost dropped the apple she was eating. "Hey," she said, looking around. "What are you do-ing here?"

"So you were deliberately avoiding me?" he surmised, as he sat down. "Why else would you be so surprised to see me on a day you knew I wouldn't be in school?"

She didn't say anything.

"To answer your question," he continued, "my mother wants me to keep studying outside Ms. Lucci's office until I've taken the SAT. My question to you now is, why are you avoiding me?"

"I know about the conversation you had with my Dad."

"The one where he asked me to stay away from you?"

She nodded.

"So you knew about it Sunday when we talked?"

"I knew about it Saturday when I stopped by my house while you were unconscious. I tried to tell you back in your room, but couldn't. Then my mother was going to tell you when she came for me, but I stopped her. I figured I'd be able to convince my Dad to change his mind when he got home that night. But he didn't. I told him I wasn't going to stop seeing you, so I guess that's when he decided to talk to you instead."

He waited for her to continue, but when she didn't, he spoke.

"He told me that I had put your life at risk. That I had made you an easy target for John to kidnap. He wasn't malicious in his delivery of his opinion. In fact, he was quite astute about it."

"A trick he has perfected, I suppose." She smiled.

"Touché. The accent helped soften the delivery too," he said, smiling back at her. "I still don't understand why you avoided me if you already knew about our conversation."

"You said you wanted to talk to me in person about what he said. It doesn't take a genius to know you're going to break up with me."

"Oh," he said. "You have to admit, he does make a really compelling case why we should."

She remained silent.

"And you thought that delaying this conversation would…" he prompted.

"I thought it would give me more time to get him to change his mind. All he needs is a good distraction and he'll forget about this whole kidnapping thing. Or, *maybe* you could change his mind for him?"

"I'm not going to do that."

"I knew you wouldn't. I guess I just needed to hear it rebuffed out loud. He told me you agreed with his assessment of the facts," she continued. "And that you said you can't be selfish and put your needs above my safety."

Alex didn't have a reply.

"Alex, just give him some time. This whole thing will blow over soon. He has a trip coming up next Tuesday. I'm sure by the time he returns from resolving some diplomatic crises abroad, you and I will have moved down on his priority list."

"So let's say you're right," he said. "And in a month or two, your dad is like 'fine, date whoever you want.' Do you think that would resolve the real problem?"

"Of course, because by then my dad—"

"Amanda, your dad saying to stay away from me is not the problem. I am. The problem is if you stay around me, you will always be at risk of getting hurt. And not only from outside threats like the John Fischers of the world, but from me too.

"I am a ticking time bomb that can explode at any minute," he continued. "I literally exploded in my room in front of my mother when I heard about your kidnapping. I threw you into a wall when all you tried to do was surprise me."

"But that was an accident!" she said.

"Accidents happen when you least expect them. That's why they're called accidents."

A tear rolled down her cheek as she shook her head. "Don't do this."

"I don't want to."

"Then don't."

ACKNOWLEDGMENTS

Thanks to my son who has been my inspiration throughout this entire process. You are truly my little superhero.

Thanks to my sister, Angela, for all her support in making this project happen. Thanks for being my sounding board. You will always be my first and most critical critic.

Thanks to my editors, Crystal and Kelsey, for doing an amazing job with this project. Crystal, your suggestions were invaluable.

Thanks to Melchelle Designs for a fabulous cover and flexibility.

To everyone who purchase and/or read an authorized edition of this book, thank you for your time and patronage.